DRAINERS II INFINITY
Book One

by
Ronald James

PublishAmerica
Baltimore

© 2005 by Ronald James.
All rights reserved. No part of this book may be reproduced, stored in a retrieval system or transmitted in any form or by any means without the prior written permission of the publishers, except by a reviewer who may quote brief passages in a review to be printed in a newspaper, magazine or journal.

First printing

ISBN: 1-4137-7061-4
PUBLISHED BY PUBLISHAMERICA, LLLP
www.publishamerica.com
Baltimore

Printed in the United States of America

FEBRUARY

Four pairs of eyes looked down. At first, there was excitement, but the feeling quickly faded. The finger had moved, prompting a flow of adrenaline from the watchers but it had been short lived.

"Is there no hope, then?" the woman asked.

"Oh, there's always hope," a kind voice said, "but I'm afraid—"

"It moved again, Mom!" a younger voice chimed.

The man in the white smock looked down, sighing. He had tried everything he knew, but had failed at every turn. He had even gone so far as to bring in his .45 automatic, and had placed it in the man's hand, but to no avail. He had even loaded the clip, trying to make it seem authentic, but still he had evoked no response. Maybe he should have brought in his new pump shotgun instead. He would try that tomorrow, and maybe the man would remember the same kind of weapon that almost ended his life. Anything was worth a try. He vowed to try it again if the man showed any response at all.

"Doctor?" a new voice interrupted.

The man in the smock turned. "Yes, nurse?"

"The new intern? Doctor Redfern? Do you know where he is?"

This new internee sure had something, but damned if he knew what it was. Half of the nurses on the floor were oozing animal lust every time he was around, including the married ones.

"As a matter of fact, I do. He's borrowed my new car, and has gone out to the auto center to get some stereo speakers for that fancy truck of his. The battery was dead in the truck, so I imagine he'll get a new one of those as well. Maybe the reason his battery was dead was because of that stereo; I don't know, but he'd sure as hell better not dent my car up!"

"Oh, I'm sure your car is safe with him, Doctor," the nurse shyly said. "He is...he seems to be a very good driver."

The doctor smiled, thinking he was a very good 'driver' indeed. "I'll take your word for it. I only got it back from the garage yesterday, after the fire I had under the hood. They had to replace all the wiring.

Your Doctor Redfern said he'd be gone about an hour, but he's already a half hour late."

Unaccustomed fire flashed in the nurse's eyes. "I'm sure he'll be back soon, Doctor," she defended, "and I'm also certain your precious automobile will be all in one piece!"

He smiled to himself when the nurse unloaded on him. Whatever this Redfern had, he wished he knew the ingredients.

The nurse left then, still fuming over what had been implied against her Chuck. They were going to be married; he'd said so last night when they'd made love in his truck. She picked up the watering can and watered the plants that ranged around the room, thinking what she and Charlie were going to do that evening.

"I think we'll leave now, Doctor," the woman said. "The senator is waiting for the boys and me out at his place, a pool party or something. I wish we could stay longer, but the senator's bodyguards are waiting for us in the lobby."

The doctor nodded. "No problem, Mrs. Benner. I'll take good care of your husband."

"Thank you, Doctor. Come along, boys, the senator is going to show us his new pool."

The woman leaned over and whispered in the doctor's ear. "It has a tunnel that goes around the perimeter of it. The pool has glass sides, but you can only see through it from inside the tunnel. We are able to see what goes on in the pool from the tunnel, but the people in the pool can't see the tunnel. We're all so excited about it, but the boys haven't seen it yet."

One of the boys was reluctant to leave his father, but his twin prodded him after the woman. The white-coated figure watched the trio until they were out of sight, shaking his head.

Maybe it was a blessing the man in the pod was deaf to everything. The woman was a real piece of work, more interested in a pool party with her father than she was in her husband's welfare. What was that old saying? What comes 'round goes 'round? Yes, that's what it was, and maybe some day she would be in worse shape than her husband was now.

He closed the pod, watching for some sign from the man that would signify awareness, but as always there was nothing. He looked for the nurse, but she had gone into the solarium after tending to the man's plants the police department had sent.

The silence of the room closed in on him, the only sound coming from the vibrating pod. He walked down to the nursing station then, pulling out the admittance information on the man. There was something he wanted to check. He heard the jangling of keys before he was finished, and turned when his name was spoken.

"Sorry I'm late, Hank, but I had a little trouble putting the battery in."

"That's quite all right, Doctor, but I suggest you go into the solarium and speak to the nurse. She seems to be a little upset at something."

Both men smiled knowingly. The intern walked into the solarium to placate his latest conquest, and the older doctor left for the recreation room.

The television was blaring, and he noted there was a silly soap opera on. To his way of thinking, these programs were almost enough to destroy a man's brain. He just couldn't—for the life of him—see what women got out of these idiotic love stories.

Were all women the same? Were they all suckers when it came to men who had a fast line to shoot them? Like the intern was doing right now to that nurse in the solarium? He thought not, but he hoped for the intern's sake that she never found out about the other two nurses that had seen the ceiling of his fancy truck.

He watched the screen for a while, remembering parts of another old adage. *Something about a woman being scorned. In this case, it would be three of them, and the good doctor would be fortunate if they didn't rip his gonads out.*

He realized he had a splitting headache, but blamed it on the television. He reached for the remote to shut it off, just as a news bulletin pre-empted the program. At first he thought it might be something about the *TWELVE GAUGE KILLER*. There had been a rumor that a copy-cat had killed that store owner, and that they hadn't actually seen the last of him.

Earlier in the week, another twelve-gauge-killer had been shot by another store owner and the media, together with the police department, had been ecstatic. He watched the screen as his pain worsened, but found it was not about the killer after all.

There was a riot or something going on in New York; he could see the fires raging behind the reporter that was on the scene. The pain in his head was past the migraine level now, and he could hardly make out the screen. He endured the agony and watched further, mesmerized, then he saw the reporter clutch at his own head. Hank screamed in pain—and watched in horror as the reporter turned and walked into a solid wall of flame!

DISCOVERY

The silence pushed its force down the long deserted corridors. It searched all the rooms, sliding up the dusty windows and around the walls. Finding nothing of interest, it returned to the corridor and desperately roared down to the very end.

Where before there was nothing, a red light now started blinking. It paused, waiting. Perhaps now there would be something to absorb its lonely quest. A final resting-place. Icy tendrils shot up to the blinking red eye, touching and caressing it, ever searching.

It kissed the crimson orb, swirling around, waiting hopefully for a reaction. Nothing. Always nothing. Its full rage reached, it blasted back down the corridor from whence it had come. It screeched to a halt at the broken window, intent on its purpose and screamed again, venting its rage.

Out it went, tearing down each dark street, finding ever nothing. No dogs. Not a cat or a rat. Down long dead alleys it roamed, slowing to investigate all the shadows, all the nooks and crannies. As before, there was nothing. If only it could have entered where the red light had started blinking—

CHAPTER ONE

The finger twitched again, more pronounced this time and the eyelids opened. Not fully, but enough to see the myriad collection of wires and tubes, issuing from a central region and culminating somewhere out of his vision.

He lay there, not daring to move. He did not know where he was. Even worse, he did not know who he was? Who was he? Where was he? What had happened to him? Why? There was complete silence around him, and then he discovered why. Above his head, he saw a canopy covering the bed he was enclosed in. *But enclosed for what? From what?*

He opened his mouth and roared out his frustrations. Silence met him. He tried again, and this time was rewarded with a squeak. Damn—he couldn't even talk. He closed his eyes and tried to think. Flashes of light coming so fast, but leaving just as quickly. Opening his eyes again, the flashes bringing only pain, he clenched his right fist and found he couldn't even do that. Maybe he had moved too fast. He tried it again, going much slower this time.

The fingers curled, finally touching his palm. The fingernails dug into his pale skin. Good. At least he was still alive, and could at least move a little. He tried the left hand and found that it was the same.

Perspiration beaded on his forehead from the exertion, running down the tubes and wires that seemed to be growing out of his body. He looked down at his right arm and saw that there was a tube in it, running out of the enclosure.

As he lay there, not able to move, his whole body began to vibrate.

It frightened him at first, and then he accepted it, trying not to think about it. After a moment it stopped, and he wondered what had happened. Could it have been an earthquake? But no, nothing else had moved, and there had been no noise. Just a slight buzzing sound that hurt his ears.

Thoughts came to him then that he wasn't deaf, nor was he blind. And if he did it slowly he was able to move. He closed his eyes again, but opened them right away, the flashes bringing pain.

As he tried to trace each umbilical to their source, a screen in front of him burst into life. He had not noticed it before, but now he gave it his undivided attention. Greens and reds leaped out at him, depicting, he thought, what must be his vital signs. The screen was split, and he decided that the top area was depicting his brain activity. The bottom area showed a regular heartbeat, the beeping the first real sound that he had heard. It also displayed blood pressure and lung activity. When he removed the cap taped to his finger, part of the sensor went dead.

The top part of the screen was something else again. There were a mass of zigzags, highs and lows, no two the same. This had to be his brain pattern, but he thought it to be erratically inconsistent. Mesmerized, he watched the screen,

Three minutes later, both screens winked out, but the row of lights at the bottom stayed on. The screen came to life again, beeping, but this time there were words on the whole screen, pulsating on and off. He mouthed the words, wondering at their meaning. They burned their pattern into his brain, forcing him to look down. Thirty seconds of this and the screen went dead again, the imbecilic beeping stopped and all of the lights at the bottom of the screen went out.

He listened for a moment; the silence deafening after the beeping noise had stopped. He remembered the words he had read on the screen, his brain sorting out the letters that had made them.

Push button.

Push button? What push button? How? He couldn't move; he could barely make a fist. He tried closing his hand once more, and discovered it was much stronger now. He tried his left hand, but had to relax his grip when the nails dug into his soft palm once more.

He tried moving his head—experimentally at first—and found

that he could. He felt pain in his shoulder, but found he could tolerate it. The vibrations started again, this time stronger, making him wince. When the vibrations ended, the screen came on again, showing a much stronger heart. The brain waves on the top screen had lessened their impossible severity now, and a much more uniform pattern was emerging.

The screens winked out, but the words came on the screen again, this time with an added message. He read what the screen was displaying. *Pushbutton—right hand* and then he waited for the screen to shut off again.

Looking at his right hand, he saw a soft, green luminescence emanating from the capsule that surrounded him, bathing his hand and the interior with an eerie glow. He flexed the hand then turned his head to watch it move. The pain in his shoulder was easing, and as he watched his fingers opening and closing, his eyes locked onto another light panel. But there wasn't any pushbutton there, just a dead light panel. He tried moving his arm, but his elbow screamed at its lack of use, protesting vigorously.

He had been reaching for the light panel when his arm balked, causing him to rest it. A second later he tried to move his arm again, but this time the pain was not as grating as it had been before. He ran his hand over the panel, his fingers splayed out, caressing the bolt that held the panel in place. A twinge of pain in his elbow caused his arm to twitch. He heard a click; the light panel jumped to life and the screen—in total darkness until that moment—blazed out at him.

"Hello, Stephen," a voice said. "I hope you slept well."

On the screen, a slight, balding man was speaking. His eyes were very bright, as though he was on drugs, and this would prove to be the case. A truth was about to be revealed to "Stephen" that he would find very hard to believe.

"A little levity, there," the man said. "I hope you don't mind. I fear you will need more than a little humor in your life in the coming days, if you have survived to this point. If you have, in fact, returned to *the land of the living*, so to speak, before the generator dies, then perhaps all is not lost. I must tell you first where you are, and also who you are."

At last. Some answers.

"This facility is in Atlanta. You were brought here from the *COMA CENTER*. Your doctor had to come here to survive, and that is why you are here. I know you will have many questions, and I must tell you now that I was your doctor. I say was, because soon I will take my own life."

This was some kind of joke! It had to be. Here was a supposed doctor, talking to him via video, telling him that this same doctor was going to commit suicide?

As "Stephen" watched the screen, a hand came out of the air and raked the doctor's face, the fingers clawing at the eyes. Another hand came up and held it away, but with what seemed considerable effort. This second hand then held the first one from inflicting any more injury. The murderous hand lay still then, seemingly reprimanded.

"You see, Stephen," the figure on the screen said, "I have no control over my body. Not my body, really, but my brain. What you are about to see might shock you, but it is what the whole world has come to. What is left of it!"

Stephen watched in utter amazement as the doctor pulled a syringe from his vest pocket, and then sunk it into his arm.

"Something has happened to the world, Stephen. It is not as it used to be. Something has happened to our brains."

The doctor injected the contents of the syringe into his arm as he went on speaking. "What I am injecting into my arm will control my brain, but only for a short time. At night I hook up to an automatic affair that continuously feeds my brain. Otherwise, my own body would probably kill me as I slept."

"You are likely wondering why you have not been affected, but I'm not sure if I can answer that question. What I *can* tell you, is that when you were brought to the hospital in New York City; you were more dead than alive. Your head had been ripped away across the top. Does this surprise you?"

Stephen was more than surprised—he was shocked.

"Stephen, you were shot in the head with a shotgun, and it took the top of your head off. The neurosurgeons that operated on you inserted a protective plate over your skull. It covers your whole head, almost down to your ears. You were injured before the world went crazy, and that silver plate may have saved you from going mad; it's the only explanation I can offer."

Stephen was beginning to believe what this man was telling him, but still found it a little hard to swallow. He remained silent as the man on the screen continued.

"You were shot attempting to stop a robbery in a drug store in New York City. You were a policeman in New York, Stephen, but you were off duty. That was back in January. January seventh, to be exact."

A policeman? He had been a cop!?

"New York City is gone now, it is completely burned up. If you have a hard time believing that, let me show you what happened!"

He watched in growing horror, staring at a scene out of a nightmare. The eye of the camera denoted scenes of complete insanity. A mob setting fire to a grocery store, and then setting fire to themselves. A cabdriver sending his vehicle through a plate glass window after driving down a crowded walkway, killing hundreds! A world gone mad. The police shooting innocent citizens, and then turning their weapons on themselves. Firemen burning their own trucks. Madness everywhere! Killing—killing—killing!

"The cameraman who shot that footage just laid his camera down and walked into a blazing wall of fire," the speaker narrated. "God only knows how the video was saved. I taped this from a network program, but that was before the worst had happened. And now that I have your attention, Stephen, you will be told what has been done to save you, and why."

The speaker then told him that the vibrations he had felt were his muscles being exercised. In the event that he recovered from the coma, he might be able to walk and move with very little therapy.

"There is a catheter connected to remove all of the excess body fluids, but it should be a relatively simple matter to remove the tube."

Curious now, Stephen tried to move the blanket covering his body. After some pain, he had the blanket raised up enough to see the tube. He also saw that he was very nude.

"Be careful when you pull the tube out,"—the voice on the screen warned, as though he could see Stephen—"for it will feel like it has grown to be a part of you. A sharp tug and it should come free."

Stephen experimented with it, testing the pull. The pain hit him at once and he stopped to rest. He squeezed on the tube as he rested, and felt the pain recede. Experimenting further, he squeezed the tube again. Unknowingly, he had released the "bubble" that held the catheter from coming out of his bladder, and then the catheter pulled out with comparative ease. With this accomplished, he faced the screen again, ignoring the pain he felt coming from his penile area.

"The sensors on your head are taped on. It could cause some pain when these are pulled off, for they have been there for quite some time."

Stephen reached up and received more pain. He worked the shoulder around until he could reach up with a modicum of anguish. Ten sensors were connected to his head, and one by one they pulled off, leaving a dark, angry ring. If he had been able to see himself, he would have thought that an octopus had attacked him.

With the sensors on his head gone, there was only the intravenous in his arm. There were sensors in his ankles, but he hadn't been informed of this yet.

"There are also sensors on your feet. Two on the ankles and two on your toes."

He laboriously removed the blanket, sliding it over the intravenously punctured arm.

"I must caution you about removing the I.V. before you are able to move your legs, Stephen. It is quite possible that starvation could kill you. This would be ironic, for the stores of the world are yours to pick and choose from. Anything you desire will be yours if you are patient and resourceful."

He tried moving his legs and found that they wouldn't budge. He tried again, but the result was the same. Frightened now, he tried moving his left knee. The pain that shot up to his brain told him it had moved. When he tried his right knee, the level of pain was greater yet.

"Do not be alarmed if you cannot move your legs right now, for the sensors will not let you. These must be removed first."

He listened some more. This doctor seemed to know of his every problem and movement, so he had better listen to his directive.

"The sensors on the toe are simple, but the ankle sensors are quite another matter. The toe sensors are only caps and will easily slide off. What you must realize is that the sensors on your ankles are wired right into your central nervous system, and cannot be removed."

Stephen tried his voice again, wishing to vent his anger. A roar escaped his lips, the vocal chords starting to lose their rust. "Why me?" he roared. "Dammit all to hell! Why me? Why didn't you just let me die?!"

The pain in his head became greater than the suffering his body was experiencing. The video went on, his pain and suffering unnoticed.

"There are plugs on your ankles that can be pulled apart. Once that is done, you will be able to move your legs. You must be very careful when you pull these plugs apart; do not break the wires that go into your body. When the plugs are removed, they must be taped over, or your whole nervous system could be affected. Remember, Stephen, your body has grown around these wires now, and is a part of you."

He would remember this day. His body and brain had betrayed him; had awakened him.

"There is a huge generator in the basement of this place, and that is what has been keeping you alive. It is fueled by two diesel tankers that I brought in, and these tankers are located in the building adjacent to these facilities." The speaker paused, perhaps assembling his thoughts. "The date of this video you will see on this screen, and it is also the date that I died. I plan to take my life as soon as this video is completed."

"No!" Stephen cried suddenly. "You can't *do* that!!!"

The speaker continued with his explanations, oblivious to Stephen's ranting. "I have fought this thing as long as I can. I grow weary of this constant losing battle. Better to die like a man than to live like an insane slave."

"You're not a man!" Stephen cried out. "You're a coward! A damned coward!"

"When you have freed yourself, you will find the date that you awakened on a clock just outside your pod."

My "pod"? Oh, yes. I've been growing in here, just like a damned vegetable.

"When you are able to move your legs, you will find the pod exit button just over your left shoulder."

He pushed himself to a sitting position; the pain was so exquisite he almost enjoyed it. After moving back and forth for a few minutes, the pain lessened to a tolerable level.

Now for those damned plugs.

The plugs pulled apart easily once he learned to put pressure on the sides of them. The caps on his toes slid off then and he was almost free. He started to turn, looking for the escape button, but it was too high for him. He would have to work for it.

"You will find videos and books on various subjects, and also any medical supplies you may need. There are antibiotics labeled, for you should have some when you are finally free of the pod. The medication is at the nursing station on this floor, as are the library and gym."

Stephen started to work on his legs and found that they *would* move! This gave him heart, and he worked his knees back and forth, up and down. The pain was severe, but he ignored it. Now, he thought, time to get rid of this portable food bank!

The I.V. was taped on, and he winced as the tape came off, taking some skin with it. When he pulled the I.V. out, blood came out with it. He staunched the flow with his left hand, applying pressure to it.

"Everything you will need is just outside of the pod. Wheelchair, crutches and a cane. You will find food that could last you for six months. Mostly canned food, but you will be able to use the refrigerator and freezer as long as the generator keeps going."

Stephen put the pain out of his mind as much as he could, then laboriously ripped a strip from the sheet that had been covering him. He wrapped his wrist with it, effectively bandaging the hole the I.V. had made.

"All of your identification and personal belongings are at the nursing station on this floor. Everything else you need to survive is there as well."

He had been working his legs while he'd been watching the screen, feeling more strength and power flowing into them. He still didn't know if he could walk, nor if he could even stand up.

"You may find, Stephen, that you have limited motor use, for we don't know how much of your brain has been damaged. Maybe you will have powers that you never had before. You will not know until you try." There was a short pause. "I hope you have been watching this video. It is my hope that everything I have done has not been in vain." Another pause as the figure on the screen reached down for something out of the camera's view. "If you wish to see my body, it will be at the nursing station on the first floor."

The figure stayed on the screen, looking at the camera morosely. Another thought must have come to his mind, for he spoke again. "Stephen, do not think too harshly of me for taking my life. I have been alone for over two weeks now, and I think everyone in the city is dead. Except for you, my friend, maybe the whole world is dead! I have come in here every day to sit and talk with you, for you were my last link with humanity and sanity!"

The man looked down at something unseen. Stephen had been feeling sorry for himself, and now his compassion spilled over to include the man on the screen.

"I hope I have done something for you," Stephen's benefactor said. "For the world, for the human race. If you have survived, please go on from here."

The doctor broke down then, crying into the camera. "I…I must go now. Maybe we will meet again on the other side. Good-bye, my friend."

Complete silence invaded the pod as the screen blanked out.

He searched his thoughts, rewarded with a feeling of utter despair. Then his thoughts turned to the man who had just been on the screen, and he was ashamed of himself.

Here he was, feeling sorry for himself. But the man on the screen—the man who had done so much for him—was going to his death. Correction—had gone to his death! When? How long ago?

The thought galvanized him into action, all feelings of despondency turning to anger. He pulled his knees up toward his chin and rolled over. This action he immediately regretted as pain in his knees blasted white fire into his brain. He stayed in that position, rocking back and forth, waiting for the agonizing pain to decrease. Finally, when the pain receded to a dull roar, he reached up and punched the pod release. He fell back and straightened up, the pain in his tortured knees being relieved somewhat. When a whirring noise started, he watched in tearful glee. The two sections of the pod slowly parted, revealing a bright, sunny room, with windows set into the ceiling.

As the pod's sides swung down and away, then moved to either side of the bed, his senses recorded a terrific blast of heat. He looked around, trying to see everything at once then slowed his staring eyes. He was impatient, and that would never do. It might be days before he could walk, maybe longer.

Looking over the side of the bed, he saw that the pod had been on rails. The rollers connected to the pod moved out, allowing horizontal and lateral capabilities. A limit switch attached to the rail had stopped the pod from going any further and had shut it down.

He thought it was an ingenious device, but then, even the simplest things had seemed that way to him when he had been—what? His protector had said that he had been a cop. Something tugged at his mind, and he remembered something the doctor had said. "You will find the date you awakened on a clock just outside of your pod."

His eyes searched, and then he found it.

It was another ingenious device. The clock was not only showing the time, but also the date. He looked at the clock, checking the time— 9:54 a.m. And the date... the date was June eleventh!!

The ramifications of the time differential slammed him between the eyes. He did the math, and discovered that he had been *sleeping* for five months! "And...and ..." he stuttered, "the doctor has been dead since the fifteenth of March! My God!!"

He would have to move, but at this moment he was too stunned. He had been "sleeping" for five months, and his doctor/protector had been dead for—what? Some three months now?

A light suddenly went on in his brain. "I remembered!" he exclaimed out loud. "Okay, I can remember. But why in hell can't I remember what happened to me? Why did I have to be told about it? Why, for God's sake, can't I remember last year? The last thing I can remember is... when I was sixteen, and I had just learned to drive...and Dad had given me that old car for my birth—"

He relaxed then, knowing almost exactly what he had lost. He figured it out as he looked at the clock and rechecked the date. He had lost eighteen years. Eighteen years of his memory gone. Eighteen years of his life wiped out. Even his name was gone, erased, as if he had never been born. He could remember almost everything up to the time he had been sixteen, but nothing after that. But why couldn't he remember his name? Surely he'd had a name when he had been sixteen? He tried to remember until it hurt.

He could even remember being in first grade. His mind recounted the memories, holding on to them, needing some sort of reality. Some kid had laughed at the pants he was wearing, and he had pushed the kid down. The kid had run away, crying, and had come back with an older sister. She was going to *box his ears*. She was, until she saw the knife. The knife that he'd found. The knife he'd carried in his pocket all the time.

He'd found the knife down at the town dump, the tin handles broken off and the rivets sticking out. His Uncle Frank (Uncle Frank had fought in the war, and had returned home a drunk and a cripple. He had never married, and lived down the lane from them) had fashioned a wooden handle on it for him. He'd stuck it reverently in his pocket, and had carried it all the time.

The girl and her brother had backed off then, and the teacher had come out, demanding the knife. He had once told a friend that he would never part with his knife, but that day he lost it to the teacher. He had never laid eyes on it again, but for years after his teacher had experienced broken windows in her house. She had blamed him for it, but there had never been any proof. The day that Eddy Belcher got caught going past her house with a rock in his hand, she had called for him to stop. She'd blamed Eddy for all the broken windows, and Eddy's mother had paid for the windows just to shut the old teacher's vindictive mouth.

After that, Eddy had become his friend, and he'd found out that some of Eddy's ideas had been almost as good as his. Miss Childon had not been a very good person—they had both decided—and when she had awakened one day to find her prize roses cut off at the ground, she had flipped out. Maybe the dead cat on her front step hadn't helped.

Stephen remembered more of his childhood after that, especially his punishment. When his father had come home from work the day his knife had been taken away, he'd become very angry. He remembered how his father had "punished" him. He mostly remembered how his mother had saved him from his irate father. Maybe it would have been a lot better if he had just let that girl *box his ears*.

When his father had cooled down, he'd apologized, but the damage had been done. He had given a lecture then, but it had never changed Stephen's mind about anything. "If you have to defend yourself, son," his father had said, "use your hands. If you had hurt those kids today at school, they would have come and taken you away from here!" Stephen remembered that his father had never said who *they* were, and he had never asked, but he *had* learned how to use his hands.

He remembered all that, and a lot of other things until the time that he became sixteen, but nothing after that. He even remembered his birthday. According to the date now, that would make him...thirty-four. Great! A thirty-four-year-old body, in a sixteen-year-old mind. Just what he needed. He gave himself a mental slap, reminding himself that he was still alive.

But what he needed now—whether or not he could do it—was to accomplish what he had started out to do. Get out of the damned bed. Looking around, he saw the wheelchair. If he could make it to the chair, he could at least get around, even if he couldn't walk yet.

He was talking to himself now and he knew it, but the sound of his voice reminded him that he was still alive, and that he was going to give this his best shot. His voice also reminded him that this was a wide-awake nightmare, not the sleeping variety.

Rolling over onto his stomach, he slipped his legs over the side of the bed, crying out when his knees took all the weight of his legs. He tried to grab the bed and pull himself back up, but the sheet came with him, dumping him unceremoniously on the floor. He lay there for a moment, assessing the pain. His back, hips and knees were on fire, but not as bad as before.

"Well, Doctor," he said aloud, "I'm out of bed."

He dragged his body around the half pod, pulling his body to the wheelchair. The dust on the tiled floors helped him make it to the side of the chair with relative ease, and the only problem left was getting his body into the seat. He pushed the chair over to the wall, and then positioned his body in front of it, facing away from the chair. He pushed up with his knees, holding the chair with his hands. The agonizing pain was like a solid blow to his temple and he promptly fell to the floor.

It was as if someone had chopped his legs off. Tears came to his eyes so bad he couldn't see. It had been like molten lava flowing through his brain. When the pain had subsided, he cried in despair. "It's no use! No use! I can't do it!"

But he knew he had to. He positioned himself again, and willed his brain to forget the pain. Slowly, his legs and back took the tremendous strain, until at last he was sitting in the chair. He relaxed his body and mind then sat back.

This time, the pain was a living thing, tearing at his nerve endings, stretching his capacity to overflowing and his brain shut down. Mercifully, he passed out. When he came to it was almost dark. His thoughts of before were a jumbled maze he had to thread his way through to return to near-normalcy. His head throbbed with a *thrum-thrum* sound he could actually hear. When he opened his eyes, he thought the pressure behind them might blow them out of his head. Gradually, the ache in his head receded and he was able to think once more.

He had made it to the chair by blocking out the pain, concentrating on no pain. When he had slumped into the chair and relaxed his concentration, the blocked out pain had returned with a vengeance, hitting him with the force of a freight train.

Was that what had happened? Had he actually blocked out the pain in his tortured body, enabling him to climb into the chair?

Refusing to think about it any more, and wanting to explore his new *"home"* he grasped the wheels and pushed off. The wheelchair moved easily, rolling up to the doors. He discovered that as he used his arms, the pain lessened. Realizing this, he pushed his chair through the doors. They opened easily, swinging both ways and closing when he had pushed through.

Once out in the corridor, the view he received of the outside world shocked him.

The corridor was actually a glass-covered bridge, a causeway from the main building to where he had been kept. This explained why there had been dead plants hanging in large pots around the room. That part of the complex must have been a terrarium of sorts, or some kind of plant room. He wondered how long the care of it had been abandoned.

He tooled along, checking the rooms, looking only into the opened doors. The closed doors had a foul stench emanating from them, and he knew what they must contain. Holding his breath, he looked into one of the rooms and discovered it had been a laboratory of some kind. His eyes picked out the dead, still in their white smocks, but splashes of red denoted they had died violently. He closed the door when he could no longer hold his breath and continued on. Reaching an open area, he approached with caution. He had no way of knowing what he was going to find.

On a hanger, above the desk was a nameplate that read: NURSING STATION SECOND FLOOR.

This was what he was looking for, what he had been told about. Behind the desk sat a cot, and behind the cot a fridge and freezer combination, both in one unit. A machine of some kind lay silent, the intravenous tubing coiled around a peg and pinched off with some kind of clamp. He wondered silently if this was what his doctor had used.

He backed his wheelchair up to the fridge and tried to open it, but the doors opened from the center. He would have to push the cot ahead and out of the way. Merely pushing his wheelchair into it did this, for the cot was on casters. He opened the fridge door and looked inside. Everything he would need was there, including condiments of all sorts. The freezer, he found, was filled with bread and pastries, enough to last him for a very long time. Under the desk he saw canned food of every description, again enough for a long time.

Beside the fridge, unseen until now, stood a two-burner hot plate. Below that there was some kind of oven that he couldn't remember ever seeing before. There were some instructions tucked in beside it; he learned it was something called a microwave.

The nursing station was split in two, with medication on the other desk. A filing cabinet graced the far wall, drawing his attention. His doctor/protector had said that his name was Stephen, but had revealed no last name. Maybe the filing cabinet held some answers.

He opened the top drawer and tried to stretch up to see what was inside. It was loaded with files, but not knowing what his name had started with he reached up and pulled the whole mess out. With them all in his lap, he backed over to the cot, dumping the pile onto the blanket.

He opened a file and tossed it aside. Some woman with a brain tumor, unable to walk after surgery, had died in a fall. The next one was of a young boy. A bicycle accident had left him a paraplegic. Nobody knew how he had slit his wrists. He went through the whole pile before he found the one that he wanted. His had been on the top, but he had thrown the pile upside down on the bed.

BENNER, STEPHEN T., he read, sounding the name over and over, but nothing came. Farther down he read of his injury. Long, foreign sounding names that he had never seen before. When he got to the information that he wanted so desperately to see he stopped. It was all going to be revealed to him now. His name, who he was, or rather, who he had been. He gathered his courage and read on.

BENNER STEPHEN*** T***

DATE OF BIRTH... OCTOBER 17 1957... OCCUPATION: POLICE OFFICER...NEW YORK CITY... DISTINGUISHING MARKS: V SCAR BASE OF LEFT THUMB... MARITAL STATUS: MARRIED WITH TWO CHILDREN ... TWIN BOYS... SPOUSE: MARIE BENNER...NEE PATERSON

The information unfolded before him, telling him everything but telling him nothing. No pictures of his family, just meaningless words. He found out that he had been a married man with two children, but it was a vague idea in his mind. He read on.

*NATURE OF INJURY: SHOTGUN BLAST TO THE HEAD
TOP OF CRANIUM TORN OFF
SURGICAL PROCEDURE — FUSED NERVE ENDINGS
SILVER PLATE OVER BRAIN CASE
PLASTIC PLATE OVERALL — IMITATION HAIR IN SECONDARY
PROGNOSIS — UNKNOWN*

Stephen reached up and tapped on the top of his head. He heard a hollow sound but felt nothing. The hair on the top of his head felt very coarse, almost like wire, but the hair at the side and back was fine and smooth. These findings told him there was evidence of what they had done to him. He *HAD* lost the top of his head! He thought they must have used a horse's tail for hair. But if the top of his head had been blown away, surely his brain must have received severe damage. He would die in this place without ever being able to walk. What an end to such a glorious awakening.

He flexed his left leg, finding that it moved with a minimum of pain. The pain was brutal when he tried the right leg, his knee hurting the most. He knew if he was ever going to save himself he must be able to walk. To do that, he must find the gym and start his therapy.

Reading on down his file, he found there was an address in New York that he didn't remember and not likely ever would. There was no need now, for the whole city was a burned out husk. If this was the case then his whole family was dead.

He was alone!

CHAPTER TWO

It staggered his imagination. *Every person in New York City dead. Millions of people burned alive, some jumping out of windows from high places. Still others jumping out in front of wayward trucks, the drivers chuckling in frenzied glee. Anarchy and murder all over the city. Maybe the world.*

He had been a cop, and had been shot with a shotgun; the world going crazy while he had slept. That's all he knew. A notation at the bottom of the page caught his attention: See news clipping in sections G to J.

There were four drawers, and he had emptied the top one. He set his file down and opened the second drawer. Inside, he found news clippings that someone had laboriously cut out, preserved, probably, against the day that he would awaken. He picked up the first one, wincing from unknown fears as a clean-shaven face popped out at him. The caption read:

POLICE OFFICER SHOT
NEAR DEATH IN HOSPITAL
   A New York City police officer was gunned down late last night. The officer was off duty, and had entered an all night drug store, hoping to have a cold remedy prescription filled for his wife. As he was talking to the store owner, a lone gunman rushed in and stated that he wanted the cash box

"emptied." Complying with the gunman's demands, the pharmacist did as he was told. The gunman cautioned the police officer to "stay cool."

The robber handed the pharmacist a brown paper bag. When the paper bag was passed back over the counter, with the contents of the cash register, the gunman reached out for it. The officer grabbed for the barrel of the sawed-off shotgun, attempting to wrench the weapon away. The large bore gun discharged, sending deadly missiles toward the officer's head. The lead pellets took the officer down, shearing off the top of his skull. The gunman fled then, taking the paper sack with him.

The pharmacist is credited with saving the officer's life when he packed his head in ice. At this writing, the officer is still alive, but only barely. The assailant is still at large, and police are asking the public to...

The article went on to describe the thief, as described to them by the pharmacist. A composite picture was sketched, inset beside what he took to be his own. Two faces he didn't know.

He would have to find a mirror to see what he looked like. He knew he had a beard now, but had once been clean-shaven. He picked up the next clipping and saw a young, attractive, black-haired woman, standing behind two young boys.

FAMILY OF DOWNED OFFICER DESPONDENT AFTER HORRENDOUS ACT

Marie Benner, wife of injured police officer, is shown here with her two sons, Daniel and Darryl. When asked how she felt, she replied, "I hope they catch the bastard that destroyed our lives, and tear his heart out the way he has ripped our lives apart!"

When the boys were asked, Daniel spoke first: "I just want Dad back. I miss him terribly!" Darryl's reply was more vindictive. "I want my Dad back, too. But I also want that rotten criminal caught! I wish someone would tear his head apart, just like he did to my Dad!"

Stephen thought it was interesting. One boy meek and mild, the other more like the mother, seeking revenge. He wondered if he himself had been aggressive or if he had been meek and mild as his son, Daniel, had been? The next clipping showed only his picture.

> FAMILY OF OFFICER DISAPPEARS
> A spokesperson from Senator Paterson's office has said that the family of the stricken man will be unavailable for comment. The family has been moved to an undisclosed location. Senator Paterson is the father-in-law of the downed police officer.

The clippings that followed had to do with more robberies, involving a shotgun-wielding killer. Three store owners had been shot to death with what seemed to be a double-barreled shotgun. The perpetrator had been dubbed: "The- Twelve- Gauge- Killer." The last clipping showed a picture of a stranger.

The caption read—*REST EASY STEVE*—The story followed:

> *"At three a.m. this morning, a man was shot while attempting to rob a liquor store. The robber was pronounced dead when police arrived on the scene. The robber's head was completely destroyed when the store owner shot him with his own shotgun. The robber had a twelve-gauge shotgun as well, with the handle sawn off. The store owner has been detained pending further investigation. Police Chief, Joseph Donner had a comment—"Rest easy, Steve! We got him!"*

The rest of the column followed—*"If this was, in fact, the twelve gauge killer, then officer Benner has been avenged. Perhaps we will never know for sure."*

So that was it, his whole life. He felt no animosity or pity toward the dead killer. How could he? These clippings were a story of his life, but he couldn't remember any of it. That life didn't matter to him anymore. The present one was all that mattered, and he had better get moving if he was going to survive.

He looked up; noticing that the dark had swallowed up the

daylight. He hadn't noticed that the fluorescent lights above the desk were on, had likely been on for months. He'd been so immersed in the clippings that he hadn't seen the daylight slip away, hadn't noticed because of the overhead lights.

A rumbling at the pit of his stomach told him that he was hungry, prompting a smile. He laughed aloud. Of course he was hungry; he hadn't eaten a meal in over five months.

He scanned under the desk and found a can of peaches. On a shelf beside the stove, he found a can opener and opened the can. With a fork, he speared a piece of the fruit and was about to put it in his mouth when a thought struck him. "Uh, oh," he said aloud. "This is solid food, and solid food has a by-product. A nasty by-product!"

He put the fruit back in the can and drank some of the juice. He thought he could go for a whiz anytime, just wheel into some corner and let it go, but a bowel movement was something else. He had no idea that the juice he had consumed would start a bowel movement.

He put the can on the desk then wheeled over to the shelf to replace the can opener, and discovered something that he hadn't seen before. He hadn't noticed it because he had backed up to it; there was a cupboard under the shelf. He turned around, replaced the can opener and checked out the cupboard.

It was equipped with a sliding door, and held all sorts of wonderful things. The most important item to him was the flashlight. He reached in and picked it up, pushing the button on the top of it. The light was dim, but it came on, illuminating the inside of a treasure chest. A hammer, some screwdrivers, wire cutters, pliers and more, a veritable treasure trove, worth their weight in gold. At the back of the cupboard, something shiny glinted in the light's glare. He reached in for it, but it was too far in for him to grasp. Using a screwdriver, he hooked it out, bringing it within reach. He recognized what it was then. It was a familiar sight, even though he had never seen it before. Picking it up, he held it, turning it over in his hand.

It was a pleasant feeling. Somehow, he felt comfortable and knowledgeable with this object in his hand. He released the clip and pulled it out, checking the loads. The clip was full, and he banged it back in, laying the .45 in his lap.

He had been a cop, that much he knew, and this was likely the kind of weapon he had used. Maybe his doctor/protector had stored it here against the day he would awaken. Probably wanted it around for self-defense. Maybe there were still crazy people around who had survived. He would keep it with him at all times, just in case. To have survived this far—just to be murdered by some insane animal—would be criminal.

He wheeled out into the hall with the flashlight and gun in his lap. He turned right, shining the light around, looking for a washroom. Two doors down he found it, a sign above the door proclaiming *Patients Only*. Well, that was him all right. But now it should read: *Only Patient*. He smiled when that thought crossed his mind.

The door was wide, a swinging door, as he would find all the doors to be. He pushed in on the door, and was surprised to find that the light was *on*. Releasing the door, it swung back, closing fully, and then opened again into the hallway. The door hit his wheelchair and started his knee up again. He had gotten careless and paid for it, but he would try to be more careful in the future. But at least he knew that the door would swing both ways, and that he couldn't be trapped inside.

He pushed the door open again when the pain in his knee subsided to a dull throb, wheeling himself into the washroom. The doors swung shut when he was inside, and for a moment he panicked. Then he remembered that the doors would swing both ways.

His thudding heart slowed, and then he saw the huge interior for the first time (he had been here before, but was unaware of it). The whole room was an open concept, containing a huge bathtub that was equipped with a hoist mechanism. He thought this must be used to gently lower the patients into the water. He saw that there was a toilet but no urinal. Clearly this was a boy *and* girl bathroom, used specifically for patients of both sexes who could not navigate under their own power.

There was an identical lifting device, positioned over the toilet, but it was much smaller. It appeared to be designed for someone to be lifted onto the toilet seat, and then back into the wheelchair. The whole affair was connected to overhead rails.

Now he could eat those damned peaches, and any thing else he chose to.

He noticed that one part of the lift was missing, and that he would have to find it. The part he would have to sit on, the part that had the rings that these hooks would fit. Immediately another thought struck him. What if these things didn't work any more? There was a small box with an umbilical that attached to each lifting device, but there had to be power to it or nothing would work.

He had to find out! He had to know!!

He wheeled over to the toilet and grabbed the box, pushing the up button. He waited, but nothing happened. It wasn't fair, he whined. It just wasn't *fair*. To have come all the way back, just to be thwarted like this. He let go of the box, and as it swung back he noticed a switch on the side. He grabbed at the box again, his heart pounding.

It was a slide switch, and he quickly pushed it up. A loud snapping noise told him that something had happened, and with trembling fingers he reached for the up button again! His heart almost stopped when he saw the lift slowly rising. "Oh boy! Oh boy—oh-boy-oh boy!" he cried aloud.

His world was right again. He shut the switch off, relinquishing his death grip on the control box. Happy now, he checked out the rest of the room. He saw a sink, set very low. There was a window over the sink, but a man was looking in at him. *A madman!*

Instantly, instinct taking over, he reached for the .45 in his lap and brought it to bear on the figure in the window. The man in the window had his own gun, and was aiming at him! He pulled the trigger, expecting an explosion, but heard nothing. The .45 was not cocked.

When he looked at the window again, expecting to be shot, he noticed that the madman's gun had misfired as well. He pulled back on the barrel, cocking the gun, and...started to laugh. He laughed so hard he almost fell out of his chair. When he had calmed down and wiped the tears from his face, he wheeled over to the window.

He had almost blown a friend away, would have if the gun had been cocked. He looked into the mirror at his bearded face, not recognizing it. But he smiled quickly.

"How in the hell stupid can you get? Trying to shoot your own face out of a mirror!"

Still grinning, he spied some scissors and shaving gear on a ledge beside the mirror. "You must have been a smart man, protector," he said to the mirror. "You seem to have thought of everything."

Warning bells started clanging in his brain. "Whoa, now. Wait a minute. I need water to do this. How can there be any water?"

He opened the tap, surprised when water came out, the lights dimming as it flowed. When he closed the tap, the lights returned to normal. Deep in the basement, the compressor shut off as the pressure gauge reached the shut-off point. When a water tap was opened again, the compressor would kick in, trying to keep the pressure in the tank. The water tanker was still almost full, and was relatively easy to keep pressurized. One of the diesel tankers was empty, but the other one was still half full. Stephen had no way of knowing it, but he still had about thirty days of power left. Water would not be a problem, but he had no way of knowing that, either. But his mind made the connection between the power drain and the water supply.

"When I turn the water on," he said aloud, "the lights dim. When I shut the water off, the power returns to normal." Somehow, the water was supplied electrically. He would have to use the water sparingly, for it seemed to take a terrible toll on the hydro. He would use water only during the day, shutting all the lights off before he opened a tap.

Picking up the scissors, he trimmed as much of the beard as he could. He thought he would shave the next day. There was no rush for that now, but maybe then he would recognize his own face. He remembered a sixteen-year-old face, not one of thirty-four-years. He replaced the scissors and backed away from the sink. Somewhere, the seat part that he needed was hanging. He would find it, for it meant his survival.

Getting through the doors was no problem. He simply pushed the chair up to, and then through them. Once through, he turned left, going back to the nursing station. What he was seeking was not there, so he would have to look elsewhere. He was starting to panic again, so he stopped to still his fluttering heart.

"Stop it!" he said aloud, commanding himself to slow down. "It's here some place, it has to be. You've only looked a little, slow down and think. Think of where it might be."

If it had been him, he would have left it with the chair. It had to be under you to—"That's it. It has to be in the room where I woke up. I'd better start using my brain a little more."

He wheeled out into the corridor, then down to his *pod* room. The door opened just as easily as it had before and he rolled in. He shut off his flashlight, not needing it. He had noticed when he had regained consciousness in the chair that there were lights on in this room, recessed pots in the walls and fluorescent fixtures hanging down from chains. The light in his pod must have been coming from these. He didn't see any wires coming into the room, so he deduced this area must somehow be connected to the nursing station. Although he was unaware of it, the lights had been designed for the plants in the room. The pot lights were incandescent, and the hanging lights were fluorescent, imitating the sun's rays to a certain degree.

He pushed himself over to where the chair had been, but the harness wasn't there. He searched the whole room, saw that the crutches and cane were the only items that he might be able to use, and then looked elsewhere. The only place left to search was in a wardrobe at the end of the room. There were two doors on the wardrobe, and these opened out from the center. He backed up to them and opened one. Then he moved over against it and opened the other door.

There was a light switch inside, but he used his flashlight. His eyes roamed over the contents of the closet greedily. There was enough room to wheel the chair in, and after he did this he could see much better.

Hung on hangers were all kinds of clothing. Pants, shirts and jackets, but no sling. He calmed himself when he felt the stirring of panic rearing its ugly head. If he couldn't find the sling, he would make one. Maybe out of a sheet or a blanket. He checked out the clothing, thinking that maybe they might have been his, but they looked too big. He tugged some pants and shirts down from the hangers, and then backed out of the closet with them.

"One of these shirts might do," he said out loud. "Better yet, a jacket. Yes. A jacket. A large one." He wheeled back in and found a large jacket, then wheeled back out with it.

"Yes, this might do it," he said. "It looks strong, and I must have lost a lot of weight."

Stephen didn't know it, but he had lost over fifty pounds. If he could have weighed himself, he would have found that he weighed one-hundred-and-twenty-four. At the time of his injury, he had weighed a firm one-hundred-and-eighty-three.

He wheeled over to a couch that sat beside the clothes closet and plopped his booty on it. Picking up the jacket, he tried to stuff it under his thin buttocks but was unable to. He looked down to find out why, and a silly smile came on his face. Still smiling, he dropped the jacket onto the couch and picked up the two rings on either side of his hips. He thanked his lucky stars that his doctor/protector had had the good sense to place it on the wheelchair, out in plain view. He just hadn't seen it.

"I've been sitting on it all this time," he exclaimed. "There is a dead man on the first floor with more brains than I'll ever have!"

Turning the wheelchair, and picking up the rest of his booty, he wheeled out of the room and down the corridor to his new home, pushing the clothes up onto the desk. Then he returned to the *pod* room to retrieve the crutches and cane, taking them down the corridor to his quarters. He had a little trouble getting the crutches through the door, but managed it. All this time he kept the gun and flashlight in his lap.

Going back to his old room, he found the light switch and turned off the power to the lights. There was no need for these lights to be on now. Halfway back to his new quarters, he stopped on the glass-covered causeway and turned his flashlight off. When he looked out at the city and saw only darkness, fear began to gnaw at his brain. It brought to mind an old Christmas rhyme, but he couldn't remember the words.

The enormity of it struck him, making him feel infinitely small. Quite possibly, he was the last man alive in the city, maybe the whole world! The thought made him tremble, and this caused him to thumb the flashlight back to life. The small beam of light made him feel better, and he hurried back to his brightly-lit quarters.

He felt hungry now. His stomach had been rumbling ever since he had swallowed the peach juice. He reached up for the canned peaches and gobbled one down, picking it out with his fingers. He drank the rest of the juice and ate all of the peaches, tilting the can to his lips to get them all. It made him feel better, stronger. It also made him feel tired, and for the first time since he had *awakened* he started to think about sleep.

Should I? Do I dare? Will the coma take over again?

He thought not, and proceeded to fashion a rope out of a sheet that lay over the cot. The other end of the sheet was looped around his neck, and he pulled the cot out into the corridor and down to the washroom door. Once inside the washroom, he positioned the cot close to the lift. It took some doing, but he succeeded in lifting his body out of the chair and onto the cot. His right knee pained considerably, but not as much as before. He hardly felt the left knee at all, but there was a slight tingling sensation in it. He untied the knots in the sheet and draped it over his emaciated body. He was asleep almost at once.

CHAPTER THREE

The thing had been a man once, but had no recollection of that. It had no memory, except that of being driven away from the pack. They would have killed it, but it had fled.

It was completely insane, snapping at the air and growling at shadows. It wore a semblance of clothing, but most of it was in tatters. Instinct drove it on, not knowing direction or purpose, only feeling of movement.

It moved deeper into the city, knowing only that it must feed; it did not care what it fed on, and had no sense of taste. It was now only a hating, killing machine. It turned its head, sniffing, and changed direction. A new scent came to it, the spoor of live food. Hunched over, it followed the new scent, knowing soon it would feed again.

CHAPTER FOUR

He awoke with a start, cursing when the pain hit him. He had jerked his legs, and his right knee had flamed into existence with a wave of fire. His body felt broken, the joints stiff after having little or no movement all night. He thought he must have slept too long, and rose to a sitting position. It came to him what his protector had said. Antibiotics—medication—out of the pod.

He reached for the control box, and raised his miserable body from the cot, positioning himself for entry into the chair. Eventually, he was sitting in his chariot, but not without banging his right knee once more. The pain in his knee started hammering at his senses then suddenly shifted to his head. The knee was painless now, but his head was pounding. Involuntarily, he brought his hands to his head, trying to stem the brightly-colored agony in his pulsating brain. As suddenly as it had started, the pain left his head when a loud, demanding voice entered his mind.

Danger! Something is coming for you! It draws near each day!

A dull pain entered his right knee again, but at a tolerable level.

What in the hell was that all about? Who in the hell was that?

Afraid now, he reached under the pillow on the cot and retrieved the .45. He looked around the room, releasing the safety he had put on the night before but saw nothing. There was nobody.

Was there someone out in the corridor?

He wheeled over to the door and listened. After a careful moment he pushed through, reaching for the gun as soon as he was out of the room. The corridor was vacant. He looked both ways, but found only emptiness. Rolling soundlessly up to the nursing station, he peered around the corner. He found nothing, and then realized that nobody had spoken at all.

It had been a voice inside his head! But—that was impossible!

He had heard of mental telepathy before, had actually participated in a school group. Nothing had come from it. Some of the kids had made lucky guesses, but that was all. ESP, precognition and telekinesis, they had tried them all. It had included paranormal psychological phenomena and psycho kinesis. What had happened to him had been something like telepathy and precognition together. Then a thought came unbidden to his mind.

Maybe I will have powers I never had before. There is no way of telling until I try!

Until you try! The words rang in his head. He put all thought in the back of his mind then concentrated on the rumbling in his stomach. "What I'm going to try now is some of that peanut butter I saw at the nursing station. I loved it when I was a kid; let's see how it is now."

Completely forgetting the mind warning he just received, he reached in and found a jar. Twisting the top off, he sniffed the contents. "MMM, sure smells good!" he crooned. He dipped a finger in and tasted it. "Oh, it still tastes the same. Now, if I only had some bread."

Then he remembered the freezer that was stocked with pastries and bread. He opened the door and pulled out a loaf, but it was frozen solid. He thought it would take some time to thaw out.

This decided, he went back into the washroom and shaved. With only cold water, it was torture. He thought he had endured the worst until he splashed on the after shave. He looked into the mirror when the tears finally left his eyes. Some semblance of recognition came to him, but he would have to get used to this new face.

He replaced the towel in the holder at the side of the sink, then thought of finding the library and gymnasium. He knew he had to start walking soon, even if it was some kind of shuffle. Pulling the sheet from the cot, he draped it over his body and legs, subconsciously concealing the .45. He didn't know if he had ever been a prude, but he sure hadn't been lately.

He found a roll of skin-sensitive tape and secured the wires at his ankles, then promptly forgot about them. He had remembered his doctor's words, though, and didn't want the wires getting snagged on anything when he started his therapy. He also took the bandage he had fabricated with part of a sheet from his wrist and applied an adhesive bandage. He decided against the medication.

Once out in the corridor, he turned right and began looking at the signs on the doors. Recreation room — Arts and Crafts. More patient doors, some open. He glanced in at these and felt relieved that they were empty. The closed doors all had odors coming from them, so he didn't even slow down. Nine doors down from the nursing station he found the gym. The library was right across from it.

Stephen pushed in to the gym, checking for foul odors. He looked around when he was inside, marveling at the most complete set of gymnastic equipment he had ever seen. He saw what he wanted and wheeled over to it. It was designed for people in wheelchairs. Two hoops were hanging down, attached to ropes that were then attached to a tripod affair over a padded bench. At the end of the bench there were two leg holders, and these holders had adjustable brackets. The holders were attached to cables that ran over pulleys, up across the frame and down again to two steel weights. The user simply inserted his (or her) legs into the holders and pulled down, raising the weights. Simple, if the user had legs to stand on.

He knew his right leg wouldn't hold him, but he didn't know for sure about his left leg. He lifted his left leg from the footrest and sat it on the floor. Next, he grasped the hoops and tested his arms. They were getting stronger, and the pain had lessened considerably.

He hated to do it, but he thrust the .45 behind him and grabbed the hoops, putting some weight on the left leg. The pain was there but manageable. He sat down again and lifted his right leg to the floor, keeping his left hand under the knee. There was a slight tingling as his foot touched the floor, but little pain.

Hoisting himself up, he experienced more pain when he put full pressure on his left leg. It was at a tolerable level, but he rested there for a moment before going on. The pain subsided, and he hoped it was only the stiff knee joint complaining over lack of use. The right knee was quite another matter, and when he began to straighten the leg, his knee protested vigorously. He kept it coming, however, and soon had it resting on the floor. All of his weight was now on his left leg, and he swung his body over to the bench, pivoting to sit on it.

Letting go of the hoops, he grasped his right leg and pulled it up. The pain in his right knee was only a dull throb now, and he squirmed down the bench. With his legs in the holders, he sat up to adjust the straps, and then let his upper body fall back to the bench.

"Now for the moment of truth," he said to the ceiling.

He flexed his left leg, and watched as the cables moved, lifting the weights considerably. His right leg moved involuntarily, the movement of his left leg pulling it down. He knew pain then, but he also knew that he must keep on exercising this bad limb. Stephen stayed on the bench, pulling and lifting, lifting and pulling until he was almost exhausted.

At first, it was sheer torture to move his right knee, but gradually the pain lessened. When he finally stopped to rest, he found that his body was soaking wet. But now there was only a slight tingle in his right knee, and the pain had all but disappeared in his left knee.

He disconnected the clasps on the leg holders, sliding them up and away. He pulled his knees up to his body and sat up, swinging his legs over the side of the bench. As his left leg descended to the floor, he experienced a slight giddiness. He passed it off as excitement, and took the weight of his body on his left leg, slowly and experimentally. When he tried putting weight on his right leg he cried out in pain.

"Okay," he groaned, "I hear you. You don't like it yet, but you will!"

His right leg wouldn't take his weight yet, but it seemed that his left leg would. This meant that he could walk if he used the crutches.

Showing disdain for the hoops, he stood on his good leg and pulled the wheelchair over to him, gratefully sitting down. He thanked his Maker for allowing him to walk again, and special thanks went out to his doctor/protector.

I couldn't have done it without you, friend. Without the pod and vibrator, without your insight.

Tears came to his eyes then, and soon he was crying unashamedly. Crying for his protector, for himself—and for the world. When his eyes cleared, he wheeled out of the gym, the .45 safely out of sight under the sheet again. He wheeled across the corridor and into the library, stopping dead in his tracks when he saw the television set.

His doctor/protector was speaking on it, as he had been when Stephen had been in the pod. This thought made him realize he didn't like his name. He didn't care for "Stephen." Then he remembered the clipping. That police chief had called him Steve, and that was what he would think of himself from now on.

He had seen a VCR before; the school had borrowed one on several occasions to show science films but had never purchased their own. The screen went snowy, and he watched as the tape rewound itself. He wheeled over and found the button that would shut off the rewind. He removed the cassette and vowed he would treasure it for the rest of his days. He found the *power off* button and shut both machines down.

He was planning to look for books on different subjects, but decided to have something to eat first. After all, he had plenty of time to investigate the library. He returned to the washroom and picked up the jar of peanut butter, taking it back to the nursing station. The bread had thawed a little, so he spread the gooey stuff on a slice and enjoyed his first lunch.

He wanted some coffee, had wanted some for quite a while and decided to pull the plug on the fridge before he turned on the stove. He found the coffeepot and filled it with water from the bathroom. The lights weren't on now, and neither was the fridge so he had no way of telling how much the *invisible pump* had drawn on the power.

He spilled some of the water on the way back to the nursing station, but decided this to be a minor inconvenience. He found the coffee and spooned some into the aluminum basket. Turning the stove on, he set the pot on to *cook*. While he waited, he searched for milk but found none. He looked for canned milk, pawing through the canned goods, but was unsuccessful. He found a jar of something called *"Coffee Companion"* and read the directions. "Well—well," he beamed. "Technology."

When the amber liquid bubbled up into the small glass top, he guessed that it was almost ready. He found a cup and pulled the pot from the stove, immediately learning another lesson. He dropped the pot back to the stove, sucking on his finger. Looking around, he found an oven mitt and tried it again; he would be a little more careful in the future.

Trying the powdered creamer experimentally, he finally had his first cup of coffee in over five months. He sipped at it, savoring the brew, and thought of the crutches. When he finished the coffee, he wheeled over to the crutches, leaving the gun and sheet on the chair as he stood on his good leg.

He tested the crutches, getting the *feel* of them. The first step he tried to take almost put him on the floor, but he experimented with them until he felt good enough to go for a *stroll*. When Steve thought he had mastered the crutches enough, he used them to go to the library, pushing the wheelchair along in front of him. When he arrived there, he rested. It was harder than he'd thought it would be.

When he felt refreshed, he moved into the library and selected some videotapes and books. He piled them into the wheelchair and pushed over to the television set. Popping in a tape, he turned the machines on and watched the screen light up. He removed his treasures from the wheelchair, putting them on a reading desk and gratefully sat in the chair.

He watched videotapes all day, learning more and more, exercising his knees as he sat. Finally he rose to his feet—making sure that he could—and crutched over to the machines. He pulled the last tape and sat it on the desk with his other choices, and then shut the television and the player off. The tapes were all left on the desk, but he took the books with him, crutching and pushing back to the washroom.

Steve felt a strange sensation. He knew without a doubt that he had to use the toilet. He was a little apprehensive, but he crutched in and found out that all of his plumbing was working. He had been a little worried about this, but was elated when it had finally happened. He finished the paper work, pulling tissue from a new roll and wondered if this was more of the doctor's work.

He used the wheelchair when he left the stall to get to the sink. He washed his hands, and then wheeled to the nursing station. He replaced the sheet over him and the .45, deciding it was time to get some clothes on. He had been moving around like an animal, and his rear end was sore. He definitely needed some padding.

Steve stood up and pawed through the clothing he had put on the desk, choosing the smallest pair of pants there. Gingerly, he put the right leg in first and sat down to pull the left leg through. The pants were too big, but would suffice. Next he decided that what he needed was a belt, and some shoes and socks. Steve stood again and tried one of the shirts. It wrapped around him like a shawl, but would serve its purpose. Later, when he could get around, he would go on a *shopping* trip. He thrust the .45 in the waist of the pants, taking up some of the slack. The shirt he left out, covering the gun effectively. He still didn't understand this furtive obsession.

The pants were made of a harsh blue material, the shirt a uniform type and it seemed to be comfortable to him. Quite possibly he had worn this type of shirt before, but that had been in another time. Another life. But he did like the two pockets.

In the wheelchair again, he rolled in to the bathroom and retrieved his flashlight, then tooled down the hall and into the pod room. It wasn't dark yet, so he left the lights off. At the rear of the clothes closet, on the floor, he found some shoes. There were some socks on a shelf just above the floor. Steve almost fell out of the chair picking out what he thought would fit, but caught himself and backed out with his possessions.

When he tried them on, the socks felt soft and wonderful. The shoes were a little big, but comfortable. They looked like shoes, but were padded and came up to his ankle. There was a name on them that he didn't recognize, and a lightning bolt logo emblazoned on the backs of them. Except for his right knee, he was now ready for the world.

In this much elevated state of mind, Steve returned to his cot. He rested on the cot, picking up one of the books. He fell asleep reading it, and was awakened sometime in the night with a pounding headache.

It is much closer now, and you will have to fight it to survive. It has a terrible anguish and fights to live, but wishes to die. Beware!

Again, another message, another blinding headache. What in hell was doing this? What was coming for him? Why him?

As Steve mulled this over, another drama was unfolding just three miles away.

The old man walked out of the dark alley, and it granted the old man's fondest wish. It tore the old man's throat out with long claws that had once been carefully manicured fingers, and then fed on the corpse, not caring about the stench. It must eat to survive, and must kill to eat, and so, it killed.

All of the old ones wished to die. It wanted to die as well, but also had to preserve its existence at all costs. If it were not already insane, this thought alone would have made it so. It gorged itself, caring only for the pain in its stomach to ease, but there was no way to ease the agonizing white-pain in its head.

CHAPTER FIVE

In the days that followed, Steve read many books on many different subjects and watched many videos. He exercised his right leg until he could not only stand on it, but could walk on it as well, slowly at first, but he was definitely mobile again. He still never went any place without his .45.

One morning, he awoke and decided he was ready for a little excursion. He hadn't tried walking up or down stairs yet, but today he was going to try. He had to get to the first floor nursing station, had to go down to the basement, had to go out into the city and find some new clothes. He had many wants, and now he was going to find out if he was equal to the task.

He tested his legs as he slipped them over the side of the cot. He always had some discomfort first thing in the morning, but after about twenty steps it went away. He found very little pain today, and padded to the toilet. He washed up when he finished and slipped his clothes on, tucking the .45 into the waistband of his pants.

He had started taking pastries out of the freezer when he retired at night, and this was what he had for breakfast every morning. The coffeepot was always fixed the night before, so all he had to do was to pull the fridge plug and turn the stove on. He had a second cup of coffee and made his plans for the day.

His first objective was the first floor nursing station. He took the cane and the flashlight, making some peanut butter sandwiches to take with him. These he rolled in a jacket and he was off. The elevator door was wide open, but he didn't think this would work as there were no lights on.

He found the stairs and started down, and it was then that he found out the difference between walking on the level and negotiating stairs. Walking was one thing, but steps were quite another. As he placed his left foot on the first step, he received a sharp pain in his right knee, and quickly brought his right foot down. A surprised look came on his face, and after that he took one step at a time. It was slower going, but there was no pain. He thought that perhaps later he would be able to walk normally on stairs, but not right now.

He opened the door cautiously when he reached the bottom of the stairs, peering around the edge of the door casing. Finding silence and no movement, he edged through and into the corridor. This was the main floor, and it was a little different from the second floor, but he still had to turn right to get to the nursing station; he could see it down the hall.

Putting his hand on a railing, Steve walked towards his objective. He didn't want to see death, but felt he had no choice in the matter. As he neared the nursing station, he smelled something pungent. It was a sickly sweet smell, and his olfactory senses identified it. Steve was about to meet his doctor!

The body was sitting in an easy chair, the arms flung wide. On the floor in front of the body was a shotgun. His doctor/protector had taken the quick way out, but it had been messy. The ceiling had been splattered with his doctor/protector's diseased brain.

Steve was saddened that a good friend and a great mind were gone. Then he noticed a sheet of paper on the desk, weighted down with a box of twelve gauge shells. He picked the paper up and started to read a message that had been typed over three months before.

"Welcome, Stephen," the words read. "Glad you made it. I don't suppose I look too good right now, but death is better than total insanity. Besides, the body is nothing. It's the soul that is all-important. It is my fondest hope that wherever I am going will be a much better world than this one. At least that is my belief."

Steve had to stop and wipe his eyes. The pain he read between the lines threatened to engulf him.

"I have only one thing to ask of you, and that is that you cremate my remains. This chair is on casters, and if you wheel it out through the main doors you can safely incinerate it. If you had not been here, I would have burned this whole building to the ground. You will find a two gallon can of gasoline just inside the main doors, and some matches as well."

"My name is on the tag pinned to my lapel. Say a prayer for me, Stephen, for the whole world if you want to. I fear it is all gone now, or soon will be. So, hello Stephen, and farewell."

Steve had a hard time reading the last words, his eyes blurring from the stinging in his nose. Tears coursed down his cheeks, but he was not ashamed of them. He wiped his eyes and nose on his shirt sleeve, and looked up at the corpse, realizing that the top of the head was almost gone. He supposed his own head had looked a little like that.

"For a little man," Steve muttered, "you sure had a lot of guts! I only hope I have even a small spark of your courage."

He read the name tag, and a smile tugged at the corners of his mouth. Doctor Henry (Hank) Gibson. Steve would remember this man as long as he lived, but would only remember him as *Hank*.

Steve walked around the desk, then picked up the shotgun, placing it on the desk beside the shells. It was a pump model, and he tried it, not surprised when a new shell entered the chamber. He envisioned Hank putting the barrel into his mouth and pulling the trigger. He didn't think that he himself could have done it, no matter what.

I hope I never have to find out, Hank.

Steve left everything on the desk except his .45 then walked around the chair. He started pushing the grisly load, heading towards the reception area. He made a left turn there when he saw the doors to the parking lot.

The gas can was where the note said it would be, and a carton of matches lay beside it. Steve stopped and unbolted the doors, opening them to the world. With the doors propped open, he pushed the chair outside, bumping over the small ledge of concrete that held the door casing. Once outside he looked for a suitable spot to grant a friend's last request.

To the left of the parking lot stood a flowerbed, with a red brick sidewalk flowing up to it. Steve noticed the heat as he pushed the chair, a living thing that tried to suck the very blood from his body. The flowers were all dead, as was the grass, and the sky looked strange and free of clouds. By the looks of things, it hadn't rained in a long time.

Steve pushed the chair to the burned-out flowerbed then returned for the gas and the matches. Dousing the figure and the chair with the highly flammable liquid, he stood back and lit a match.

Goodbye, old friend.

He threw the match, and the gasoline erupted with a *whump*, instantly turning the chair and corpse into a blazing pyre. He whispered a childhood prayer, and watched as the flames consumed both chair and occupant. It was a bright sunny day, as he would find all the days to be, but he endured the heat until the fire had burned itself out. He heard the hissing and crackling as it burned, but he tried to put it out of his mind.

Steve went back inside, breathing a small sigh of relief to be out of the glare of the sun. He wandered around the floor, up and down the corridor until his legs felt like lumps of mud, then sat down in the reception area. He thought he could still smell the corpse, but decided it was just his imagination.

The thought struck him then that the fire might have attracted something, so he returned to the doors and locked them. Retracing his steps, he returned to the chair and sat down, trying not to think but it was useless. He had to do something to take his mind from the flames, he knew, but what?

And then he knew. He would go to the basement. *But how? Where was the door?* Then he saw a door behind the information desk. He opened the door and saw only a broom closet, and then wondered if the stairs were back at the elevator. He retraced the route he had first taken, and found what he was looking for.

BASEMENT—NO ADMITTANCE

When he opened the door, a roar greeted him. He jumped back, his heart thumping wildly, and then he remembered that this was where the generator was. Steve waited until his heart slowed, and then he proceeded into the bowels of the hospital. The steps seemed to go on forever, but finally he was at the bottom.

A light gleamed dully to his left, but to his right all was in darkness. Steve moved towards the lighted area, and finally knew where his power was coming from. He thought he had heard a *pom-pom* noise when he opened the outer doors, but hadn't been sure. This was what he must have heard.

The din was too much for him, prompting him to go back to the main floor. He found that he could navigate the stairs normally; there was no pain in his knee when he walked up the stairs, his knee only pained when he walked down. He reached the top and closed the door behind him, shutting off the terrible noise. He would not go down there again, there was no need to.

Returning to the nursing station, Steve picked up his belongings, intending to go back to his quarters. It was too late to go out in search of clothes now; he would wait until tomorrow. With the barrel of the shotgun stuck through the jacket/knapsack, he picked up the box of shells and headedfor the stairs. He remembered the typed note and returned for it. After all, the last will and testament of Doctor Henry Gibson should not be forgotten.

Later that day, he checked out the shotgun, ensuring that the gun was fully loaded again. He pushed the safety on and put the gun on the desk, covering it with the extra clothing that was still there.

Steve watched some more instructional video, paying particular attention to the more important themes. He thought the video on weaponry was very interesting, showing different types of hand guns and automatic weapons. Something about them seemed vaguely familiar, but it was a fleeting and intangible sensation. A quick flash in his mind, then gone again.

That day he learned something about welding, carpentry, plumbing and electronics. Even how to drive a school bus, but he didn't think that particular occupation would ever be used again. Everything was on video, but there were books on those subjects as well. He would keep the tapes and books on practical subjects, as well as several *"HOW TO"* books he had come across. He had to begin living again, and he had to have some kind of teacher.

It was an easy task to prepare supper; canned meat on bread, followed by a can of cherries. He was starting to settle into a routine, but that was going to change—sooner than he expected. That night he fell asleep reading about gardening.

CHAPTER SIX

It touched the hot metal, its ruined fingers tracing the silver letters. It did not know what the letters meant, did not, in fact, even remember letters. But it knew what this thing was. But this one was quiet, not like the one that had roared at him

It watched from behind the white car as Steve pushed his burden out of the hospital. It had been frightened when the flames erupted, and had huddled on the blacktop of the parking lot. It had been terrified of the all-consuming flames that had belched from the ground.

There was a time when it had almost been burned alive, but that had been a long time ago. It had escaped when a wildly careening machine had thundered down on its attackers. It was something like the one it was hiding behind, but had made a terrible noise when it had smashed into its enemies.

The fire was almost out when the thing that had once been a man peered out from under the bumper of the car. It saw that the man's back was turned away from it, and it scampered across the blacktop on all fours, racing into the building and hiding behind a couch in the reception area. It knew there was food in there, could smell it all around him. It also knew that the man would have sweet, red juices flowing through his body. When the man sat down over its hiding place it had almost attacked, but instinct had stopped it.

CHAPTER SEVEN

Steve awoke in the morning, his bladder crying out for relief. He used the toilet and felt immediately better. *Make your bladder gladder.* Now where had he got that from? Oh, well, he might remember later where he had heard it. Maybe he'd read it in one of the books.

He felt alive and refreshed after a good night's sleep, even after the headache and the voices that had woken him in the night. He was at a loss to explain what was causing the voices, but he hoped they would soon go away.

He put it out of his mind, and then decided that today he was going to learn about mechanical things. He would need to know something about cars and machinery if he was going to be able to get around.

He had his usual breakfast, taking a cup of coffee down to the library. He watched a video called *Mechanic Man* as he sipped from the cup, learning all sorts of things he thought he would never need. If a vehicle developed a problem of some kind, he would simply choose another one. The world was his storehouse, Hank had said.

He had the overwhelming urge to see the weaponry video again. He gave in to the desire and popped the tape in.

Why am I so damned obsessed with weapons? Hasn't there been enough killing?

Steve settled down and watched it again. He thought there was enough fire- power in that video to satisfy an army. Automatic rifles, grenades, and a large gun with a sight that just couldn't miss. There was a special section on handguns, and his .45 was featured.

After pulling the tape, he shut the machines off and headed for the gym. He toiled with his right leg, stretching and pulling until the pain stopped him. This was the only area he had a problem with now, but he felt it was getting better.

When he left the gym, Steve thought he saw movement out of the corner of his eye. He thought he had seen something down by the nursing station, but when he looked he could see nothing. "You're getting jumpy, old man," he said aloud. "There's nothing but shadows and memories in here."

Curious, and slightly apprehensive, Steve pulled the .45 from his waist and moved down to the nursing station, checking his belongings out when he got there. Everything was as it had been, nothing had been moved. He thought he smelled something, but decided it was only his imagination.

He turned to look back towards the gym, and a sound froze the blood in his veins! A low, menacing, animal growl sounded behind him, and he couldn't move. He had seen something after all, he knew that now, but it hadn't been at the nursing station. It had been in the room *past* the nursing station. Steve turned slowly, not wanting to startle whatever it was. As his head came around, his eyes picked out an apparition he just couldn't believe! His mind balked at what his eyes were looking at!

The growling was coming from a man, or what had once been a man. The clothes were all in tatters, dirty and blood caked. Mixed with the blood and dirt there was something else he didn't even want to guess at. This, then, was the odor he had smelled.

Steve was turned fully around now, facing this caricature of a man. He raised the .45 in his hand, but couldn't bring himself to shoot. This poor creature in front of him was a man, even if he looked and smelled like an animal. The man advanced on him, crouching, but still he didn't shoot. His hesitation almost killed him.

The crazed, crouching figure leaped, saliva drooling from the opened jaws, the man's long nails reaching for his throat. Steve was knocked to the floor, sending the .45 spinning through the air. The gun hit the floor and went sliding down the hallway. The wild man's leap carried him over Steve's body, bouncing the bedraggled torso off of the wall. But the creature was instantly on its feet, coming after him again.

Steve withdrew until his back was against the desk. He remembered the shotgun, and reached under the discarded clothes, but couldn't find it. He realized it was closer to the center of the desk, and inched along, praying he had time. His hand felt the etched butt and he grabbed the gun, then lurched away.

The thing that attacked him was advancing again, and Steve knew he had no choice. He would have to kill this yesterday man or be killed himself. He released the safety and waited. The madman leaped at him, and Steve pulled the trigger!

A bright crimson balloon burst against the far wall, splattering the peaceful blue surroundings. The noise of the blast was deafening, and Steve found himself on the floor again. The thing's momentum had been enough to reach him, and it had knocked him down, its blood pumping out of the headless torso.

Steve pushed the dead man away from his blood-drenched body and stood up. He leaned against the wall, trying to calm his shaking hands and screaming nerves. When his heart slowed to less than racing, he wiped his eyes and surveyed the carnage. His stomach threatened to erupt, but with a supreme effort he held it in check and walked to retrieve the .45.

He would never come that close to death again, at least not in this place. He would leave in the morning, carrying everything he could with him. Whatever happened to him from now on, he would not hesitate again. He would use the guns if he were ever threatened.

He had noticed a pick-up in the parking lot, and with his new knowledge it would be relatively simple to *hot wire* it. He had thought of taking the white car parked next to it, but the truck would serve his needs better. Once away from here he would look for a new truck, one that had keys. It was still early enough to leave right away, but he didn't want to get caught in the dark this close to the city. He would clean up today and check out the truck, and then leave in the morning.

He pulled the fridge plug and went in to the bathroom to clean up. He threw the clothes away and came back to the desk. Sifting through the clothes he had put there, he found another pair of pants and a shirt. They were bigger than the bloodied, discarded clothes, but would have to do until he could get some new things. Using the butcher knife, he cut a strip from the jacket and tied it to the belt loops, pulling the pants together. The shirt he left out of the pants, covering the .45 he had retrieved. With the shotgun wiped off, he thrust it under his arm and headed for the stairs. He remembered the tools and came back for them. He knew they would be needed in the parking lot.

Once out in the parking lot he opened the hood and looked into the engine compartment of the truck. According to the video, he would need a wire to go from the coil to the battery. But where was he going to get the wire? And then his eyes locked on to the white car, baking in the impossible sun. He smashed the side window on the expensive car with the hammer, and then opened the door. He was sure the owner wouldn't mind and pulled the hood release. He cut a length of wire from the car and returned to the truck. He ran the wire from the battery to the coil, and that was supposed to give him ignition. Then, using two screwdrivers he crossed the solenoid with them. The motor turned over, but wouldn't start. Steve grasped the linkage on the carburetor and pumped the gas. When he tried it again, the engine roared to life.

How long? How in the hell long has this truck been sitting here? It couldn't have been too awfully long, because the battery has really turned the engine over quickly.

Steve went to the driver's door of the truck and smashed the window in with his hammer. Then he walked around the whole truck, checking for more *crazies*. If there were any more around like the one he had shot, he'd better have more firepower than what he had. The shotgun was excellent for in close, but he'd just as soon not let anything get near enough for him to have to use it.

Steve sat in the seat and kicked the gas pedal sharply, letting the engine throttle down to a slow idle. The person who owned this truck had taken the trouble to install gauges, he saw, and had disconnected the red *"idiot"* lights he had seen depicted in the book. After he scanned all of these, his eyes went to the fuel gauge. The truck's fuel tank was almost full, but he wouldn't be using all of it. He would find a new truck, and then he would get away from this part of the country.

He got out of the truck and checked the immediate area again, then picked up the shotgun and laid it across the seat. "Too bad I don't have a set of keys for you, old girl," he said to the steering wheel, "but maybe I can have second best."

Why is it so hot? Could this be the reason for all of the insanity? Could this be why the world went mad? Constant sun all day long?

He revised his thoughts. The sun always went down at dusk. This would have given everybody some respite from the abominable and terrible heat. There was something about a layer of gas that protected the earth from the ultra violet rays of the sun—he remembered from a video—but the name escaped him.

He worked well into the afternoon, cutting wires from the white car and wiring them into the truck. When he was finished, all of the ignition wires had been extended into the truck. Steve had fixed two sets of double strand wires. All he had to do was connect the two on the left, and he had ignition. When the two wires on the right were touched together, it would cause the engine to turn over. He must remember to hold these two wires by their protective coating, and not to hold them together too long or he would burn his fingers. He remembered something the video had shown him, and he quickly looked at the ignition switch. He breathed a sigh of relief when he saw what he had been looking for.

"Good thing you're an older lady," he said, as he lovingly patted the steering wheel. "You don't have a locking steering wheel." He was thinking out loud more often now, but even his voice was better than no voice.

The truck had a radio and cassette player, and with a trembling hand he turned the radio on. He got what he expected to get; the airwaves were dead. He picked up a tape and pushed it in, immediately regretting the action. His eardrums were almost destroyed when an inhumane screech came out of the unseen speakers, and he quickly killed the sound.

What in the hell was that? No wonder the world was gone; if this was any indication of the music they had been listening to. If, indeed, that's what it had been.

He stepped out of the truck and pushed his tools under the seat then reached across and retrieved the shotgun. He returned to the second floor and tried to decide what he was going to take. He remembered that he had left the fridge unplugged, but he wouldn't need it anymore. He hauled all of the canned goods that he could, loading them in the ruined jacket. When he had everything he wanted, he went back to the second floor once more, and took some things from the freezer. He took only what he could use up quickly, for he knew that they would rapidly spoil once thawed.

He took the half-used loaf of bread and all of the utensils. He remembered that he didn't have a knife, but the knife he had used when he wired the truck would suit his purposes quite nicely until he could get a good one. Although he didn't realize it, he still had a thing for a pocketknife.

He left then, trying not to look at the bloody mess in the hall, but couldn't help himself. He hadn't wanted to kill that poor creature, but he hadn't had any other choice.

Going down the stairs, he drew his .45 and advanced slowly. If something—or some thing had gotten in—and found the shotgun that he had left beside the couch, he would be prepared. Never again would he disregard the precognition he seemed to have inherited.

He sprawled on the couch that night, the shotgun beside him on the floor. The .45 he kept in his hand and the flashlight was within easy reach. He knew he wouldn't sleep, but he closed his eyes for a moment. When he opened his eyes again, it was morning.

Surprised, he rolled off of the couch and picked up his gun; the .45 had fallen out of his hand when he had fallen asleep. He unbolted the main doors, and returned to eat some of the pastries he had taken from the freezer.

This finished, he went out to the parking lot and brought the truck up to the doors. He had to drive over the long-uncut and dead lawn in order to bypass the card-operated exit barrier, but he didn't think anyone would protest. "A little levity there, Hank," he said aloud as he pulled up to the doors.

He labored then, loading all of his possessions into the truck. He looked over at the burned remnants and saluted when he was finished, bringing his hand up to the side of his head. "I'll never forget you, old friend." he murmured."

With the butt of the shotgun on the floor, and the barrel resting against the seat, he climbed into the cab. When he sat down, the .45 dug into his body, prompting him to pull it out and lay it on the seat. With a last look and a wave, he pulled the truck in gear and drove away.

He didn't know where he was going yet, but his first stop was definitely going to be a clothing store. After that, he would look around for another vehicle and some heavier weapons. When those items had been attended to, he would decide what he wanted to do, and where he wanted to go.

Steve didn't know it, but it had already been decided where he was going, and what he was going to do. And it would be done in such a way that Steve would think it had been his own idea.

CHAPTER EIGHT

Has the beacon been arranged? the thought boomed.
Yes, Commander! came the answering hue.
Has the man moved yet?
He is moving now, sir!
And does the man seek weapons?
And apparel, sir. He thinks clothing a priority.
Maybe there is hope yet, the thought waves transmitted. *Perhaps this one will be our salvation. We will direct this one to the war ship and see if he proves to be capable. Do you understand?*
Yes, Commander! the thought returned.
Keep in mind, Captain, the thought continued, *that we are responsible for the catastrophe that has caused this world to go mad.*

They had experimented with time, and, inadvertently, had caused the protective ozone layer of the planet to suddenly *disappear* for an instant. This *instant* had been all it had taken to make the blood boil in men's minds as the ultra violet rays of the sun had shone through. Unprotected, the lucky had died instantly. But what had caused the most damage were the horrendous objects that had been drawn back with the crippled ozone layer. These objects were what had caused global insanity, and even the aliens who had caused this problem had not been able to devise a plan to rectify the wrong. There had been some who had been unaffected, and The Co-Existent Planetary Commission had ordered the offending nation to undo what they had done, and to start the sane beings back to some semblance of normal life. Failing this, they would be banished, relegated to a nomadic existence in another solar system.

There are others of this man's beliefs?

Yes, Commander, the captain answered. *We know of several groups that have escaped with their minds intact. Some are warlike, but there are many that wish only to live out their lives in peace. We learn of more every day, but not all are gracious. In some cases, a great distance separates many of them*

Listen well, Captain, the commander directed. *We will protect the peaceful ones as much as we are able, and guide them with thought. Does the man still transmit his thoughts to this woman?*

Yes, Commander, but he is unaware that he does so. And his thoughts cause the woman much agony. He has projected to her what he does, but not his location or what his features are.

We will direct him to her. You will monitor the thought waves and soften them before they enter the woman's mind. She will still know pain, but at a lower level.

Yes, Commander, the captain agreed. *What are we to do if the antagonistic ones attempt to do the woman and her family harm? Even as our thoughts speak, they are being watched!*

In that event, the commander directed, *you will temporarily cause their minds to be "simple" for a time. Do not interfere otherwise, for that would surely doom our race to perpetual wanderings. In any event, the woman must not be harmed.*

Yes, Commander! the answer was instant. *I will issue the proper orders.*

No words were spoken. The communication between the two beings had been accomplished by thought transference. The Commander turned his thoughts inward so none could *hear* him.

If they had not attempted the time theory, this would not have happened. Their technology had grown too sophisticated, and they had been lulled into a false sense of well being.

They had thought that they could repair any and all damages they wrought. How sad it was when they had almost destroyed a whole race. A planet that teemed with life was now reduced to a precious few, and the outcome was still uncertain. All the hopes of his race now hinged on a plan of survival for the unfortunate beings of this ruined world. And all of his dreams were pinned on one being, who had only a short while ago "awakened!"

His was a simple plan. Find some beings who were spared the awful devastation, and start them back to the civilization and culture they had once enjoyed. It would be a gigantic undertaking, even by their standards, but it must be accomplished. But before this could begin, they had a greater problem to solve.

The unwanted—and potentially lethal gases that now ringed the planet—must be disposed of, and this must be accomplished in such a way as to not damage the ozone layer further. This problem was insurmountable, but they must do it. And even though it might cost the powerful one—who had only just awakened—his life, it must be attempted. They had exhausted all other avenues, and now had no other options. It was an unpretentious procedure, and only their old nemesis would decide it.

TIME!

CHAPTER NINE

Steve pulled out onto the street with mixed emotions. He was elated to be finally doing something on a positive note, but at the same time he felt sadness creep into his soul. It was mind-boggling that there were no people living in all of the buildings he was passing.

The street was getting cluttered with burned out and wrecked vehicles, but he was able to pilot the truck around them. There was no indication of any stores yet, but he would keep going. Strange name for a street, he thought as he read the street sign. North Druid Hills Road. He drove under an overpass, finding more and more derelict cars and trucks. It appeared to him like some giant had tossed his toys around in a fit of anger.

Ten minutes later, he came to a shopping complex. He wheeled in, dodging the abandoned and destroyed vehicles. He pulled into the fire lane, and then shut the engine off by pulling the ignition wires apart. If there were any more crazies around, they would be here. He grabbed the shotgun as he got out of the truck.

It was deathly quiet, so he eased the door shut; it wouldn't be a good idea to advertise his presence. As he walked towards the main entrance, many eyes followed his progress. Although he looked left and right he could see nothing moving, but he stopped dead when a voice boomed in his brain!

"You are not alone here!"

As if to lend credence to the voice, a disheveled old man appeared, followed by four other yesterday human beings. Steve shot into the air and immediately pumped another round into the chamber. He didn't want to kill these dregs of humanity; there had been enough killing and death. He would kill only as a last resort. He didn't know how prophetic his thoughts were. He had been thinking about weapons ever since he'd watched the videos. There was a chance he could be overpowered by sheer numbers, and his shotgun and .45 would not be sufficient then.

The five almost humans disappeared back into the complex, scattering in all directions. He knew that he would have to be very careful in there, and trust in his new found powers religiously. He'd thought at first that the voices in his head were a result of his head injuries, but now he knew otherwise.

The sign over the complex read: L—NN-X SH-P—-CE-T-R. Some of the letters were missing, the plastic on the hitherto lighted sign broken out. This complex boasted that it had more than four hundred stores, so he should have no trouble getting what he wanted here, except maybe the armament that he felt necessary for survival.

He entered the huge establishment carefully, looking both ways. Broken glass lay everywhere, and decaying bodies were strewn as far as he could see. He thought it must have been a terrible way to die, because everything that a person could want was here for the taking, yet all they had wanted to do was kill each other.

He wondered again—for the hundredth time—what had caused the world to go mad. He had escaped it, but only because there was a steel plate covering his brain. He shuddered when he thought what he would have become if he had not been lucky enough to be sheltered. But maybe he would have been better off if he would have died in that damned holdup.

He looked both ways again, and decided to turn right. It seemed there were fewer bodies that way, and with all of these stores he should hit on what he wanted. He saw that all of the windows and doors had been smashed as he threaded his way down the body-strewn hall, and he stopped at one shop that displayed a white wedding gown when he saw that someone had described an *X* over the abdomen with red paint. Or was it blood?

Twenty stores later, he located a men's shop and found what he wanted. A shopping cart from some grocery store had been wedged into the window of the shop across the hall, and he loaded all of his *purchases* into this. Steve was selective, choosing practical rather than pretty. Boots, pants, shirts and belts. Socks and underwear went into the cart, as well as anything else that he thought he might need. He never tried any of it on, for he had been afraid to put the shotgun down.

He continued on down the hall, ever on the lookout for movement. Nothing moved, and the voice in his head remained silent, prompting him to let his guard down. He stopped to look at a new car display, amazed at the size of them. He remembered cars as being a thing of beauty, but these things looked ugly and small, unsafe vehicles that would likely crumble if they hit anything larger than a mosquito. He walked on when he saw the bones behind the cars

Steve shuddered; cold tendrils of fear creeping up his back. The hair at the nape of his neck stood straight out. He continued on, thankful to be away from that particular area. What a horrible end the world had come to.

Who had caused this terrible thing to happen to the human race? Could a world government have devised a weapon? A secret weapon, designed to wipe out mankind, while they lived in luxury on some south sea island, their every whim catered to? The Special Elite! Genocide perfected! The bastards!

Steve's imagination went wild; conjuring up all sorts of atrocities visited on a slave world. He shook off his foolish thoughts, and came away from the land of imagination to find half-men barring his way. They were snarling and snapping at each other, and he saw that they meant to kill him! Given a choice, he would have turned and fled, but when he turned he found more *new people* behind him. While he had been stupidly wool gathering, they had crept up on him. He raised the shotgun without conscious thought and fired into the *crazies* that barred his way back, destroying a large part of them. He pumped and fired again, tearing the life from the rest of the insane throng. He turned and fired at the group that confronted him, taking over half of them down. Then Steve watched in awe as the *leftover crazies* turned on their comrades, tearing at them with grotesque fingernails!

Tearing his shocked gaze away, he turned and fled, going back the way he had come. He pushed the buggy as fast as he could, veering around his *kill*, and when he chanced a look back he saw only animals, indulging in a grisly, cannibalistic act!

When he was back at the entrance, and safely out to the truck, he reloaded the shotgun. He vowed he would never be caught like that again; he would shoot at anything that dared move. But there was no movement anywhere, so he decided to chance laying his gun down long enough to change clothes. This he did with both guns lying on the hood within easy reach. When he had his new clothes on, he thought it strange how it made him feel so good.

The truck started easily, and without looking back he peeled out of the parking lot, steering around the ruined vehicles that seemed to be everywhere. Two hours later he came to Interstate 75 and headed north; at times steering around obstacles that were blocking the road.

He had planned to go south, so why had he turned north? Maybe he was subconsciously heading back to New York? Whatever the reason, he would turn around the first chance that presented itself.

He continued on north, passing more shopping plazas but was unable to get to them. He kept driving, and then he saw something that looked promising. The huge sign told him that this could be just what he wanted. He had come across a naval station and air force base. Steve thought if he couldn't find firearms and transportation here, then he'd never find any. He wheeled off of the northbound lane and entered the south bound, driving until he came to another highway. He cut cross-country with the truck, bouncing over anything that was small enough, going around others that were not. He almost missed the access road to his objective and had to back up to get to it.

He found the big steel gates locked when he arrived at the base, but the .45 made a great key, and soon he was driving on U.S. Government property. He wanted to find the armory, but the first thing he saw was the chaos that had struck. Everywhere he looked he saw death, the machines of murder strewn in all directions. Automatic weapons abounded, some with skeletal fingers still wrapped around their triggers, frozen there in death! He passed these all by, knowing he would find an arsenal inside the buildings. All of these weapons would be useless; he knew that all of the clips would be empty. His mind envisioned the battle that must have been fought.

An operations hut lay straight ahead, and Steve pulled up to it and killed the engine. The first thing that struck him when he stepped out of the truck was the silence.

Why was it so quiet? Why were there no birds? No insects? Had everything on earth been destroyed but him? And the heat!? Why was it so damnable hot?

It was maddening, the only interruption coming from the Truck's cooling engine, and after checking for movement he left the safety of the truck. The shotgun was pointed straight out in front of him in case he met up with some more *crazies*, but he found nothing to threaten him. He advanced cautiously, stepping carefully up the stairs and opened the door. He looked in, and then turned his face away.

The gag reflex was strong, but after swallowing several times he breathed deeply, drawing new air into his lungs. It seemed to work, for he didn't lose the contents of his stomach. He'd thought he would when he left the building; the carnage inside had been so devastating. Bits and pieces of men and women had been scattered around the room, making it look and smell like a slaughterhouse. A machete was still stuck in a rotting skull.

He negotiated the steps slowly when his stomach settled, still not sure of himself. To his left, he saw what looked like a hangar, but the doors didn't look as high as he had remembered hangar doors being.

When he had been barely a teenager—he suddenly remembered—his teacher had taken the whole class on a tour of the Yuma…The Yuma Air Station! He had been…going to school in…San Diego…California! He had been living in California, and going to school in San Diego! He had not been living in San Diego, but in a little town called…some valley. Spruce Valley? Not Spruce Valley. Pretty Valley? Yes, that was it! And he'd gone to school with some Indian and Mexican kids!

Putting this memory out of his mind—as much as he could—he walked to the hangar and found a side door. It was locked, so he tried his *special key*. The lock refused his efforts, and after he had used three rounds, with the lock still holding, he put the handgun back in his belt. A couple of rounds from the shotgun proved effective, and the lock fell apart.

Someone sure wanted this place closed up tight! What was so important to have a lock like that on it?

It was dark inside, the only light coming from the door he had just opened. There was an abundance of dark places in the building, and that meant that there were a lot of places to hide. Steve thought he'd better go get his flashlight; it was just too dark in there to suit him.

He returned with his light, but found the building's lights had turned on. He looked around, but could see nobody, then thought that he must have activated some kind of timer when he had opened the door, and then he stopped dead in his tracks. What he saw inside made his senses reel!

The big door had been opened before with a button, but there was a chain hanging down and he gave it a tug. The huge door moved a little, and he decided to open it more. If he would have just pushed the *up* button, he would have saved himself a lot of work, but he didn't know then that the whole place was *live*.

Setting the shotgun against the doorframe, he put both hands on the chain, holding the .45 in his right hand. The door moved, and soon it was part way up, flooding the interior with super-heated sunlight. He picked up the shotgun again and turned around. What met his gaze was even more intimidating in the sunlight than it had been in the glare of the electric lights.

The thing was huge, sunlight making it shine like an idea. He looked at the front of it and was enraptured. Steve whistled in appreciation, and thought that if ever there had been a weapon of destruction, this was surely it! He noted the armament on the front of the craft, and started around to the other side. There were more weapons there, and he thought that this machine had been designed either to start a war or to stop one.

Marveling at what he saw, Steve walked all around it. He looked for wheels of some kind but could see none. The walls of the thing came down to the floor, so they could be hidden, he decided, but there had to be a drive train of some kind. He tried to guess at its dimensions on the way around the strange craft. About fifty feet long, he judged, and about sixteen feet wide. The top of the invention swept up at the back, making the rear even higher than the front. He looked for a door but could find none. Not a fold or crease showed, and he had searched the hull from front to back. Steve put his hand on the side of the huge object, feeling cool metal and a slight vibration.

Damn—this thing is alive! But how in hell had the owners gotten into it? He retraced his steps, running his hand all along the sides of his discovery. Still, he could find no opening, nor evidence of one. When he returned to where he had started; finding nothing, he heard a beep and his hand was pushed away from the side.

A small panel had pushed his hand up, opening when he had run his hand over it. Inside the panel he saw two rows of buttons, and he wondered at their purpose. The first row was marked from zero to nine, and the second had only letters, running from A to E. He thought them a combination for something, but what?

Would this craft—or whatever it was—explode if the wrong buttons were depressed? Well, he was living on borrowed time anyway, so he thought he might as well find out. Maybe it was controlled from an external source, and there was no way to get into it.

Steve saw no windows on the machine, not even a windshield. This made him wonder how the thing had been operated. Taking a deep breath, he pushed a random combination of numbers and letters, and another panel lit up. A display showed him that he had guessed wrong, but at least he had not been blown up. Steve had not seen this display panel before, and now, as it winked out, the panel became invisible again. Try as he might, he could not see where it had been. The panel had read: *NO ENTRY*

He tried other combinations, but got the same *No Entry*. After countless tries, he gave up and walked around the machine again, and then noticed some letters on the front of the craft he had not seen before. Where there should have been a bumper, lights appeared. In these lights he now saw letters. The right side of the craft proclaimed the letters: *U.S.A.F.* The letters on the left side spelled out: *G.R.A.A.V.* In smaller letters, the message *prototype* came through.

Prototype! This vehicle, if that's what it is, was the only one made. There are no others like it. He had stumbled onto a weapon of some kind, a weapon that had been locked in here for God knew what reason, but he couldn't get into the damned thing!

Steve returned to the panel, determined now to find the correct combination, but after an hour of countless variations he was still no wiser. In exasperation, he slammed his hand against the panel. The same NO ENTRY came on again, but another message took its place.

ENTRY CODE ABORTED DEPRESS E-7 TO REPROGRAM

Steve's eyes lit up. This was more like it. He pressed E, and then 7, but nothing happened. Maybe he had to push them together. When he did this, the screen changed. It was not flashing now, and he got a READY message. He punched in five digits, all numbers, but still nothing happened. He watched as the READY returned to the screen, his numbers disappearing.

Now what? The screen had said to use E-7 to reprogram. Maybe I need seven digits. He punched in one to seven, and as an afterthought punched the letter E. The screen changed again, the letters ERR replacing his code. Steve used the E-7 again to return to the READY mode, and this time he punched in the numbers one through six, and then added the letter E. To his amazement, the screen changed yet again, and a *BEEP* sounded.

TO INITIATE DEPRESS C

Excited now, he pressed the letter "C" and the beeping stopped. The screen went blank, and six feet away a door started to open, the bottom rising and swinging out. As soon as the door reached that apex, a set of steps pushed out. It was at that moment that his head began to ache, and a voice boomed into his mind.

"Beware! Insanity looms at your back!"

The headache disappeared as quickly as it started, and Steve looked behind him. He had gotten careless again, had been so involved that he hadn't heard them tearing his truck apart. If he moved to roll down the hangar door, they would see him and attack.

Thinking quickly, he vaulted into the war machine and immediately looked for some kind of button with which to close the door. To his left he saw a big red button marked *HATCH*. He pushed it and the steps rolled in. The door closed silently, and he was completely locked in.

CHAPTER TEN

The house stood at the southwest corner of the lake. Everything about the place was clean, and everything was neat as a pin. A new van sat in the driveway, gleaming in the scorching, unreal sun.

"Another one, Jessie?" The man had just awakened; sleep still showing in his eyes.

"Yeah, Dad," the woman replied, "almost the same as before."

"The same vision?"

"No, Dad, this one had some huge machine in it."

"Oh?" the man asked. He was afraid his daughter had something wrong in her head that couldn't be fixed. Not now, and not ever.

"The other one only showed a shopping mall," the woman continued, "and some poor man was fighting for his life. He had to shoot some of *them* to get away."

"Are there still some of *them* left? I thought they would all have been killed off by now. It's been months since it happened, you know." Around the same time she started getting the headaches. The visions had only started a couple of weeks ago, and now he feared for her life.

"Your shoulder giving you trouble?" the man asked, breaking his train of thought.

"If we stay here we'll be safe, Dad," the woman said, ignoring her father's question.

The man was bothered that his daughter had ignored his question. She still didn't want to talk about it, or maybe she couldn't! He changed the subject abruptly. "Uh, what was this machine?" The woman cocked her head, as if listening to something. "It was a war machine, Dad, a terrible war machine! It had big guns all over the front of it. The man was hiding in it, trying to get away from them."

"You get a good look at the man this time?"

She shook her head. "He seems to be in a shadow, like something is hovering over his head. I can't understand it."

The woman's father nodded. She couldn't see this man, but she could see everything else around him. All in her head, of course. "Uh, you need anything from town? I have to get some nails and things."

"I'll go with you, Dad," the woman replied. "We better get a load of canned goods. You never know when some of *them* are going to show up. Maybe we should pick up some more ammunition, too. I've been having some funny feelings lately."

Doctor Peter Lindell looked at his daughter, a frown on his face. His *nails and things* were actually more guns and ammunition, anything he could lay his hands on to defend their little world. He found it strange to be thinking about taking life, because he had always tried to save it.

He had enjoyed a lucrative practice in Salem, coming to his daughter's home on holidays and weekends, to help with her veterinary practice. His first kill had been his own son-in-law, and his mind went back to that day.

That weekend he had talked Keith into letting Jessie and their eleven-year-old son, Kevin, come with him to the Cascades on a camping trip. Keith had begged off, claiming he had to get the engine rebuilt in his old truck, but Peter had known differently. Keith hated camping. He had voiced his opinion before that it was a waste of time. They had gotten Keith to come with them once, and he'd griped about it the whole time. Keith hadn't been able to help it, though. Keith was a workaholic.

"Maybe you should trade that truck in," Peter had taunted. He'd packed Jessie and Kevin in the van then, chuckling when Keith responded. Keith had loved that old truck and would never part with it.

They had driven as far as they could, and then backpacked into an old campsite at Crescent Lake. After they'd set up camp, they'd fished until Kevin had tired of it. Kevin had wanted to go exploring in the afternoon, so they had packed their fishing gear away. With their backpacks strapped on, they had started out. They all loved to hike and Kevin had been a natural born explorer.

Mid-afternoon had found them a little tired, but exhilarated. Jessie and Peter had wanted to head back, but Kevin would not hear of it. They had trudged laboriously behind him, opening their eyes when they heard a squeal of delight.

"A cave, Mom," Kevin had cried. "It's a cave!" Kevin had bounded ahead, his mother's warning unheard.

"Wait, Kev," Jessie had cried, "don't go in th—"

Kevin had been a normal, eleven-year-old boy, and very active. At times, his wondering mind had been more active than his body, but it had not been so that day. Peter and Jessie had rushed up to the cave mouth, expecting to find Kevin running back out, some animal hot on his heels. They had peered in and saw Kevin on his knees, his hands on the cave floor.

"Kevin!" Jessie had cried in alarm. "What are you doing?"

"It's a dog, Mom," Kevin had replied. "He's hurt!"

Jessie had rushed in to the cave. She'd known what rabies could do, and that it wasn't a pretty sight. "Don't touch him, Kevin!" Jessie had screamed, fear choking her words. "Stay away from him!"

As if to confirm her fears, the dog had started growling, snapping at her son's fingers. Kevin had pulled his hands back, and had stood up just as Jessie had arrived at his side. She had pulled him away from the dog, checking his hands.

"He didn't bite me, Mom," Kevin had explained. "He only snapped at me, 'cause I hurt him. He's all bloody on the hind end."

Jessie had turned back to the dog. It was a German shepherd, and it was in terrible pain. "Easy, boy," she had soothed as she approached the animal. She had seen the bloody flanks, and bent to examine them. The dog had growled, but made no attempt to bite.

"Dad?" Jessie had called. "Would you come here a minute?"

Peter had been standing with Kevin, his hands on the boy's shoulders. He trusted his daughter's instincts, however, and had come to bend down beside her.

"Looks like he's been shot, Dad. Can you hold his head while I have a look?"

Peter had stroked the dog's head, rubbing behind the ears and using his most soothing voice. A low whine had come from the dog, but it hadn't moved. Jessie had probed gently with her fingers until the dog growled, and then she had pulled her hands away and stood up.

"I think the bullet went right through; there's an entry and exit wound." she'd said quietly. "I don't think it hit any bones, but it sure made a mess coming out. Did you bring the first aid kit?"

"Hah!" Peter had exclaimed. "Do chicken have teeth?"

He had turned his back to her, telling her that it was in the outside flap. She undid the strap and pulled out the plastic case, and had then spoken to her father again. "Hold his head again, Dad, and I'll see if I can patch him up."

Peter had held the dog while Jessie worked on the wound. The dog had lain passive, as if knowing it was among friends. It whined, but as before made no attempt to bite. Jessie had finished the dressing and stood up.

"Good boy," Peter had said when Jessie had signified that she was finished.

"He's not a good boy, Dad."

Peter had looked at her questioningly.

"*She* is a good girl," Jessie had explained. "The dog is female."

Jessie had started to go towards the cave mouth then, leaving Peter and Kevin alone with the dog.

"Will the dog be all right, Mom?" Kevin had asked, but surprise had shown on his face when his mother's throat emitted an ear-piercing scream. Peter and Kevin had turned towards Jessie, to find her on the cave floor, her hands clutching her head.

"Jessie?" Peter had called—his fear a living thing.

Jessie had curled into a ball, unable to speak. She was out cold. Peter ran to her, cuddling her head in his lap. A moan had escaped her lips, and she'd opened her eyes.

"What happened?" Jessie had asked.

"You fell, honey!" Peter told her. "Did you trip on something?"

"No...I don't think so," she faltered. "It's my...my head, Dad. All of a sudden I got a blinding headache. My eyes are still blurry."

Peter had thought of several complaints that might have caused those symptoms. "Kevin! Go check on the dog."

"But Mom is—"

"Your mother is fine," Peter had lied. "She just tripped and knocked herself out. Now go!"

Kevin had gone obediently, his eyes still wide with fear.

"Honey," Peter had asked Jessie when Kevin could not hear them, "are you pregnant?"

"No, Dad," Jessie had said. "At least, I don't think so. Keith had a vasectomy, and he—"

"Don't bet on it," Peter had said. "A vasectomy isn't foolproof, there are no guaranties."

Jessie had smiled then and Peter had asked if she could get up.

"Sure, I just tripped and banged my head, like you said."

Peter had smiled back and rose to his feet, supporting her in case she fell. He had thought of another possibility, but dismissed it. The idea was too frightening. Jessie had walked out of the cave then, under her own power, and had come back with some tree branches.

"I need your camping knife, Dad."

"What are you doing, Jessie?"

"Making a travois," Jessie had explained. "I don't see any other way of getting Miss Muffet out of here."

Kevin had left the dog, and rushed to his mother's side, looking very hurt.

"What's the matter, Kev?" Jessie had rumpled his hair.

"Nothing!" Kevin had groused.

"Must be a pretty big nothing, almost big enough to be a something." She had waited, and Kevin had blurted out what was bothering him.

"I thought we didn't have any secrets from each other! That's what you and Dad told me! You said I was big enough to be included in all the family decisions."

Jessie had winked at her father. "Doctor Lindell, I think we have struck a nerve here, and I think we also have a young man on our hands. Yep, passed right over being a teenager, and went right ahead to being an adult."

Peter had fielded Jessie's wink, and understood immediately. "I think you might be right, Doctor Barlow," he had said with a poker face. "How do you think that happened?"

"Could be the altitude, Doctor. Air is a little thin up here, you know."

"Aw...Mom," Kevin had muttered. "You know what I mean. Granddad sent me back to the dog so he could whisper somethin' to you. I ain't stupid, you know."

Jessie had then soothed Kevin's ruffled feathers, telling her son that his grandfather hadn't meant anything by it. That he was just concerned about her falling. It had worked admirably, for soon Kevin was bringing in branches for the travois. When they'd left the cave with the dog-laden travois, none of them had known that the world had gone insane.

"Dad!" Jessie cried, bringing her father's mind back to the present.

"Uh...what?" Peter acknowledged his daughter when he was able.

"I saw something flash up there," Jessie said, pointing toward the edge of the forest. "Like the sun was glinting off something."

The sun and heat had been impossible since the world had changed, and it had not rained a drop. There were no animals or insects in evidence, not even a bird to mar the paint on the new van.

Peter scanned the tree line. "I don't see anything, Jessie."

"I could have sworn I saw something?"

"It could have been a stone, Jessie. The sun could have caught it just right."

"I guess you're right, Dad," Jessie agreed. "This damnable heat is making me a little jumpy."

They heard a dog barking then, and Kevin and Miss Muffet came bounding out of the trees.

"There's what you saw," Peter said, smiling faintly. "Probably the sun glinting off of one of Kevin's shirt buttons."

Jessie nodded, smiling when she saw her son running down toward them. When the boy and dog came up to them, all four climbed into the van and went *"shopping"*.

The man in the camouflage suit backed into the trees. The dog hadn't smelled him, because he had been downwind.

The woman had seen something, but it looked like the man with her had talked her out of it. They hadn't been wearing masks of any kind, and they didn't seem to be crazy. Maybe he could get out of this monkey suit. Better not, just in case. The Colonel would bust his ass if he ever found out.

The man had been keeping watch on the people at this residence ever since a patrol had found out that they were there, but now they were going somewhere else, and he thought he'd better get on back and report.

He returned the same way he had come, finally getting back to the Armored Personnel Carrier. He would be glad to get back to base and get out of the monkey suit.

CHAPTER ELEVEN

Steve turned around, gaping in wide-eyed awe!

He had never seen anything like this in his life. From outside, he hadn't seen any windows at all, but now as he looked over the curving, unreal control panel—he couldn't call it a dashboard—he could see outside. The whole machine had *windows* set all around the walls, and there was even a *window* set into the hatch.

He could see that his old truck was being mobbed now, apparitions ripping everything out of it, tearing his new clothing to shreds. He knew he had to scare them off before they got to his books and tapes, but how? This fantastic machine had more firepower than an army did, but he didn't know how to use it?

He looked at the control panel, overcome by the many computer screens. He had been introduced to computers in high school, and again when he had gone to... *The Academy!* "The Police Academy," he mouthed the words, "before I..."

His memory left him there, disappearing into the mists of yesterday.

"There must be a main terminal that powers all of these screens," he mumbled, trying to forget what he couldn't remember. "Maybe in the *driver's seat* I can see more."

He sat in the seat and saw the terminal. It was set at an angle to aid the driver, and that's why he hadn't seen it before. He had seen only the back of it. A soft green light was flashing in the upper left-hand corner, waiting, it seemed, for a command.

"Aha!" he exclaimed. "That's called a cursor! I remember that!"

But what had the instructor said about operating a computer? Something about when in doubt...when in doubt get help!

"Help!" he said aloud, almost shouting. "Find the help button!"

The *help* button was located on the right side on a separate panel. He punched it and waited. The screen lit up, and he could see the options on the monitor, showing all of the programs that he could use. He was now looking at a *"menu"*.

He moved the cursor, over and down to the program he thought would actually help him, and entered it. The screen changed, and he read all about the armament and its capabilities. He didn't understand any of it until he came to the bottom of the screen.

Steve punched the menu up again then entered M.A.O. He heard clicking all around him, and realized that he had just punched up *MANUAL ARMS OVER-RIDE*. He looked around then, and spotted a row of buttons on the other side of the machine marked: *FIRE*. They were all covered with silver flip caps, and when he walked around to them he flipped a cap open marked: *AUTO*.

He hesitated, unsure of himself. He saw on the small screen—that was set in the panel—the hangar door that he had opened, and he also saw the insanity tearing at his belongings. With his finger on the "FIRE" button, he hesitated, and then, throwing all caution to the winds, he pushed the button.

When he saw the holes appearing in the hangar door, he released the button. He heard nothing, but the things that were tearing his truck apart apparently did. As he watched in glee, he saw that they had all jumped from the truck, and were running off in all directions.

"Just like children," he murmured. "Make a loud noise, and they are terrified."

Steve pushed the button again, letting off a longer burst. He watched in awe as a larger hole appeared in the door. Then he sat down in the chair directly in front of the weapons control panel. His mouth was open, and a silent *WoW* framed on his lips.

Steve just sat for a moment, mesmerized at what he had accomplished. "If this one gun was aimed properly," he said to the console in front of him, "I could wipe out an army!"

The thought prompted him to look for the control that would aim the gun, but his searching was in vain. He became puzzled, and his fingers started drumming on the arms of the luxurious leather chair. He tapped his fingers idly, thinking, and then he saw a screen change its picture. The screen that showed the hangar door had now moved to the right.

Curious now, he looked down at his fingers and saw the four buttons. He hadn't noticed them before, because they were covered with the same material as the chair was. The buttons were flush with the flat arm of the chair, and he had to concentrate to see them.

The buttons made a North-South/East-West pattern. He wondered about it, and pushed the *North* and *East* buttons simultaneously. The screen changed, showing an area higher and more to the right. He touched the other two buttons and the screen swung back to the *West* and down, showing the nose of the machine. He stopped the west travel and held the *South* button down. The picture remained the same.

Steve pushed only the *West* button, and the picture changed again, showing that it was pointing directly abreast of the nose of the machine. He used the *East* button then, and brought the weapon back. Now the weapon was pointing straight ahead again.

He left the seat and returned to the *driver's side*. A screen had lit up there, too, showing what the smaller screen on the other side was showing. Nodding his head, he returned to the smaller screen, snapping the cap over the "firing" button. When the screen went dead, he thought that he could have operated all this from the other side, and he knew he had guessed right when he looked. He was elated that his assumptions were correct.

His stomach started rumbling, telling him that he was hungry. He would have to go to his truck anyway if he wanted his books and tapes, so he would take the chance and see if the *"crazies"* had left any food there.

Steve picked up the shotgun and pushed the hatch button. The door swung up and out, the stairs pushing out again. He had guessed correctly that the red button would also open the door, and he felt a little smug about that. He checked around for stragglers, and then walked warily to his truck. He thought that if it would still run that he would drive it into the hangar. He reached the truck and peered in. A voice stopped him dead, and his heart came up in his throat again.

HATCH WILL CLOSE IN THREE MINUTES—THREE MINUTES

A loud speaker had activated, and a woman's voice had issued from it. He quickly started the truck, noticing that some of his tapes and books had been destroyed. Steve drove the truck into the hangar and parked it against the door with the ruined lock. The two-minute warning blared out of the unseen speaker when he closed the big hangar door. He returned to the truck and removed his things, transferring them into the wondrous machine he had found. He didn't feel safe again until he was back inside his newly acquired home.

Steve picked up the treasures he had tossed through the opened hatch, and stacked them against the wall behind the driver's seat. With the bread all gone, he feasted on canned fruit and peanut butter, scooped out of the jar with his fingers. He thought he would have to get more of the gooey stuff.

He felt the need to urinate, and opened the hatch. He walked to the hangar door and relieved himself, glancing at the gaping hole near the bottom. "Anything small enough to get through that I should be able to handle," he uttered to the hole. Then he giggled. He had enough weapons to destroy the damned moon.

He wondered again where the power was coming from. He thought there would be time to find that out when he was safe from the outside world. He finished up and went back inside, just ahead of the closing hatch.

A thought tugged at his mind, that he would probably never hear a train whistle again. One of his earliest memories had been the time his parents had taken him down to the old train station. When the train's whistle had blown, he had been terrified. Later, when he had started going to school, he'd lost his terror of trains. He'd even skipped school at times to watch what the other kids had nicknamed *The Peanut Train*. It had probably been one of the first diesel trains around, and all the boys had liked to watch it as it went by, yelling and hooting, and brandishing their contraband cigarettes.

If he had smoked when he was young, was he still a smoker? He didn't feel any urge to smoke, so he must have ended the habit when he'd joined the police force.

Thoughts continued to bombard his senses, causing him to remember playing a game that all the boys his age had participated in. There had been a large train trestle, and he and his friends had walked to the center of the bridge and had waited for a train to come. The bridge had been equipped with "barrel stands"; water barrels had, at one time, been placed at certain intervals on the train bridge. He remembered how they would wait until the train was almost upon them, and then race like mad to get into a "barrel stand". It was a race they'd had to win, because if they didn't make it to the safety of the stands, the train would have surely killed them. The only alternative would have been to jump off of the bridge into the water below, but the bridge had towered at least 60 feet above the water.

Losing the thought, he decided it was time he explored this strange machine. Nothing could get at him now, certainly not the brainless occupants that seemed to have inherited the world. At least not this part of the world. As he walked down the hall past the driver's seat, he saw a door marked *HEAD*. Upon opening it he discovered a toilet and sink on the one side, and a bathtub with a shower on the other side. The shower curtain was pulled back to reveal the gleaming walls of the enclosure. Outside of the head/bathroom he found a desk. He rummaged in the drawers, finding instruction booklets on all of the various controls and control panels. He thought these papers worth their weight in gold, and he replaced them, planning to look at them later. Continuing on, he found a door marked *R&R* and opened it.

To his complete amazement, Steve gaped at the most plush living quarters he had ever seen. Everything was here that a man could want. To his right stood a stove and refrigerator, and upon opening the bronze-colored door he found it to be filled with all kinds of food and soft drinks. There was also another one of the magic ovens he'd seen back at the hospital.

There was a television set, with what looked like a built in VCR. It looked as though someone had planned to stay in this machine for quite some time, and when he opened the freezer part of the refrigerator, he was sure of it. Steve thought someone sure must have had a sweet tooth, because it was half filled with bread and frozen cakes. The other half of the freezer was completely filled with ice cream. He wondered if someone had planned a victory celebration.

Steve closed the door, and found the power button on the television set. He was rewarded with a perfectly blank screen, with static coming out of the speakers. He killed the power on the set, thinking that he could use this to run his videotapes. He had to learn again all that he had once likely known and even things that he probably hadn't known.

A flash of memory came again, showing a white house. He remembered having flashes like this before, but this one was showing a lake and trees. Was it a memory? Could it be a scene that was yet to come, or was he looking at the home he used to have? He knew he had more unanswered questions as the scene faded.

He turned to the countertop, and saw all of the things needed for a day-to-day existence. Under the counter he saw shelves filled to the brim with canned and bagged goods.

This thing was designed to be on its own for…how long? Could he live out his years in this machine? Or would it suddenly die for want of a battery charge? He had to find out.

He noticed the bunks on the way out, as well as the table that sat in the middle of the room. There were four chairs pushed in to the table, and he remembered seeing more bunks over the control panel. Across the hall, he saw another door marked *Conference Room*. Steve checked it out, finding a chart and map table, with many charts stuffed into round holes beneath it. Another television set, complete with VCR, stood at one end, and there was a huge screen that looked like it might have something to do with radar. There were four armchairs in the room, all plush and very comfortable looking. He tried one out, and as he sat down the television clicked on. The scene that unfolded was of this very machine, but it was showing huge pipes coming out of it. These pipes shot upwards, and were then bent at the ends.

A camera zoomed in on an old car, and as he watched in awe, the old car just disappeared in a flash of light. The camera then panned around to the front of this now frightening craft, for he believed now it was a craft of some kind. When he saw where the lethal blast had come from, he was positive. He saw little pinpoints of light in the absolute center of the nose. The twinkling dwindled away to nothing, and then all that he could see was the unblemished metal of the craft's front end. When Steve moved from the chair, both television and VCR died.

Amazing! Just as he had not been able to see any windows from the outside, he also could not see anything of this incredible "Star Gun." *What else*, he thought, *is incorporated into this strange ship that cannot be seen?* He would learn how to operate this monster and all of her weapons. There was no doubt in his mind that he had found a veritable doomsday machine, one that was capable of great destruction.

Out in the hallway again, he turned to the rear and entered an unlocked door. He negotiated a short corridor, and found himself in what he believed to be some sort of engine room. Steve could see that all of the guns were fed from here, also, for he saw ammunition belts that fed the guns. These were all in separate bins, and the larger missiles—that he had not seen until now—sat in a spring loaded affair, much like a clip in a smaller gun. When he looked around, he could see smaller bins attached to the auto loaders. These contained small arms ammunition. Though he searched through them, he could not find shotgun shells. He would have to look elsewhere for these.

Following the curvature of the ship—glancing at the varied and death-dealing projectiles—he came at last to the heart of this creation. Before him now, he read the words that explained where the vast amounts of power were coming from. And it was a ship, he discovered. An atomic powered, death-dealing ship! Steve read the words out loud:

CAUTION
NUCLEAR REACTOR
THIS PROTECTIVE CASE MUST NOT BE OPENED

Making certain that nobody could tamper with it, the casing was completely sealed.

Anyone that did would be inviting sure death, so who in their right mind would? But there aren't any people left in their right mind. Well, I sure as hell am not going to open it!

Another thought hit him, and he paled.

What happened to all of the nuclear missiles that had been scattered all over the world? But...no...all of the insanity I was attacked by used only their hands and teeth. They did not use weapons, even though they could have. There had been exceptions, but they were all dead. All dead! But, what if...what if...what if there are still military personnel, waiting at their command posts, ready to use their keys? Ready to fire off the deadly missiles?

Steve turned away from his morbid thoughts, and then returned to the desk that held the instruction books and sat at the desk to read them. He read for a long time, oblivious of time and space. When he stopped reading, he was ready to try out what he had learned.

It was simple. A person only had to know what program to call up, and the computer did the rest. The only problem, he could see, was in knowing how to call them up!

He smiled and tapped the sheaf of instruction books marked: CLASSIFIED. The computer was in control of everything, including the lighting in the ship and the hangar, and he had an unlimited supply of juice with the atomic power from the reactor. There was a program to put all of the lighting on manual, but he would leave it where it was. When he left here, all he had to do was disconnect the umbilical that powered the hangar. Simple. As long as he had the instruction books.

Steve laid the books beside the computer, and then tried out the various programs he had seen in them. Everything he tried seemed to work, even the hatch. The timer incorporated into the hatch would be bypassed when the computer was used to open it, and would stay open until the computer was told to close it. Using the red button could close the hatch, but then the computer wouldn't know it had been closed. He decided that it would be best to open and close it the same way, so as not to cause any problems.

He consulted the book, and used the upper case on the keyboard to get the asterisk. He punched in the three digits—C.L.S.—then hit the return. The hatch closed, sealing him off from the outer world once more.

He remembered some sort of control panel, on both sides of the short hallway that gave access to the reactor room. He had to check that out, and then he would get some rest. In the morning, he would try to find out how to run the ship.

Steve returned to the reactor room, reading the names on what seemed to be control boxes. There were three letters stamped into the face of the boxes, and then the long form below that. As before, he read them aloud. "Programmable Logistic Controller." There was something about that in the manual. The computer sent a signal to the controller then the signal returned to the computer, telling it that the proper signal had been sent and initiated. Amazing! He didn't understand it, but then, he had never been able to understand computers and how they worked. He only hoped that nothing went wrong with it, because he didn't have the knowledge to repair anything on this ship.

Suddenly, a blinding pain in his head slammed him to his knees! He could hardly see now and the pain was unbearable! Steve clasped his hands to his head, trying to still the agony. His mind felt like it was on fire, but he could see something there even though he was almost blind. The pain abruptly subsided to a tolerable level, and though he couldn't see too much through his eyes, the vision in his mind remained.

A woman, an older man and a young boy. In front of some store, loading guns and ammunition into an already overloaded vehicle. The woman talking to the man at the opened door of the vehicle. The boy running up to them, a dog bounding up beside him. A big dog! German shepherd, it looks like. Something like the ones I trained at the...I trained dogs like that to sniff out drugs and explosives!

The vision left him then, taking the rest of the pain away and returning his sight. He was still on his knees, holding his head when the realization came to him. He dropped his hands and rose to his feet, still shaking from the incident.

"Oh, my! What in hell is happening to me? What was *that* all about? Who *was* that?"

He hadn't seen these people before, at least not that he could remember. The only one that had looked familiar was the dog. The experience unnerved him, and he decided to rest for a while. Someone, or some thing was trying to warn him about something, or he was having flashbacks to his past.

Steve walked back to the control room—as he now called it—and started to climb up to the bunk over the control panel. When he turned to lay his tortured head on the inviting pillow, he saw a face peering into the hatch window!

CHAPTER TWELVE

Colonel Jeremy Francks was a military man who issued orders like a vending machine spewed out coffee. He expected these orders to be carried out to the letter, and woe to the man who failed. Colonel Francks could be a very vindictive and terrifying man.

Since the end of the "civilized world", he had ordered over a dozen men executed for being *delinquent of duty*. Some of his officers tried to reason with him, and they were never seen again. The colonel's new aide told the other personnel that the officers had been called back to *Home Plate*, the code name for the base in Arizona.

Colonel Jeremy Francks was blessed with an aide, a brutish man who had no peers when it came to brawling, using his fists with devastating power whenever he chose to. And now he chose to whenever Colonel Francks told him to.

Private Billy Tanner pulled in to the domed camp and parked the two man A.P.C., anxious to be inside and out of his confining survival gear. The colonel insisted that all personnel wear the garb when they were away from the Dome.

"Can't be too careful, soldier," the colonel always reminded. "Until we find out what happened, we don't dare breathe the outside air."

They had been ordered to a secret location, ostensibly to undergo survival training, and the Dome had been built to make everything seem realistic. There was enough food and water for a full year, and the air they breathed was being manufactured in the huge underground laboratory. Four scientists were living below the Dome, servicing the pumps and doing some experiments on something or other, but neither Billy nor the other men had ever seen them. The colonel was the only one that had ever spoken to them, along with Colin Soames, the base doctor. Doctor Soames carried the rank of Major, but was always referred to as "Old Soames."

Billy was used to the *whump-whump* of the air pumps, as were the other grunts. The one thing they had never gotten used to, though, were the disappearing officers. The only officer left now, except for Major Soames was their C.O., Colonel Jeremy Francks. Originally, there had been thirty-two army personnel ordered to the Dome, and the number had fallen to nineteen. Even the colonel's aide had disappeared, and now Sergeant Pilke filled that spot.

Billy shuddered when he thought about Pilke. He was sure the sergeant had been instrumental in the disappearance of the officers, but he had no proof. He had to keep his mouth shut about it, though, or he might join Jerry and Ray in the infirmary. Pilke was a mean and thorough bastard, Billy knew, and had put both of his friends there at the same time.

Once inside the outside doors, Billy stripped. He hung his suit in a cabinet and turned a valve. The suit was bombarded with foam, effectively destroying any microbes that might have clung to it during his outside recon. From there he entered the showers, where his body was cleansed, first with a chemical spray, and then with a soapy solution. Billy hit the button that would shut off the cleansing segment and a dryer automatically turned on.

When his body was completely dry—and free of all possible outside infection—yet another door opened and he was permitted back into the *bull pen*. He went straight to his shirt pocket, lit a cigarette and inhaled deeply. His brain enjoyed the blast that went straight into his lungs. Billy exhaled, and exhaust fans turned on, dispelling the smoke. There were similar devices in the Dome, keeping the oxygen to a minimum of over twenty-percent. He was glad that the scientists had thought to put these in, because the colonel smoked very long—and very smelly cigars. When he was properly attired—Lord help the grunt with a button or crease out of place—he entered the detox chamber. This took only forty seconds as he was scanned for any foreign matter. He got the all clear from the computer, and was then admitted into the main building.

The long hall was deserted; the enlisted men (grunts) would be relaxing in the recreation room. But then again, they could be in the infirmary if any of them had crossed the colonel or his new aide. Billy was going to do just that, he knew, and he was certain of what Pilke was going to do to him.

Billy had decided on the way back that he wanted out. There had not been any orders from *Home Plate* for almost three months, and Billy was of the opinion that there wasn't a base there anymore. There hadn't been any radio or television transmissions for over two months, and the only thing that came out of the civilian stations had been static.

There had been no contact with the outside world, and the only other people he had seen alive, and reasonably sane had been the family at the farm. It had appeared to be a farm, but he'd thought it strange, because the surrounding land appeared to be timber country.

One other thing bothered him, but he was aware he could do nothing about it except wonder. The colonel and his aide had been out together in the large A.P.C., but if they knew what had happened they were keeping mum about it.

Billy had to report to the colonel now, as he had been ordered to, but he was going to lie through his teeth. He would not likely have many teeth left, he decided, when the colonel figured he was lying, but it was a chance he had to take. Billy had devised a plan to get away from the Dome, but he was going to take Jerry and Ray out with him if they were still alive. He took a deep breath and knocked on the door.

CHAPTER THIRTEEN

"That's about it, Dad," Jessie said. "We can't pile any more in here and still drive it."

"All right, honey," Peter agreed. "Better call Kevin and Miss Muffet."

As though they had heard, Kevin and the dog came running around the corner of the van. Kevin was out of breath, but the dog was still raring to go.

"Kevin!" Jessie was surprised. "I was just going to call you to co—"

Jessie doubled over, the pain in her head like a tooth being pulled. Peter tried to pull her hands away from her head, bending over to look at her face. Her eyes were shut, but he could see the grimace of pain on her features.

"Kevin!" Peter yelled. "Help me with your mom!"

Wide-eyed and afraid, Kevin came over to stand beside his mother, not knowing what was expected of him.

"Help me lay her down, Kevin," Peter said. "Your mom has another headache."

Peter and Kevin laid Jessie on the ground and Peter told Kevin to watch her while he went to the van for a pillow and his bag. He returned with the pillow and put it under her head, then fumbled in the bag for a syringe. He found the bottle he wanted, and filled the syringe, pumping the air out of it. Peter plunged the needle into Jessie's arm, emptying the contents into her blood stream. Reaching back into his bag, Peter produced an ampoule and broke the end off. He then waved it under Jessie's nose. She coughed, and opened her eyes. They were glazed, but there was understanding in them. She tried to raise herself up, but Peter pushed her back down.

"Uh, uh," he warned, "don't get up yet. Wait until that shot starts to work."

"But, Dad—" Jessie began to complain.

"No buts!" Peter was adamant. "Listen to your doctor, he knows better than your dad does."

"But I saw him, Dad!" Jessie blurted. "Clearly!"

"Easy, girl," Peter said. "Just lie back for a minute."

"But, Dad!" Jessie insisted. "I saw him. All of him. He was sitting in that machine, reading something. He looked familiar, somehow, like I'd seen him someplace before."

"You sure you're all right?" Peter asked, not listening to something he considered foolishness. "Can you sit up now?"

"Of course, I'm all right!" Jessie fumed. "Just need a little boost." Jessie sat up, expecting her head to spin around but found it was clear. The terrible pain was gone, and she felt great.

"Help me up, Dad."

She raised her arms to him, and Peter helped her to her feet. Kevin, still crying, rushed now to hug his mother, crying all the more. Peter reached to pull him away, but stopped when Jessie shook her head.

"I'm all right, Kev," she told her son when she saw his tears. "I did something stupid and fainted, that's all."

"Oh...Mom! You're not stupid!" Kevin came to her defense.

Jessie laughed, the tinkling sound making Peter's heart smile. Maybe she was right. Maybe she'd just fainted, but he hadn't heard her laugh like that in months.

"I didn't say I *was* stupid, Kev," Jessie beamed. "I just *did* something stupid! You remember that time you bent over to tie your shoes? And you fell right over and banged your noggin?"

"Uh, yep."

"Well, that's what I did," Jessie lied. She looked at Peter, shaking her head again. "When I bent down, the blood rushed to my head and I fainted. It was a stupid thing to do, and I won't do it again. Okay?"

Kevin stopped crying, and raised his eyes to his mother's face. He was smiling now, but his cheeks were still wet. "You're gonna think I'm a sissy now," Kevin blurted. "Cryin' like a little baby!"

Jessie was about to say something, but her father saved the day. "You're no sissy, Kevin. I've cried before, and I'm a grown man."

"You, Granddad!?" Kevin was surprised to hear that from the man he thought of as being a *tough old coot*.

"Yep. When I went to med school, and passed out the first time I saw blood, actually saw my first operation. I cried half that night; I was so ashamed of myself. When I found out that I wasn't the only one who had passed out, I was okay again. And you will be, too!"

Kevin seemed to rise up when he heard this, and at that precise moment he began to grow up. He didn't know it right then, but in the coming weeks he would grow up fast.

Jessie drew her father aside, and asked him if that story about his first operation was true, and she smiled when her father lied again. She knew her father even better than her own mother had, and she knew his drive would never have permitted him to do a thing like that. But she was happy to see that her son was all right again, thanks to this rough old man, who was really a *"pussy cat"* when it came to matters that counted.

"Now, young fellah," Peter said, "let's get our butts in gear and get on home. We got a heap of things to unload when we get there."

Kevin was his old self again, and climbed into the van. "Come on, Miss Muffet," he called. "Let's get going!"

The dog leaped in after Kevin, tumbling cans and guns over. Kevin hugged her, and indicated he was ready. Jessie climbed in and Peter started the van.

On the way home, Jessie felt exuberant. Her eyes were shining, and Peter asked her about it. When she answered him he was shocked.

"I remember where I saw that man, Dad."

"What man?" Peter asked, as innocently as he could.

"The one in my vision."

"Oh?" Peter was worried about his daughter's mental state now, as well as her physical well being. How could she see a man in a dream, so to speak, a man she had never seen or known before? And now, when she was awake and seemingly lucid, she claimed that she knew who he was? It all seemed rather ludicrous to him. "And where was that?"

"Well," Jessie began, "you remember that time you came down with the newspaper clippings? The ones about that policeman who got shot?"

"No," Peter said. "Can't say as I do."

"Oh, you know," Jessie reminded. "The one from New York City. The one who was still in a coma."

Peter remembered now. It had been happier times, and Keith had still been alive. "Yes, honey, I remember."

"Well, it's him, Dad," Jessie followed up. "I'm sure of it!"

Peter was astounded! " But… honey, how could you see a picture of a man in a rough newspaper photograph, and then recognize him months later? From a dr…uh, vision, no less?"

Peter stopped the van. The smile went out of Jessie's eyes when he questioned her, but the fire was still there. He could only hope that he hadn't sent her back to that place she had climbed into when Keith had tried to kill her.

"It *is* him, Dad!" Jessie was resolute. " I know it. And another thing, he's coming here. And I won't have any more killing headaches! Now, don't ask me how I know all this, I just do. I feel it."

Peter was speechless, perhaps for the first time in his life. He turned to his daughter with a retort on his lips, but stopped when he saw the dazzling smile on her face. Something was going on here that he didn't quite understand, and he doubted very much if he would find the answer in any medical book.

"One more thing, Dad," Jessie said, lowering her voice. "I know Keith had to die, and I accept it now. I'm only sorry it was you that had to shoot him. He would have tried to kill us all, you know."

Peter knew that very well, but he also knew that he now had his daughter back. She had finally accepted the fact that her own husband had tried to kill her.

It must have been the cave that saved them and the dog that long ago day. Jessie had been going to the cave mouth when the flash came. She had received a partial shock, but not enough to fry her brain, as it had done to Keith and others.

The only thing he could figure out was that the sun had been the culprit. A solar flare, perhaps, or some other kind of explosion on that super-heated star. It had simply fried everything on earth. Animals, birds, it had even destroyed all of the insects. Peter's mind returned to that awful day.

They had returned to the farm that day, but found it deserted. They'd searched the house after Jessie had patched up Miss Muffet and found it empty. Outside, there had been no movement. Peter had thought it strange that there was no sign of animals around, but he surmised that Keith had put them inside, out of the staggering heat.

The barn doors had been open, and Jessie had walked towards them, calling her husband's name. As she passed through the opened doors, she had become lost in shadows, and then she had screamed.

Peter and Kevin had run through the doors, but were unable to see right away. When their eyes had grown accustomed to the gloomy interior, Peter had been shocked to see Jessie on her back; the screwdriver embedded in her shoulder. Keith had been standing over her, a raised pitchfork ready to descend through her unprotected throat!

Peter had yelled at him, as had Kevin. Keith had turned his head to them, and Peter had seen then that the man had become insane. Slobber drooled out of his opened mouth, and the eyes had looked like golf balls. Peter had seen that Keith's eyes were wide open, but he hadn't been able to see any color except white.

Keith had laughed, loudly, insanely and had turned back to Jessie's inert form. Peter had run for the .22 rifle that was kept in the barn to shoot the occasional rat. He'd yelled again, but Keith either couldn't or wouldn't hear him. Peter had aimed for the shoulder, but Keith chose that precise moment to lunge downward with the pitchfork. Jessie had tried valiantly to roll out of the pitchfork's deadly thrust, but one of the tines had buried itself in her body beside the screw driver, glancing off of her collarbone. The small .22 bullet had missed Keith's shoulder, and had ripped out his throat.

Keith had dropped to the floor immediately, and Peter and Kevin had rushed to Jessie. After a quick look, Peter had pulled the pitchfork out of her shoulder, but had left the driver untouched. The driver had gone in to the hilt, and Peter had been afraid to touch it for fear of causing more damage.

Jessie had been conscious and crying, a low whine coming from her throat. Peter had talked to her, trying to calm her down. He'd glanced at Keith's still body and knew he must be dead or dying; there had been too much blood pumping out of his neck for it to be a flesh wound. He had known then what damage the little bullet must have done.

Kevin had been crying, kneeling down beside his mother. He'd wanted to pull the awful screwdriver out of his mother's flesh, but Peter had told him to wait. Peter had then taken the small pocketknife out of his pocket, and had cut away the material from Jessie's shirt, discovering that the driver had miraculously missed all of Jessie's bones. He'd sent Kevin for his bag, and had yelled at him. Finally, Jessie had told him to go, and it was only then that he'd obeyed.

Peter had injected Jessie several times with antibiotics, and had removed the screwdriver, bandaging the angry-looking rips that the pitchfork and screwdriver had made. He had immobilized the shoulder, making a sling out of a bed sheet that Kevin had been sent for. The rest of the sheet had been draped over Keith's dead body, shielding it from view. Jessie had survived the ordeal, but had not mentioned her dead husband's name until now.

"Yes, honey," Peter said, returning to the present. "But I'm sorry it had to be me that shot him. I aimed for his shoulder when he moved to drive the fork into you, and the bullet hit him in the neck. I meant only to stop him from killing you; I didn't mean to kill him."

The van turned silent, and then a voice from the rear piped up.

"Granddad?"

Peter turned. "Yes, Kevin?"

"Let's go home. You had to do it, and nobody blames you. We're still a family, you know!"

Peter felt his eyes burning, but held the tears back. He hadn't cried, even when his wife had died of Leukemia, but he'd felt as helpless then as he did now.

"That we are, Kevin!" Peter agreed boisterously. "And if your mother's visions are correct, I'm afraid it might be getting bigger!"

Jessie flashed Peter her most brilliant smile. "Yeah, Granddad," she said. "Let's go home."

CHAPTER FOURTEEN

Steve stared at the hatch, but could see nothing. Had there been something there, or had it been his imagination? He stepped back to the deck and went to the hatch, looking out. His jaw dropped when he saw what had looked in the window.

"Oh my God! A kid! A little kid! Now where in hell did he come from?"

He looked around, but could see nobody else. It hit him then that the lights were still on in the hangar, and the kid must have crawled through the hole he'd blasted in the door. His thoughts racing, Steve decided that this kid was probably as demented as everybody else. He started to turn away, but something tugged at his mind and he looked out again. As he did, the small face turned up to meet his gaze, and his heart melted.

It was a queer feeling to look into someone's eyes and know that they could not see you. And this was definitely a someone, albeit a very small someone. The eyes were the deepest blue he had ever seen, and he had always been a sucker for blue eyes. Or had he? If not, he surely was now, for there was not a hint of insanity in those two bright orbs.

Not taking any chances, he grasped the .45 and slammed the hatch button, but nothing happened. He tried again; still the hatch refused to open. He went to the computer and punched the program in that would open the hatch, but only got a loud beeping when he depressed the "enter" key. And then the screen came alive.

CAUTION
HATCH WILL COLLIDE

"Hatch will collide?" he said aloud, trying to figure the message out. "With what?"

And then he understood. There must be a safety sensor in the hatch. The little boy was directly in front of the hatch, and it would hit him if it were to open. He had to get the boy away from the ship. But how?

He banged on the hatch with the butt of the .45, but either the boy was deaf or the sound couldn't get through. Exasperated, he banged on the glass that was not glass. Still nothing. He would have to wait until the boy decided to move on. As if hearing his thoughts, the little visitor stood up, rummaging in his jacket pocket. He produced a harmonica and walked away from the ship. Steve hit the hatch button again, but the computer beat him to it, opening the hatch with the command he had already punched in.

The first thing Steve heard was music. He stepped out of the ship, and the music stopped suddenly, as if chopped off. The boy saw him and turned to run.

"Wait, boy!" Steve yelled. "I'm not going to hurt you!"

Yeah-right! He was waving a .45 around and he wasn't going to hurt anyone?

He tucked the .45 back in his belt, and then ran after the boy. He caught him as he was trying to scramble through the hole in the door. The boy started screaming as Steve pulled him back into the hangar and turned him around. The boy delivered a kick to his groin area, still trying to escape. Steve endured the pain and clung to him.

"Let me go, mister!" the little visitor cried. "I won't bother you no more! Let me go an' you won't see me no more! I won't come back here. I promise!"

"I'm...ugh...not going to hurt you, boy," Steve moaned in anguish. "But you sure as hell hurt me. What did you kick me for?"

Steve sat the boy down, but held on to him, ready for another kick.

"Please, mister," the boy pleaded. "I gotta go! My mom is waitin' for me!"

Steve chewed that one over, deciding that the boy was lying. But he didn't want another kick so he held on.

"Well, okay," Steve said. "But before you go, how about something to eat? I got all kinds of goodies in my sh...uh, my motor home, and I was just going to have something."

The little eyes lit up, but just as quickly hooded over. "My mom said not to trust anyone, 'specially strangers!"

Steve wondered why the hatch was staying open, and why there were no warnings that the hatch would close? Then he remembered that he had punched the program in to the computer to open it, and that program must be holding the hatch open.

"Suit yourself," Steve said. "But I got peanut butter, and some raspberry jam and lots of bread. I got some cheese, too," he lied, "and a whole lot of other things, including some little pies."

Steve had cheese, and apples as well but they were in cans and jars. The foods he'd mentioned were too much for the boy to refuse. The boy made a pretense of thinking it over before nodding.

"Okay, mister," the boy said, "but leave the door open. My mom said that as long as the door is open, you can always scoot out when trouble comes 'round."

"Why, sure, young fellah." Steve answered, hiding a smile.

The boy smirked a little at that, but followed Steve up the steps. He led the boy into the living quarters, leaving that door open as well.

"Well, what shall it be?" Steve asked when he began sorting through his horde. "Pasta on toast? Or how about—"

"Beans!" the boy said, drooling unconsciously. "Beans and toast."

"Beans?

"Yep. Beans. You got a whole bunch of it."

Steve looked at the canned goods, and spotted what the boy was pointing at. "Beans it is, then," Steve said. "Uh, maybe you might want to wash up while I thaw out some bread? It'll take a few minutes, and you look like you could stand a good wash."

Steve wondered if the washroom actually worked. He hadn't tried it yet; maybe there was no water at all. "Come on, let's have a look. I can't remember if I filled the water tank or not."

With the boy following him, Steve left the room and entered the washroom. He turned a tap and water hissed out. "Well, guess I did fill it. Ah, but is there any hot water?" He turned on the hot water tap, but quickly pulled his hand back.

"Guess you got hot water, too, huh?" the boy said. "You forgot about that, too? My mom wouldn't have forgot—"

"Okay, okay!" Steve groused without thinking. "So I forgot!" This kid was too smart for his own good, but he relished the company just the same. "You think you can manage to have a bath by yourself, while I get us some supper? And take that stupid hat off!"

Steve reached for the hat and pulled it off. The boy reached to stop him, but was too late. The baseball cap came away, and Steve stared in amazement as the long golden hair spilled down over the youngster's ears.

"Why...you...you're not a boy!" Steve gasped. "You're a girl. A little girl."

"I'm not a little girl!" the visitor cried. "My mom said I was a big girl, and I am! I am!!"

The tears rolled down her cheeks, and Steve could only stare, dumbfounded.

"Give me back my hat, mister? My mom said never to take it off. She said—"

Steve handed the hat back to her, then she quickly jammed it on sideways and Steve had to laugh. The girl stopped crying then stared at him.

"It ain't polite to laugh at people, mister!" the girl scolded. "What are you laughin' at?"

"Come on, little one," Steve said. "Pardon me, big girl. Let's go get some supper. You can wash up later, and have a real bath for a change. And why don't you call me Steve instead of mister? That's my name, you know."

The girl looked at him like he had two heads. "I gotta wash my hands before I touch my food, mister?!" she objected. "My mom always—"

Steve thought in his heart that the girl was all alone, but he had to know for sure. If the child's mother was actually out there somewhere—maybe hurt or starving—he had the means to help. "Uh, where is your mom, little one? Is she close by?"

The girl turned towards the sink, concentrating very hard on the simple task of turning the water taps on. "No," she replied slowly.

"No?"

"No," the girl repeated. "I lied to you, mister. My mom ain't waitin' for me anywhere. My mom is...my mom is dead."

The words came slowly, deliberately, almost spit out of a mouth that didn't want to say them. Steve said nothing, hating himself for his damned curiosity. He was still silent when the girl started to explain.

"My daddy killed her a long time ago," the girl began. "He hit her, and hit her with a big wrench...then he came after me! My mom told me to run and hide, an' that's what I did!"

"You ran?" Steve asked, trying to understand. "Where did you run to, little one? Where were you when your daddy came after you?"

"Our bomb shelter," the girl replied simply.

"Bomb shelter?"

"Yep. We'd been pract...practicing down in the shelter Daddy made in the basement. He said we had to, 'cause if the bombs ever came we had to be ready. We always went down there on weekends for a few hours."

The girl was soaping her hands, the lather spilling into the sink. She kept on talking while she lathered, as though what she was saying had happened to someone else.

"Daddy went up to clear the air pipe; he said the filter was plugged. When he came back down he looked different. He had that big wrench in his hand, an' he started swinging it 'round an' 'round. That's when he hit my mom! She yelled at me to run, an' I did. I wanted to go to her, to stop my daddy from hittin' her, but I ran up the stairs."

Steve listened to the little-old girl until he could take no more. His eyes started to burn, and he felt his throat closing up.

"Daddy left the door open when he came back down to the shelter, an' I ran. I hid in the closet upstairs, but I could still hear my mom screamin'. Then there was no noise at all. I never cried, mister, not until you swiped my hat. My mom said big girls didn't—"

Steve couldn't help himself. He crushed the little body to his chest. "It's okay to cry, little one," he murmured. "When the pain is very great, sometimes a tear helps."

The girl stood there, saying nothing. And then she laughed. "Hey, mister," she giggled. "You got soap on your nose."

Steve released her and stood up. "Tell me, little one, how come you trusted me? How could you ever trust anybody again?"

"You laugh good," the girl said.

"I laugh good?" Steve was puzzled.

"Yep," the girl explained. "My mom said…my mom said a good man had a good laugh. You laugh good."

She smiled, and then started to giggle, and then she began to cry. "My…uh, uh…my mom laughed good, too! She love…love…loved me, an' I loved her. My… my daddy didn't mean to hurt my mom. Somethin' happened to him, to all the people."

"I know, little one," Steve said. "I know. But…listen; I can't call you little one all the time. What did your mom call you?"

The girl stopped crying, and a twinkle started in her eyes. "Jackie. My mom called me Jackie."

"Well! Jackie!" Steve beamed. "How about grabbing that towel over there and finishing up your wash? I'll get us some supper, and after a good night's sleep we'll get on out of here. How does that sound?"

"You want me to stay? After I kicked you?"

"Yep," Steve said, trying to form a bond between them.

Jackie smiled. "Okay, Steve. But don't burn the toast."

CHAPTER FIFTEEN

"Enter."

Billy opened the door and walked in. He never knew what to expect when he entered this room, but today the colonel seemed to be in a good mood. Sergeant Pilke was there with him, and they had their heads down, peering at some maps.

The colonel turned to look at him. Billy raised his hand to salute, the one thing that seemed to be important in this room. Jerry Scoggins had forgotten, and now he was in the infirmary. The colonel's aide had almost killed him, probably would have if the colonel hadn't stopped him.

"Billy," the colonel smiled. "How are you, boy? Oh, never mind the salute. We're all just one big happy family here. Aren't we, Sergeant?"

The sergeant nodded, his black eyes boring into Billy's skull. Billy shuddered, feeling like a bug under glass.

"Come over here and sit down, my boy," the colonel said, "and let us know what's going on out there. You know, you boys are doing a fine job, what with communications being out all over the place."

Billy sat in the proffered chair, but was very uneasy about it. He had good cause to be, for the colonel suddenly loomed over him, thrusting his nose into Billy's face.

"Now, Billy, what have we learned about the family this time? Don't lie to me, or you will be reprimanded." The colonel turned to look at his aide. "Severely reprimanded!"

Billy *was* going to lie, and he wanted the colonel to *know* he was lying. His whole plan hinged on it. Billy had to get to the infirmary to see his friends, but it was always guarded. That was one of the reasons he wanted to get out of this place; it was starting to feel like a prison. He would get in there to see Jerry and Ray, but he would have to take some lumps to do it.

His plan was not very complex. When Pilke hit him, he would bite the capsule he had secreted in his mouth and feign unconsciousness. Pilke wouldn't hit him again if he thought that he was out cold. Pilke liked to punish, but wanted his victims to feel it when he slapped them around. Even so, he would have to take at least one shot in the mouth.

"I didn't see anyone outside, sir," Billy lied. "Maybe the air is bad. Maybe they didn't want to—"

"Billy…Billy!" the colonel smirked. "I told you not to lie. We already know that the air is not tainted. You see, I had the filter removed from your suit, so you were breathing outside air all the time you were away from the Dome. Our analyzers can test for some things, but not all. You, Billy, are living proof that the air outside is breathable."

"You bastard!" Billy cried. "You made me sweat out there in that crummy suit for nothing. I couldn't even have a smoke. You rotten, stinkin' bastard!"

The words came out before Billy thought, and he catapulted up out of the chair. But before he could get his hands on the colonel's throat, Billy felt a hammer strike the side of his head! He reeled away, stopping himself by grabbing the edge of the desk. As he turned, another blow caught him in the mouth. He went down as if he had been pole-axed.

Billy had the presence of mind to bite down on the capsule, but it was not needed. Some of his teeth were gone, and he didn't know if he had bitten the capsule or a stray tooth. He lay there in a pool of blood, hoping the colonel would stop Pilke before he did too much damage.

"Easy, Sergeant," Billy heard the colonel say. "We still need him. Send him to the infirmary to get patched up. Tomorrow or the next day—when he is able to swallow again—we'll test the water on him."

The sergeant pushed a button behind the desk, and then waited for the guards to arrive. "Feisty little bastard, isn't he?" the colonel said to Pilke. "Guess that's what happens when you take a man's smokes away for a few days. Well, I don't think he'll want to smoke for a couple of days. Uh, you have the route to the silo memorized, Sergeant?"

"Yes, sir."

"Good, Sergeant," the colonel smiled. "Very good. Next week, Sergeant, all of the others are going to join the officers then we put the rest of our plans in motion. Are you sure you can, uh, take care of the gift you're going to get?"

Pilke smiled, nodding.

"Oh, one more thing. Don't forget to check the tankers. It wouldn't do to run out of power now, would it?"

Billy almost pulled the gun out of his tunic, but knew he couldn't. The .45 was slated to go to his buddies in the infirmary, and it was to be their way out. He would *arrange* the rest of the plan, and all they had to do was to get out of the infirmary and down to the outer doors.

Billy felt hands lifting him, and then he felt his body being tossed uncaringly onto a stretcher. His next stop was the infirmary, where he was *brought around*. The doctor who patched him up was the colonel's stooge, and never questioned anything. As far as the doctor was concerned, Jeremy Francks could do no wrong. Billy thought it was a good philosophy, one that had kept the doctor alive.

"Got another one for you, Soames," the guard said. "This one seems to have a busted mouth."

"Bring him over here and I'll have a look at him," Billy heard the doctor say. "Hmm, looks like he ran into a truck. Okay, leave him here and I'll see what I can do. Come back in an hour, and he'll probably be ready for some more."

Billy waited until the doctor turned his back then glanced over at the beds. He waved to his buddies, surprised when they both waved back. He closed his eyes again when the doctor returned. He *woke up* quickly when something was waved under his nose.

"Got some teeth missing, my boy," Billy was told. "Lie still until I go get some gauze and a suction pump. Sure must've been a big truck."

When the doctor turned away and went into another room, Billy leaped off of the stretcher. He pulled the .45 and tucked it under Jerry's pillow. "Right after chow tonight," he told Jerry, "use it to get to the outer doors. I'll be there with the necessary items to get us out of here, including clothes. The air outside is okay, and so is the food but the colonel and Pilke are up to something. They were talking about some silo, and they must have some machinery there, too, 'cause Francks said something about fuel tankers."

Jerry nodded, unable to speak because of the jaw that had been broken. Ray's bones were still intact, but he'd had to have his eye popped back in and stitched up. The old doctor had been afraid of infection, and had kept him there.

Billy was sitting on the side of the stretcher when the doctor returned. He suffered the doctor's ministrations, and then waited for his escort. They were not long in coming. He was advised that he was under house arrest, and not to leave his quarters until further notice.

Billy had found a cave when he had been wandering the forests around the area, and had stocked it with some provisions. He'd figured their best bet was to hide out in the cave until Francks tired of the chase, and then they could get away from the army and Francks. Billy had no way of knowing that this was the same cave that Kevin had found Miss Muffet in.

CHAPTER SIXTEEN

Steve awoke, and looked past his toes at the sleeping form in the next bunk. He had a reason to go on now. If this one little child had survived the devastation of a world gone mad, then there must be others. He rolled over, being as quiet as he could. He didn't want to wake the sleeping waif, for he supposed that this had been the first time in a long while that she'd had a decent rest.

While he waited for her to awaken, he read the instruction book on the workings of the great ship. He discovered it was totally operated by computer, and simple to use, but there was also a section on manual operation and he thought he could master the controls. Apparently, the power for the craft was always *on*, and it sat there *idling*, waiting for someone to use it. Although the computer was the *brain*, he would pilot the craft himself. He brought up the menu and found the sequence for manual control. When he punched that sequence in, two "joysticks" popped up on either side of the command module and he knew he had put the craft on manual.

The driver's seat—as he liked to call it—was really a command console. Steve knew he would learn to operate this ship, but he doubted if he would ever be able to put it on automatic pilot. He didn't know what obstacles lay in front of him, did not know where he was going, but he did know that he and Jackie were going to get out of this part of the country.

Steve saw the two red buttons on top of the joysticks and he knew that these had to be depressed in order to move the craft. Once underway, the controllers would lock into position if the buttons were released. A second push on the buttons and control would return to the operator. That would put the ship in a semi-automatic mode, and this made Steve feel more at ease.

When he had first seen the machine, and had walked around it, he had looked for wheels but had seen none. He'd found out why that was, and was more astounded than ever. He'd also found out what the letters the front of the ship stood for. G. R. A. A. V.—in the long form—stood for GROUND ROVING AIRBORNE ATTACK VEHICLE. The ship was part tank, part helicopter and part amphibian, but it was mostly lethal! He'd thought this was why it had been under wraps.

There was also a program that, when initiated, would result in a nuclear explosion. The reactor would overload, then the whole thing would vaporize but passwords had to be entered to do this. Steve knew he could never master that. But why would he ever want to? He knew this program was in the computer, and even though he knew it would never be activated it still scared the hell out of him.

The armament book was next on his list, and he found in its pages the weapon that he had termed: "Star Gun." It was actually a laser beam, and it could demolish almost anything on this planet. It was operated through the computer, and it would be indispensable to him on his trek. This was the weapon that had disintegrated the car he had viewed on the video, and this was why it was so important to his "mission." Steve thought that nothing could stand in his way now, absolutely nothing at all.

The inventors of the weapon had taken a standard principle and modified it tremendously; this war machine was capable of flight, ground and water travel—and could, if the operator commanded—travel under the water. What a boon to mankind this would have been. Stripped of the armament, it would have been what nuclear energy should be all about. Life, and people.

"What cha doin', mister?"

Steve looked around, startled. A blonde head was hanging down over the edge of the bunk. He smiled. "My name's Steve, remember?"

"Sorry, Steve. I forgot."

"Well, now that you're awake, come on down and we'll see if we can find something to eat."

"Gotta go pee first, Steve," Jackie lamented. "My tummy hurts from not goin' all night."

She dropped over the edge, and he caught her. "Okay, little one. Get to the bathroom."

She started to the bathroom. She turned to face Steve, a twinkle sparkling in her eyes. "My name's Jackie, remember?"

"Okay, I forgot, too," he said, smiling at her. She disappeared into the bathroom, and Steve went into the living quarters to make breakfast.

"Hurry up; it's going to get cold," he yelled.

"I'm comin', Steve," Jackie called. "Gotta dry my hands, y' know!"

When Jackie saw what Steve had prepared, she squealed. "Pancakes! Oh, I love pancakes!"

This made Steve feel good inside, and he watched her as she almost inhaled her breakfast. He feigned being full, and gave her the rest of his. Her eyes shone when he offered her more, and she wolfed everything down.

"Now," Steve said, after he cleared everything away, "let's see if we can get this thing on the road. I was learning how when you woke up."

"Learning how?"

"Yep," Steve mimicked. "I'm new to this too, you know."

Neither Steve nor Jackie knew they had both been shown the way to this craft, or that they were about to begin the strangest adventure of their lives.

Steve opened the hatch with the computer, and gripped the .45 in his right hand. He went down the steps carefully, checking for more *crazies*. Finding the hangar empty, he opened the big door. The heat rushed in, bringing the sun's rays with it, and he saw that it still hadn't rained.

If it doesn't rain soon, everything is going to burn up. He didn't know it would not rain again until a certain problem was ironed out, nor that he would be expected to risk his life to bring this about.

He found the umbilical that powered up the hangar and disconnected it, slightly amazed when the power line automatically recoiled into the side of the ship. He turned then, stepping into Jackie and knocking her down.

"Oh, Jackie!" he cried. "You should have stayed inside. I don't want you to get hurt again, not ever."

He helped her up, and she smiled at him. "I wanted to go with you, Steve. I like you."

Steve couldn't argue with her on that account, and they went back into the ship, hand in hand.

CHAPTER SEVENTEEN

Colonel Jeremy Francks had big plans, but they didn't include any of the personnel at the Dome, including Sergeant Pilke. When Pilke's usefulness ended, so would his life. He would then be the only one left—he would have the power of life and death over everything within a hundred miles—most especially the woman at the farm.

He had promised that Pilke would get the woman, but he was not going to share her with anybody. He'd had the farm and the people in it under surveillance, and, when the time came, he would have her. She would do as he asked, or he would kill her and her whole family. The old man would die first, and he knew that the woman would probably do anything to save her brat.

The threat of such a weapon should be enough. After he exterminated the personnel, he would proposition the woman. When he explained to her about the nuclear warhead that he had armed, she would be his slave. If that didn't work, he would fly the chopper over the farm and destroy it with the formidable weapons it sported. She would fear for her life, and would comply with his wishes.

There was a part of the Dome that was posted *OFF LIMITS* to all personnel, and he alone had access to it. Inside this restricted area sat a helicopter that he had flown here. He had landed the helicopter in the restricted area, and then closed the roof over it. The control for the roof was part of the helicopter panel, but it could also be operated from a panel inside the door of the *secret* compartment. All he had to do was to open the huge panels in the roof, and then pilot the devastating chopper out.

It was a fearsome thing. Heat seeking missiles, some charged to explode into fire on contact. Large caliber machine guns—that were capable of cutting large trees in two—and armor plate that would stop almost anything that man had devised. The chopper was his escape hatch, his personal weapon, but he didn't think he would ever have to use it.

The only fly in the ointment—Colonel Franks thought—*was that a Doctor Koessler knew about it. Koessler had been here since before the Dome had been built, and had supervised everything. He would have to be eliminated along with all of the others.*

There was another farm, eighty miles from Portland that also had a silo, but there was no corn in it. Inside this bunker nestled a nuclear missile, and the Dome had been built for the deployment of this missile in the event of a strike. He knew there were other such missiles around the country, but he didn't care about them. He had armed this particular missile, and now he could either deploy it or detonate it in the silo. He didn't have to depend on the Dome computers to energize it; he could do what he wanted from the large A.P.C. or the chopper, and he could time it so he would be hundreds of miles away when detonation occurred

Yes, he would have the woman and the Dome all to himself. He would live out his years in comfort, and have all of his hearts desires.

Colonel Jeremy Francks was still sitting there, counting his treasures when Sergeant Grimes rushed into his quarters.

CHAPTER EIGHTEEN

You have summoned me, Captain? the colors exploded.

Yes, Commander, the captain's colors answered. *The young one that we directed has entered the ship with the one who has the power.*

And does the one with the power realize what he has become? That the plate covering his thoughts have changed him?

No, Commander! He thinks he is having visions. He is aware of things that other humans do not know, but thinks it is his memory returning. He does not understand the warnings, but has guessed that his mind is doing it. He is perplexed at the woman's projections!

Captain, the commander advised, *I am positive that he is the one. He will soon be sending thought as we do, only more so. The woman will be able to transmit her thoughts, but I suspect only to this one brain. The man's brain has been heightened to send to all, so great care must be taken.*

The woman was "touched" by our mistake, and that is the reason she can project to this simple degree. I doubt she will ever be able to do more, but our old enemy will decide that. One other item before you return to your duties, Captain.

Yes, Commander?

You must be careful not to transmit undue thoughts to his mind, for he will surely pick them up and think he is going the way of the rest of his world!

He is that strong?

Yes, Captain, the commander proclaimed. *He is, and growing stronger each day. He will soon be able to bend matter to his will, simply by thinking it. Something was changed in his brain to permit this, for he has no wires in his brain as we do.*

The captain was incredulous upon learning this, as his race all had wires implanted into their brains. Some were graced to a greater degree, as his commander was. He hoped that he, too, would be deserving of a greater honor, and be rewarded with the final wire as his commander had.

His great commander could cloud his mind to all, except The Co-Existent Planetary Commission. If they wished, they could monitor all in their planetary realm, but not other systems. This was one of the reasons the aliens had been dispatched to this world, to report on the progress being made. The Beacon had been established, and now his great commander could report to the Commission.

Yes, Captain, the commander beamed, reading the captain's thoughts. *You will advance to a higher level. You have only to think "gracious" thoughts, and accept the punishment meted out to us for our transgressions on a lesser world. We have been trained from birth to think only gracious thoughts, for an unclean thought is punished greatly. All of our wires would be taken away.*

The captain knew that in his many time frames, he had heard of no such thing! All of his race were GRACIOUS, and even the very young had wires. Their race had not planned to harm this world; it had been a terrible accident.

The Commander reported to the Commission, hoping to please them. He received an answer via thought transference, a thundering order of obligation. It would now become their duty to bring the survivors of the doomed planet together, and to right the wrong they had brought to an innocent people.

CHAPTER NINETEEN

When Jessie looked out over her domain, the panorama was unknowingly transmitted to another mind. By she was also *receiving* pictures, although they were not as clear as she would have liked them to be. It was at that moment that she realized what was happening to her.

Her heart became light, her senses swam. She was not going crazy after all. She was merely picking up some thoughts from another brain. She was so exuberant she wanted to do something, go somewhere, anywhere. Maybe a shopping trip?

She thought they could probably get to Salem without much trouble, and besides, they had almost cleaned out everything in Sweet Home. There hadn't been that much left there after the mobs had gotten through with it. She remembered when she had asked her father one day about going to Portland, and how he had been visibly shaken.

"Honey," Peter had said, "in a big city like Portland we wouldn't stand a chance. Besides, I don't think we could get through. There must be cars piled up all over the place by now. You know yourself it's hard enough getting into Sweet Home."

Jessie had not pressed him on it, because she'd known he'd been right. They had ranged out to other towns and cities, but had trouble getting to them . Her father had wanted to get some automatic rifles, and that's why they had gone. She had wanted to look around at some of the stores, but he had driven them right back.

"I'm afraid we can't stay here too long, Jessie," Peter had warned. "There's been so much death that we would just be inviting trouble. Could be all kinds of disease and bacteria, just waiting to get into a person's pores. You really don't want to stay here in all this stench, do you?"

She had agreed with him on that. It had been two months after Keith had tried to kill her, but the smell of death had still permeated everything.

Jessie's father had been in Viet Nam, and knew all about automatic weapons. He had shown her and Kevin how to use the rifles, and now they carried them wherever they went. The only exception was when they were at the farm.

They had a small generator, but it was getting harder to get fuel for it; they had to travel farther all the time to find cars that they could siphon gas from. Peter had hooked up a few lights and the refrigerator to the generator, and at times he enjoyed watching a movie on the VCR.

But today she didn't want to watch a movie; she wanted to go someplace, even if it meant carrying her rifle in the stifling heat. Her father was still in the house, and Kevin was off somewhere with Miss Muffet, but she knew that a clang on the old bell would bring them to her.

Peter rushed out of the house, his face half-shaved "What the hell's the matter, honey? Why did you ring the bell?"

"Nothing, Dad," she said, smiling at him. "My, you look funny with your face half shaved. You tryin' to start a fad?"

Peter looked at her and smiled. He was relieved that his daughter wasn't in some kind of danger. "Yeah! Now…what in hell made you ring the bell?"

Kevin and Miss Muffet came racing from behind the barn, the dog way out in front. When they were all together, she told them about her theory, and of wanting to do something. Jessie made sure she included Kevin in all of their decisions now, mainly because he was growing up, but she also didn't want to hurt his feelings any more.

"But… Jessie?" Peter became anxious. "How can you be so sure that's what it is? I mean, I heard of some strange things happening, including what you're talking about, but I never, ever saw it happen."

"But it's true, Dad," Jessie said. "I...I had another vision this morning, and I hardly had any pain at all. I know he's coming here, and now he's not alone."

"Oh?" Peter said, his tone light. "How can you be so—"

"He has a friend now, Dad," Jessie said. "A child. I'm not sure if it's a boy or a girl."

Peter was stymied. Why couldn't he get this foolish notion of telepathy out of her head?

"Dad, it's the only sane answer I can come up with. I know you're a scientific man, and you need to prove what's right and wrong, and I can't prove I'm right. It's a feeling I have. Now, how about getting off of the subject and start enjoying this gorgeous day, even if it is hotter than hell! I feel I have to do something different today, even if it's only going for a walk."

A walk, yes, but not just a walk. A hike. Maybe back at that cave he would find some answers. Jessie had been walking to the cave mouth that day, had almost been outside when she had collapsed. It sounded right. Jessie had almost been outside of the cave, but not quite. Maybe she had received a part of whatever happened that day. If that was the case, could it be that her brain pattern was changed now, and she could do the things she claimed? He didn't believe it, not for a minute, but maybe he would find some other explanation back at the cave.

"Jessie? How would you and Kevin like to go for a hike?"

"A hike?" Jessie asked, unable to believe her ears. "You mean...a camping hike?"

"Yeah!" Kevin blurted. "Let's go! Me 'n Miss Muffet would love that!"

Jessie turned it over in her mind. Kevin seemed to be all for it; he was always raring to go. But it sounded like a great idea. "Okay, Dad," she said, trying to contain her excitement, "I'll get some things together and dig out the backpacks. You got any idea where you want to go?"

"I thought we'd go back to the cave we found the dog in," Peter said. "I want to have a look at the minerals in it. Maybe you're not so far off base after all."

Jessie looked at him strangely, but said nothing. She had some misgivings about going back to the cave, but she wanted to go someplace and now she would get her wish.

The cave; that's where it all started. That had been the day Keith tried to kill her, the day he'd died. The day her headaches had started, but not the visions. The cave and the visions, almost driving her crazy. Her headaches escalating, the pain almost unbearable. The cave! Maybe back at the cave they would learn something, but she had a hunch that it wouldn't be what her father wanted to find out.

"Don't forget to bring the rifles, Jessie," Peter said. "Never know what we're going to run across, and it won't hurt to be armed."

CHAPTER TWENTY

"I don't like that, Steve!" Jackie was resolute.

"What's not to like? It fits you, doesn't it?"

"It's brown. Don't like that color."

"Jackie," Steve said, slightly exasperated, "you should never look a gift horse in the mouth."

"What's a gift horse, Steve? You gonna give me a horse?"

"Skip it," Steve answered. "It's only a figure of—"

They had guns, and packs on their backs! They were going through the woods, four of them! Funny how he counted the dog as one. The man was talking, telling the woman something. They were walking single file, the man leading.

As Steve *watched*, he saw that the woman was going to trip on a fallen branch. His mind saw the danger and screamed a warning at her. She stopped in mid-stride and looked down, then stepped over the branch. She called to the man, and then spoke rapidly to him.

"I like this one, Steve," Jackie said. "It's blue, an' I like blue."

"Where are you? Who are you?" Steve spoke out loud.

"You're silly, Steve," Jackie said. "I'm right here, an' I'm Jackie."

"Oh," Steve said suddenly, losing sight of the vision. "I'm sorry, Jackie."

The vision had been clear. He'd felt that he had been in the forest with her.

"Uh, why don't you look around for a while, Jackie," he said, recovering slightly, "and pick out anything you want. I'm going to sit here for a bit. My headache is back, and if I sit here for a minute it should go away."

"Sure, Steve," Jackie said, engrossed in her shopping, "but I like this hat. Can I keep it?"

"You can keep anything you can carry," Steve told her softly, "but we can stop whenever we want and pick up new things. Don't take more than you can carry."

Jackie nodded absently, her eyes already looking at clothing. She wandered away on her quest for fashion, but became sidetracked when something else caught her fancy. Steve watched her for a moment then returned to his own curious endeavors.

He hadn't lied to Jackie; Steve really did have a headache. But it wasn't painful, more of a nuisance than a hurt. He let his mind wander, trying to bring the vision back. He had to find out who—and where—this woman was.

These "visions" are not from the past, nor the future. They are happening now, as if someone is making a movie and I am the audience. He was being drawn to this woman, and he believed that she was being drawn to him as well.

He pushed out, searching for her, seeking her energy. He wasn't surprised when he found her again for this had happened twice today. He was seeing in his mind what her eyes were seeing, but now he saw all around her. Steve pushed a thought into her mind as she walked. She stopped abruptly, and a name came into his mind. *Jessie. Her name was Jessie!*

He was surprised at this, because he had never before been able to *converse* with her. He thought she had to be very close to him, perhaps just outside of the city. He pushed again, and was shocked when he *heard* the answer. The thought waves came through loud and clear.

CASCADE MOUNTAINS ... OREGON

But...this was impossible. He was in Atlanta, using...using what? Telepathy? And she was in Oregon? But that...that was all the way to the Pacific Ocean! Even if he could fly there—which he couldn't—he was still six or seven states away!

Steve had found out that he was going to have enough trouble with the craft. He'd managed the ship horribly on the way from the hangar, and until he had more confidence in his ability he would keep the ship on the ground, even though it never really was on the ground.

"I'm ready, Steve," Jackie interrupted. "You wanna help me carry some stuff?"

Steve came back to the present to find Jackie loaded down with clothing, the blue baseball hat perched on her head at a jaunty angle, and two more hats in her hand. "I still have to carry my stuff, Jackie?"

"But... I need all this, Steve," Jackie explained. "I'll carry as much as I can, even this bear."

Steve looked at the brown bear clutched in her hand. "What's with the bear?"

Jackie looked at Steve, the pleading in her eyes not lost on him. Then she looked down at the floor. "I thought we could use a friend. I could hug him at night 'n everything. You wouldn't have to hug him if you didn't want to, but I would. I'd take good care of him, an' I wouldn't leave him where you could trip over him an' —"

"Okay, Jackie," Steve relented," I'm sold. Anyone ever tell you that you'd make a good con artist? Never mind; don't answer that."

Jackie smiled, raising her head.

"You ready to go now?" Steve asked, knowing he had been *snowed*.

"Yep," Jackie said smoothly, if you help me carry some of this stuff."

Steve knew he'd been suckered, but he really didn't mind. If he remembered correctly, all women did things like that to men. It was the way of the world.

"Okay, Jackie, let's go. We've got a trip to plan after we get back to the ship."

"Where we goin' Steve?" Jackie asked. "Ain't no place *to* go?

Steve thought of something, and pushed out at Jackie. He had to know it was really telepathy, and not his imagination going crazy. Jackie smiled at him, and then started to giggle.

"What's that all about?" Steve asked.

"How'd you do that?" Jackie answered with a question.

"Do what?" Steve feigned innocence.

She smiled at him again, looking at him in an amused way. "You said somethin', an' didn't even open your mouth!"

"Oh? What did I say?" Steve waited, holding his breath.

"You said, 'Pacific Ocean', but you never even opened your mouth. How'd you do that, Steve? Are you bein' funny again?"

So it was true! Not only could he pick up other thoughts, but he could also project his own. "You liked that, huh? It's a trick I learned a long time ago, when I was about your age. Would you like to play another game?"

"What kind of game?" Her eyes were shining, liking the idea of playing games again.

"You think of something," Steve began, "and I'll try to guess what it is."

"What cha want me to think about?"

"Oh, how about when you were little, and your mom cooked your favorite lunch?"

"My most favorite lunch?" Jackie's eyes were aglow.

"Sure," Steve said.

Jackie closed her eyes.

It was her sixth birthday, and she was going to have a party. Her mom was all over the place, fixing this, bringing that. Hot dogs were the main course, and after that there would be cake and ice cream. Her friends would be arriving soon, but her mom had given her a gift already. It was a cuddly bear, and she loved it because it was a "Special" bear.

"This is a very special friend, Jackie, given to a very special girl on a very special day. We even have your very special food. Hot dogs, followed by?"

"Cake 'n ice cream?"

"Yeah! Cake and ice cream!"

Her mom had smiled at her, and told her that this very "Special" bear would scare away all the monsters, especially the one under her bed. It would also bring luck, but she must never tell anyone about it. It was to be their secret.

"I'm ready to guess now, Jackie," Steve said.

Steve saw a slender woman with blond hair and a younger Jackie. They were going to have hot dogs, followed by cake and ice cream; he could swear he smelled the wieners cooking.

"Jackie?" Steve prompted when he became aware that she did not hear him. He shook her gently, mentally kicking himself for making her remember better times and a lost existence. Jackie opened her eyes and looked around, disoriented. She clutched the bear, holding it close to her. Steve saw the dazed look in her eyes, and remembered something he had seen when he had first entered the ship.

"I think your most favorite food is...cake," Steve told her. "And ice cream."

Jackie's dazed look faded, replaced with a look of wonder. "How did you know I liked cake and ice cream the bestest?" she quipped "Only my mom—"

Steve broke into her thoughts quickly. "I guessed, Jackie," he lied. "You know that nobody can see what's in another person's mind. Besides, everyone likes cake and ice cream, so it was easy. And you know what?"

"What?" Jackie asked, her curiosity aroused.

"Well, if we get on back to the ship, I'm sure there's some cake and ice cream in the freezer. Would you like some?"

Jackie's eyes lit up, her young mind melting at the thought. "Can I keep the bear?"

"You can keep anything you want, honey," Steve said. "Now, let's get going. We have some maps to look at after we have our cake."

CHAPTER TWENTY-ONE

Billy waited until everybody left for the mess hall, and then broke the lock on the footlocker. He knew what it contained and meant to have it. If he asked the owner for the item, the owner would have told him no, and with good reason.

He lifted the lid and pawed through the soldier's belongings, finally grabbing with both hands and dumping everything on the floor. He found what he was looking for at the bottom of the locker. He lifted the case out and carried it to his bunk. It was a shame to break this case open, but he had no other choice. He used a screwdriver from his own junk box, and pried on it until he heard a snap.

He pulled the top open, and feasted his eyes on the best automatic weapon ever made. He would get an argument from others on this, but in his opinion this was *the* best. Thirty shot clip—9MM ammo—355 caliber and selective firing. You could empty the clip in the wink of an eye, or use it in death dealing bursts. Billy didn't want to kill anyone, but he would if he had to. Four full clips rested in the case. He took the extra clips, leaving the empty case on his bunk. He had about one-hundred-and-fifty rounds for the weapon, and it should be enough to get to his objective.

Billy opened the door of the enlisted men's quarters—realizing the colonel had not posted a guard over him—and this made his exit easier. There would be a guard posted where he was going, but only one. He picked mess time purposely; knowing one of the guards would be gone to chow. This would give him a full thirty minutes to do what was needed, and more if he worked another con.

He went down the hall towards the outer doors, but turned left when he got to the suit room. They would not need suits outside; he had already proven that. He tapped on the door, hoping the guard would not be too inquisitive. The guard in question knew him, and came to the inspection window. Billy cocked the gun, putting it on full automatic, but kept it low and out of sight.

"What you want, Billy?" the guard asked. "Hey, what the hell happened to your face?"

"Little argument with Pilke," Billy said. "He won."

"Damn! He sure did. You should know better than to mess with Pilke. Never seen a meaner bastard than that."

"Yeah," Billy said, making small talk, "I found that out the hard way."

"What're you doin' down here anyway, Billy? Gonna be some good movies tonight, right after chow. All X-rated. Colonel brought some new vids back with him when him an' Pilke got back from their last little trip."

Billy leaned close to the inspection window, making sure the guard couldn't see the stolen gun and whispered to him. "Could be the colonel and Pilke are *both 'that way'*, you know?"

The guard laughed nervously at that, and then sobered, looking around. "Better not let Pilke hear you say that or you'll be dog meat for sure."

Billy smiled, noting the fear on the guard's face. "You're right there, Sarge. That's the reason I'm down here now. Last week, when I cleaned out the big A.P.C. I found a bottle of whiskey in the map room. I drank about half of it, and then I poured water in the bottle to fill it up again."

"Billy!" the guard said solemnly. "You're gonna get your ass in a sling if they find out!"

"Yeah," Billy agreed, "but that's not the worst part. While I was getting drunk I carved my initials in the label with a fingernail. I put the bottle back where I found it, but the colonel saw me before I got back to my bunk. That's how come I drew *farm* duty. I was out in that damned bush for three days without a smoke, spying on those poor people."

Billy saw that the guard's eyes were wide open in astonishment, and so was his mouth. "Oh, Billy. You're screwed! They're gonna know it was you that messed with that bottle! They couldn't have had a drink last time out; you wouldn't be standin' here now if they did. The colonel is pretty sharp, an' he would have remembered that you was drunk that day."

The colonel is insane, that's what the colonel is.

He thought about the predicament he was in, and the second part of his plan of action came to his shrewd mind. If he could pull it off, not only would he have another ally, but he would have gained precious time, too.

"Sarge," Billy began, "I gotta get into that A.P.C. and get rid of that bottle. It's my only chance!"

"Jeez, I don't know, Billy? If I get caught letting you in here, the colonel will have my ass in a grinder, not to mention what Pilke will do to my face!"

If the sarge could have guessed at what Billy was planning, these two worries would pale in comparison to the ones he would have then. Once Billy got the sarge to open the door and let him in, he would not have many choices left.

"C'mon, Sarge," Billy wheedled. "I only need a minute?"

"Jeez, Billy," sarge whined. "I can't *do* it!"

Billy put on the most hangdog face he could muster, and played his last card. "That's it, then! I might as well go outside for a stroll, and suck in a good snort of that poisoned air!"

The guard stood his ground, and Billy thought his plan wasn't going to work, but then the sarge relented. "Shit, Billy! Get your butt in here and go get that bottle!"

The guard unlocked the door and started to open it. Billy hit the door with his shoulder, sending the army man to his back.

"What the hell, Billy?" the sarge started to complain. He saw the machine gun leveled at him, and suddenly lost his voice.

"Now look, Sarge," Billy said, slightly remorseful. "I'm sorry it's got to be this way, but I got no choice. The colonel is out of his mind, and means to murder every man on this post. Me first!" Quickly, he told the guard what he had heard when the colonel and Pilke thought he was out cold.

"And they said they was gonna put every soldier where they put the officers?" sarge asked.

"Sure did. I figure Pilke and the colonel murdered them all. Look, they all went out in this A.P.C., didn't they?"

The guard sat up. "Uh, yeah."

"And only Pilke an' the C.O. came back?" Billy pressed.

"Yeah, that's true, Billy, but—"

"Come on, Sarge," Billy whined, "use your head. Why else would he send me out in a rigged suit?"

"Rigged suit?"

"Yeah," Billy answered, still enraged. "Colonel had the filter taken out, an' I was breathin' outside air all the time."

"But you...you said—"

Billy smiled. "Had to get the door open, Sarge."

"You're a bastard, Billy, you know that?"

"I've been called worse," Billy grinned slightly. "But I'm still not a killer like the colonel. He doesn't care who he kills or how many times, just as long as he gets what he wants."

"Which is?" sarge asked.

"Hell, Sarge, I don't know? Who in hell can tell what a crazy man wants? Now, are you comin' with us, or are you fool enough to stay here an' get murdered?"

"Us?" sarge asked, clearly confused. "Who's us? Murdered, you say?!?"

"Jerry and Ray," Billy replied. "They should be here any minute now."

"But...but they—"

Billy cut him off. "That's why I let Pilke work me over. I passed Jerry a .45 when that excuse for a medical man wasn't looking."

"You got guts, Billy, but not too many brains. You know what Pilke could have done to you?"

"Never mind Pilke, Colonel's likely gonna kill him after everyone else is gone. Only wish I was the one to pull the trigger."

A head suddenly poked through the door, and Billy turned, ready to fire.

"Don't shoot, Billy!" a weak voice commanded.

Billy saw that it was Ray, with Jerry right behind him. Both in the nude. Billy smiled when he saw them, unable to resist a jibe. "You guys can't hang around here like that. There's some clothes in the A.P.C., if you don't mind army issue. At least there was the last time I was in there."

The guard moved, and Billy trained the gun on him.

"Hold it, Billy. I gotta go with you now, whether I like it or not. If I stay, the C.O. gives me to Pilke for lettin' you in here. Seems I really don't got no choice. You conned me good. "

"Glad to have you aboard, Sarge," Billy smiled. "But you know, it ain't every day you get a chance to save a man's life."

"How's that, Billy?"

Billy smiled again. "I would have shot you if you hadn't opened that door; I was gettin' pretty desperate."

"Well, it's a damned good thing I opened the door then, isn't it?"

"I knew you had to come with us when you opened the door. You really were conned, but at least now you'll have an even chance to live. We all will!"

"Billy," sarge griped, "you are one conniving bastard, but I don't mind if you don't."

Billy grinned. "I got one little thing for you to do before we go. I want you to get your partner on the radio, and tell him that you don't feel hungry. Tell him to go to the movies, and that you'll handle this crappy detail."

The guard's eyes opened wide, instantly understanding what Billy was thinking. "Billy, I sure am glad that you're my friend. I sure as hell wouldn't want you for an enemy!"

CHAPTER TWENTY-TWO

You have a progress report, Captain? the alien commander queried.

Yes, Commander, the captain revealed. *It would seem there is another leader type. He sometimes has ungracious thoughts, but only when he is forced into it. He is very courageous, and not in the least is he selfish. He, and other's like him, seek to escape the one that would destroy them. Should we nullify the threat this evil one poses?*

That would not be wise, Captain! the commander warned. *We must not interfere physically. Is there not a possibility of swaying this evil one's thoughts?*

We have tried, the captain answered, *but it was a disaster. The evil one's brain is a maelstrom of ungracious thoughts, and the one that attempted to enter is now unwell, but we will erase the encounter before he is allowed back at his station. He was deep into the black pit before he realized his folly, but he is young and will survive the encounter.*

You have begun the mind wipe?

Yes, Commander. His mind is in The Raptures now, and he will remember nothing.

Very good, Captain. Now we must concentrate on bringing the powerful one to the woman and her family.

That will be unnecessary, Commander, for he comes to her now. As you have foreseen, he is now aware of his power, and has tapped into the woman's essence.

This is good, Captain, the commander's colors decreed. *You are still monitoring the courageous one?*

Yes, Commander, but we fear a confrontation between them and the woman; I see the same destination in their minds. We will monitor closely, and use our powers of persuasion if need be.

No, Captain, you will not! the commander ordered.

Commander? The alien captain became troubled.

If all is as you believe, this courageous one will do no harm. He will be seeking avenues of escape from the malevolent tyrant that pursues him.

What, then, are we to do? the captain asked. "We must protect the woman and her family."

Yes, the commander issued a thought, *but we must also learn of this new faction. Monitor all, and intervene only to avert death from striking the woman and her family.*

The captain bowed his head. He had not been excessively impressive in not thinking of this.

Do not be alarmed, Captain, the commander was quick to bring release. *I made mistakes when I was young and overly enthusiastic. Did not our own race make the gravest error of all? Raise your head, Captain.*

The Captain did as he was told, the flame growing bright in his mind once more.

When the powerful one and the woman meet, the commander continued, *their minds will become as one. Each will know what the other has looked upon. Their minds will know each other intimately. If procreation results from this meeting, then we will indeed have started a new race, one that will have no need of wires.*

These two beings are the key to that race, the key to our very own survival. We must do everything in our power to help this powerful one, for he has been set a very dangerous task, one that might very well end his life!

The captain had never seen his commander, only the beauty of his mind. The commander had never visited his troops or their minds, entering only into his own.

If the captain had looked upon the countenance of his beloved commander, perhaps he would not wish more wires. The commander was pure energy now, encased in a transparent prison and directing all through his captain. The commander did not think of it as a prison, for any sensation was his. He thought of himself as being in a gracious, elevated state, and, in fact, this is what he really was. His energy could be utilized to power a ship or an entire world. He needed no sustenance or rest as his captain did, but still he was not eternal.

The captain pulled himself up to his full height and straightened his pointed, ebony hat. The emerald fire from his mind poured into his eyes, producing pride once more.

He had been dismissed, but not admonished. He would do better, and someday perhaps get more wires that would bring him closer to his commander's status.

The ship moved from its location, hovering now over the Dome. It could not be seen from the planet below, but if any could have it would have been mistaken for a rainbow. The colors of many worlds danced on the hull, but inside all was emerald. Perhaps from the green fire emitted from the many emerald-eyed beings.

CHAPTER TWENTY-THREE

"What the hell do you think you're doing, mister?" the colonel roared. "You suddenly break your knuckles? Or do you want a little go with Pilke?"

The sergeant was shaken when he heard the name, but stammered out the message he had for the colonel. "Sorry, sir," the sergeant replied, "I guess I was so excited about the news I forgot to knock."

"News, Sergeant?"

"Yes, sir."

"Well, Sergeant," the colonel griped," you will be sorry you even woke up this morning if it is not damned well important news. Pilke hasn't had any exercise since he and Tanner had that little difference of opinion yesterday."

Sergeant Grimes brightened when he heard this, and thought he might come away smelling like a rose. "This concerns Tanner, sir."

The colonel did a double take when he heard this, starting to taste something bad in the air. He waited with baited breath for the sergeant to continue.

"Tanner's gone, sir," Grimes reported. "And so are Dusome and Scoggins."

"Gone?" the colonel belched. "What in the hell do you mean, *gone*?"

"Just gone, sir. So is Sergeant Neville and the large A.P.C.!"

Colonel Jeremy Francks came out of his chair as if shot from a cannon. "Whaaaat?!!"

Sergeant Grimes cringed when the C.O. fixed his wild eyes on him.

"When did this all take place, Sergeant?" the colonel asked.

The colonel's quiet, cool voice became a warning now to Grimes. He remembered other times that this had happened, and when the C.O. got like this someone usually had their balls wrung out.

"Uh, last night, sir," Grimes said, his heart hammering in fright. "Right after chow. Old Doc Soames screamed all night, but nobody heard him until a few minutes ago." Grimes was very nervous now, and his knees threatened to buckle when the colonel fixed his icy stare on him. "Uh, seems Scoggins and Dusome locked the doctor up in a storage closet," Grimes explained. "He's got a lump behind his ear, so they must have sapped him."

"With what, Sergeant Grimes?" Again, that cold, methodical voice.

"Uh, probably with the .45, sir." Grimes could almost hear the gears grinding in Colonel Francks brain.

".45, Sergeant? What in the fucking hell .45 was that?!!"

This wasn't going very well, Grimes thought as he began to sweat. He wished now that he had disappeared along with the rest of them. "Uh, Doc Soames said that Scoggins had a .45, sir. Said they forced him into the closet, tied him up and knocked him out. Must have cold-cocked him with the .45, sir."

The silence was maddening as Grimes waited for the wrath to come. "And the guard, Sergeant?" Francks asked softly.

"Guard, sir?" Grimes asked stupidly. He watched as the colonel's face went from ashen gray to pink, then to a deep crimson. When next the colonel spoke, it was through clenched teeth and very, very low. Grimes had to strain to hear him.

"The Infirmary guard, Sergeant? Just where in the hell was he when all this was going on?"

"He...he...he was dying, sir." Grimes stuttered. "We found him in the outside janitor's supply room. His own survival knife was stuck in his throat."

After another interval of deadly silence, the colonel smiled. Sergeant Grimes had seen this particular smile before and didn't like it one bit. This smile was reserved for the deceased.

"Tanner!" the colonel breathed.

"Pardon me, sir?" Grimes asked.

"I said Tanner, Sergeant," Francks repeated. "You deaf, as well as blind and stupid? He must have smuggled the .45 into the Infirmary. It's the only way it could have happened. I underestimated him, Sergeant; he's got more brains than I gave him credit for. And guts!"

Still smiling, he reached under his desk and pushed the button that would summon Pilke to him. Then he addressed Sergeant Grimes. "Sergeant, you will return to your quarters, and you will stay there until you are sent for. Until I get to the bottom of this, consider yourself under house arrest."

The colonel was still smiling when he said all this, and Sergeant Grimes was really starting to sweat.

"Who was the other guard on duty last evening, Sergeant?" Francks asked suddenly. "The guard working with Neville. I'll find out from the duty roster, so it won't do any good to lie."

The sergeant's face fell, and he told his C.O. about Neville telling him to enjoy the movies. That he would stand guard alone. Grimes heard the colonel utter something under his breath, but had the good sense not to ask what it was.

"Yes," Francks said. "That's what I would have done. Good tactics, very good indeed. Don't you think so, Sergeant?"

"Yes, sir!'" Grimes said instantly. He would agree with the colonel now no matter what he said. But when the knock came on the door he almost jumped out of his skin.

"Ah, Sergeant Pilke," Francks said when he saw who it was. "Come in...come in!" Grimes almost fainted, his knees threatening to buckle. He had screwed up one time too often, and now the colonel was going to let Pilke "do him".

The C.O. turned to Grimes. "You know my aide, Sergeant? Yes, of course you do. Everyone knows who Sergeant Pilke is."

Grimes almost wet himself, and could only stare open-mouthed when Francks turned to his aide.

"Sergeant Pilke, I want you to take Sergeant Grimes with you to that special place we have reserved, you know the one." He turned back to Grimes. "I've changed my mind about you, Sergeant. You've been truthful to me, and I want you to know that I'm impressed. So... how would you like to become an officer? We seem to be short of people that can make snap judgements—people to command—people I can trust."

What was this? Was the colonel going to give him a command? After he had screwed up so badly?

"Now, Lieutenant Grimes, I want you and Sergeant Pilke to find my A.P.C. and the men who have made off with it."

Lieutenant Grimes! Just like that! He rolled the words on his tongue, liking the feel of them.

"Of course, until I have filed the necessary papers you will still be a sergeant. Should only take a few days to make the changes in the computer, and then you will enjoy the rank and privileges of lieutenant. Good work, soldier!"

The colonel saluted the new lieutenant smartly. Grimes jumped to attention, saluting his commanding officer.

"Now, Lieutenant," Francks said pleasantly, "you will draw rations, for two days for two men. Then you and Sergeant Pilke will track down my A.P.C. Sergeant Pilke will be in command of this mission, and I wish to give him final instructions. Dismissed, Lieutenant."

"Yes, sir!" Grimes said. He saluted again and turned to go, confused but exuberant.

"One moment, Lieutenant," Francks called.

"Sir?" He turned back to face the colonel.

"Sergeant Pilke will meet you in one hour at the motor pool. Don't be late!"

"No, sir!" Grimes assured with courtesy. "I won't, sir! Thank you, sir!"

As he turned to leave once more, Grimes noticed the colonel and Pilke smiling, as if a private joke had been passed.

He couldn't believe his good fortune. Instead of being under house arrest—and maybe facing a court martial for being derelict in his duties—he was being promoted. He was getting a promotion in the field, no less, and all because of Tanner. He would repay Tanner for his good fortune. Oh, yes! And also for getting his ass chewed out. He hoped the C.O. would let him watch when Tanner and his boys were handed over to Pilke before they were brought up on charges. Colonel Francks almost always let Pilke have some fun before that happened, and he just knew this would be the case with Tanner. Yes, he sure hoped he was there when Tanner got his head busted up by Pilke.

CHAPTER TWENTY-FOUR

Steve and Jackie returned to the ship with their "purchases", and Steve punched in the code that would open the hatch. He had changed the code to one that he could easily remember

Once safely inside, Steve thawed the cake in the magic oven and dug out the hardened, frozen ice cream. He sat Jackie down and served up cake and ice cream for the both of them. Jackie was all eyes, and after she put the bear on the table, she dug into the long forgotten delicacy. Steve remembered another time that she had eaten this same dessert and he dawdled with his. Jackie finished hers in record time and Steve gave her the rest of his.

"You don't like cake 'n ice cream, Steve?" she asked.

"Oh, yeah," Steve was quick to point out," sure, I like it. But I can't eat too much of it. Gives me the runs."

"The runs?" Jackie repeated. "You mean it makes you go to the bathroom?"

"Yep," Steve said. "My system isn't quite what it used to be, so maybe I'll just let you eat the cake and ice cream."

He smiled at her, and Jackie licked her lips. Then she said something he hadn't expected her to say. "Maybe I shouldn't eat too awfully much of it either, an' save some of it for other people. Maybe there's other people that didn't go crazy, like you 'n me."

It made Steve think of the woman in his vision, and of the man and boy with her. It was time, he thought, to find out firsthand about them.

"Jackie, how would you like to help me plan a trip?"

"A trip?" she asked, her lips covered with ice cream.

"Yeah, a nice long trip."

"Sure, Steve," Jackie said, laying her spoon aside, "but do you have lots of gas to go anywhere?"

Steve knew it was time to show Jackie the ship and all its workings. He opened the hatch and brought her outside, and then he showed her how to use the number coded sequence.

"But... how'm I gonna remember all those numbers?" she asked, clearly perturbed.

Steve explained that it was a day, a month and a year. His birthday numbers. October was the tenth month, so you punched in a one and a zero. He had been born on the seventeenth day of that month, so the next numbers would be a one and a seven. Finally, the year of his birth had been nineteen-fifty-seven, so the last numbers punched would be a five and a seven.

"See, it's simple," Steve said. "1-0-1-7-5-7."

"But... Steve, how come you don't have to punch nineteen? That's the number in the year?"

"Forget the nineteen, Jackie," Steve interrupted, "we don't use it." He could see he was going to have trouble with this, so he tried something else. "Jackie, do you remember your birthday? The date you were born?"

"Well, sure! Everybody remembers their own birthday, for heavens sake!" Jackie was disgusted that Steve would think such a thing. She looked at him, more than just a little puzzled.

"What I'm trying to find out, Jackie," Steve held his patience, "is the date of your birthday. I want to change the access code to something you can remember."

Jackie thought of her birth date and it jumped unbidden into Steve's mind. He knew now what it was, but was amazed that it had exploded out of her mind into his. Was his ESP getting stronger?

"It was in February, Steve," Jackie told him. "February thirteenth. I 'member that, 'cause my mom's birthday was on the fifteenth. We both missed being valentine's babies by just one stupid day. My mom always had a party for me on mine, but she never did on hers. Why was that, Steve?"

"Your mom loved you, Jackie," Steve told her. "She wanted only the best for you, and to make you happy."

"I know she did," Jackie agreed solemnly, "an' I loved her, too! So did my daddy, but he hurt her, an' now she's gone! Why did my daddy kill my mom, Steve? What made all the people go crazy?"

Steve didn't know the answer to that one, and probably never would. He told her it had probably had something to do with the sun, but he wasn't sure. Then he reached into her mind and planted a suggestion, soothing the hurt.

"My mom's gone to heaven, hasn't she, Steve? She's not hurting anymore, is she?"

"Yes, Jackie," Steve told her softly, "she's gone to heaven. And, no, she's not hurting anymore. She's in a far better place than we are."

Jackie turned the mood around as only a child can, knowing that her mother was safe now and could never be hurt again. "I didn't tell you what year, Steve."

"Uh?" Steve said, caught unaware.

"It was nineteen-eighty-three. That's the year of my birthday."

Steve knew that from going into her young mind, but he couldn't let her know he already knew. "Okay," he said," let's see now. The second month, the thirteenth day and the eighty-third year. We could make the new code for the hatch: 0-2-1-3-8-3. How does that sound?"

Jackie seemed to be lost in thought, but Steve didn't interfere. He had resolved to stay out of her mind unless it became absolutely necessary to do so.

"But, Steve!" Jackie finally said. "It starts with a nothing. How can you start something with a nothing?"

Steve wanted to get this over with, but he didn't want to force it on her. He tried a little trick. "Jackie, lots of things start with a "nothing", even the way you spell out the number one"

Jackie's lips spelled out the letter "one" silently then smiled her silly little smile. "Yeah." she agreed, "It does, doesn't it? Okay, Steve, we can make the code out of my birthday."

Steve was relieved he had resolved that problem, until Jackie thought of something else. "I can remember the numbers, Steve; they're easy for me. But how are you gonna remember them? It's my birthday numbers, not yours."

Steve's exasperation level rose and he almost blurted out that he could always reach into her mind for them. He caught himself just in time and relaxed his emotions, taking his time. "Well! How can I forget your birthday? That's a pretty important day, isn't it? You just watch me and I'll prove it!"

He deleted the old code and punched in the new one. "See! It was easy."

Steve had her try the code and the hatch opened. "Oh—wow!" she squealed in delight. "It works! And I did it!"

"Of course, you did it," Steve told her. "Now, if anything happens to me, you will know how to open the hatch. Let's go into the ship now, and I'll show you how to run it, and the reason we don't have to worry about gas."

Jackie was strangely silent as she followed Steve into the ship, and voiced her fears before they arrived at the computers. "I don't want anything to happen to you, Steve! Why did you say that?"

Steve almost swore. He had said the wrong thing again and tried to appease her. "I only meant if I was hurt or something and you had to open the hatch for me. That's why I want you to be able to drive the ship, too, and use all of the controls, including the guns."

He showed her how to run the ship, and how to use the controls, but she wasn't too sure about the armament. "I can shoot the guns, Steve, but not at people. I don't want to kill people, even if they are crazy."

He argued with her about it, telling her that they might have to hurt some people. "But only to save our lives, Jackie. We haven't seen any lately, but there could still be some bad people around. People who will kill us if we don't stop them."

After several moments she said she would, but only if there was no other way out. He couldn't blame her for not wanting to kill; she had probably seen enough killing in her young life to last the rest of her life. She had to have been hiding for months just to survive, and she must have been very quick or very lucky. Steve didn't press her on it, and brought her back to the heart of the ship—the Reactor Room.

"This is what runs it?" Jackie was impressed.

"Yep," Steve said. "Seems pretty small, doesn't it? It also powers the lights, fridge and two stoves. It runs everything."

"But, Steve, my mom always had to put gas in her car. Don't you have to put gas in this thing?"

He explained to her that they would never have to put anything in it, and that it never shut off, even at night when they slept. The power would last a long time, and that maybe they could live out their lives in it if they had to. Steve also told her that the fuel that ran the ship was the same thing that made the bombs explode.

"The bombs we hide from?" Jackie asked, her brow knit in a frown.

"Yes, Jackie. That's why your dad built a bomb shelter."

"Why do people kill other people, Steve?" Jackie asked suddenly. "Why do they build machines to kill?"

Steve was trying to think up an answer to that one, when she hit him with another maddening question. "How come you call this thing a ship, Steve? I thought it was a motor home."

Steve gave her a story he didn't think she would believe, but she never questioned it. "I call it a ship, Jackie, but it really is a motor home with guns on it. Did you ever see a killer machine with bunks and a fridge?"

"No, but I've never seen a motor home with guns before, either."

He finally removed the situation by asking her if she was hungry, and the topic of food always took her mind away from whatever else was going on.

CHAPTER TWENTY-FIVE

When the alien beings attempted a time experiment, they had indeed pulled the Earth's ozone layer away. Down a long, dark tunnel that housed many other beings, times and dimensions. It was from another dimension that the horrible devastation—which killed off most of the Earth's population, and left most of the others mad—had come from.

Two other dimensions existed together on a single plane, one positive and the other negative. The gases that made up these dimensions were attracted to each other, but must never touch. For this reason, a thin line of plasma separated the two. A neutral, ionized gas was the only thing separating the world from total destruction. Without this protective film, the two dimensions would surely come together, and if this were to happen even the very heavens would be destroyed. When the Earth's ozone layer passed by these two dimensions, it tugged at the protective substance and the two dimensions were without protection.

When the experiment went wrong, the alien beings succeeded in reversing the process. They brought the Earth's ozone layer back to its rightful place, but also collected and pulled both dimensions and matter with it. This created a superheated stew that cooked most men's minds, until nothing was left but instinct. This was the reason that almost all humanoids and animal life had the unreasoning urge to kill, for each was obeying the most primal instinct of all. Each human and animal brain that had not been protected would now hold the belief that they must kill or be killed.

So now, the ozone layer was back, but it was not pure. Mixed into it were two other gases from two totally different ways of life. The only thing that kept these gases from completely destroying the galaxy—and completely destroying every mind on the planet—was the matter that mingled and intertwined between them.

Although the disappearance of the ozone layer caused the sun's ultra violet rays to shine through diffused, and some of the planet's inhabitants would have died from it, the terrible mind wrenching came from the totally alien gases that now ringed the hapless world. This was the reason for the tiny planet's beings committing the most terrible of acts. The reason Doctor Henry Gibson had died. The reason Jessie Barlow's husband had tried to kill her.

The three formless beings knew this for a fact, but they were not of the same dimension. Only one other knew of the terrible gases, and it would be the commander of the fleet that would attempt to right the dreadful wrong his race had caused.

This was why they needed beings with form, beings that had proven they could, and would use whatever force necessary, for no amount of thought could dispel the highly dangerous gases that threatened to destroy the galaxy, and, for that matter, the whole universe. For this reason, ships had been placed all around the tiny planet, in hopes of finding some vehicle or some being capable of the task. Such a being and machine was found, and they knew now that the one with the power could accomplish what they could not.

The aliens could destroy the gases, but at the same time the protective ozone layer would also perish. The planet's sun would then shine down in all of its intensity and everything would be burned to a crisp. Without the ozone layer, nothing on Earth would live, whether or not it was protected by some mechanical means. Nothing would be left alive. The only thing that would be left on the once green and lush planet would be the ancient minerals in the ground, and these would even be rendered useless.

It is agreed, the thought broke through. *The one with the power will be the one to restore these gases to their proper place, to rid this planet of them!*

Agreed, echoed other thoughts.

When will we notify the commander of this situation?

This came from the youngest of the three. Then, the eldest of the three, the most translucent, gave the answer. *This is already known to him, has been known since shortly after the powerful one awakened. We will now await the arrival of the one who has the power!*

CHAPTER TWENTY-SIX

Jessie didn't know if the voice she'd heard had actually been out loud or if it had just been in her brain. The voice had warned her just in time to avoid tripping on the broken branch, saving her from a nasty fall, maybe even a broken leg. She had told her father about it, but he had just raised his eyebrows and looked at her. He'd turned around again, and had started walking, mumbling to himself.

When the voice came again, she stopped walking, looking to see if even Kevin had heard it. Neither her father nor her son turned around, so she knew it was in her brain and had been meant only for her. She almost said her name out loud, but caught herself at the last moment. Her father would have thought she was crazy for sure.

She thought of her name, and then felt a tingling somewhere behind her ears. The sensation disappeared almost as quickly as it came, but she knew what had just happened. Whoever he was, wherever he was, he had just been in her mind. Jessie realized she had a fluttering feeling in her tummy and for the first time in months felt an ache in her loins.

Jessie blushed, and then looked at her son and father on the trail ahead of her. They had not even noticed that she'd stopped, and she ran to catch up with them. She let out her breath and tried breathing normally; slowly returning to some semblance of normalcy, but the ache in her loins persisted. She mentally exorcised herself, and gradually the ache stopped. When the voice returned—and the same thing happened again—she knew she was in trouble.

She and Keith had enjoyed a healthy sex life before he had been killed, but this was different. This was almost a religious experience, making her head swim and blurring her vision. She had to stop again, for the feelings she felt in her body made her weak. After the tingling behind her ears left her, Jessie found she was able to continue but the ache in her loins lingered.

What in the hell was happening to her? Was she falling in love with a voice? Or was she actually falling in love with the man who was sending the voice? There was no way to tell until she met the man in person. And she would meet him, of that she had no doubt.

She hurried to catch up with the others, waiting for the voice again but it was silent. All she could see was a picture of a blue hat; one like Keith had worn when he was on the ball team. The hat in her vision had a letter on it, but everything seemed fuzzy.

"Dad?" Jessie called out suddenly.

Peter turned, looking at her.

"Do you know of any ball teams that wear blue hats? With the letter "B" on them? Or maybe the letter "A"?"

Peter's eyebrows went up again and she could almost hear what he was thinking. If she had really concentrated she could have, but she didn't know yet that she had this power.

"Uh, well," Peter fumbled, "there's Baltimore and Boston. Lots of them wear blue hats, too. There's even a team way up in Canada. Blue Birds, I think. Some team that plays out of Toronto."

Jessie tried to see the hat better, but there was a haze in front of it. She didn't think it was any of the hats her father had just mentioned, but she couldn't be sure. "Do you know any with the letter "A" on them?" She could see another hat now, like the wearer had changed them."Uh, no," Peter stalled, trying to think. "Not that I recall. Could be California. What's this all about, Jessie? Why all of a sudden are you so interested in ball hats?"

Peter remembered that Keith had worn a ball hat, a black one with yellow lettering. He remembered Keith kidding him about it.

"You should wear a hat like this, Peter."

"Why's that, Keith?"

"See the letters on it?" Keith had answered. "Know what they stand for?"

Peter had known, and had said so. The O.F. had stood for Oregon Farmers, although there hadn't been many farmers around in a country where timber was the main source of employment. Even his daughter's "farm" was not really a farm; it only appeared that way because of her veterinary practice. He had told Keith what the letters stood for, as he knew them.

"Nope!" Keith had answered. "Got nothing to do with farmers."

"Well, if you're so danged smart," Peter had said, bristling. "What's it stand for?"

Keith had grinned. "Old Fart!"

Peter remembered that day, and remembered Keith laughing until he'd cried. But that had been a million years ago, it seemed.

"Because I can see one in my mind, Dad," Jessie said, breaking into Peter's reverie. "It's blue, but it has a different color peak. Anyway, it looks like a letter on it"

Icy stalactites of fear bombarded Peter's brain, causing excessive adrenaline to flow, causing yet more fear. Here they were—out in the almost burned out forest, a good possibility the only sane people left alive in an insane world—and his little girl was seeing pictures in her head. He had seen some kind of army installation up towards Portland, he recalled, on some kind of maneuvers, but he hadn't seen any signs they had survived.

"Uh, there's a team back east," Peter said, "not too far away from that Toronto place. It was in Buffalo, as I recall. The name on their hats escape me for the moment, but it could start with a "B". First part does. Come on, Jessie," Peter prodded, "let's get going. Maybe I'll think of something along the way."

He started out again, not thinking about hats or ball teams. He was thinking of his family, his grandson and his daughter, and of his little girl's apparent condition. What in hell was going to happen to them when they could find no more fuel for their generator? What was going to happen when they ran out of canned food? And what, especially, would happen if another sunspot—or whatever had happened to make everyone crazy—came back and happened again? They would have to move on soon, but he hated to leave the house. Kevin and Jessie would probably have a fit, but he could see no other way to survive. They had to find a new source of food, and with everything burned up, and no rain for months they certainly couldn't grow any! Well, they would have to be brave, and try to—

"Jessie!" Peter cried, suddenly turning to face her. He stopped so abruptly that the dog ran into his legs, almost knocking him down; Kevin had her on a rope so she wouldn't run off.

"Yes, Dad?" Jessie answered, and then warned Kevin about the dog. "Kevin, shorten up that rope, will you?"

"It wasn't her fault, Mom," Kevin came to Miss Muffet's defense. "Granddad stopped so fast she stumbled into him!"

"Never mind, Kevin," Peter said, taking the blame, "it was my fault. Should have given you some warning. Now, Jessie, there's another team I recall, and I saw a logo of theirs someplace. Not on a hat, but I think it was on a shirt. And there is a "A" or a "B" on some of their hats. Could that be the one you're searching for?"

Jessie closed her eyes and tried to see the hat again. Then she asked her father what the "A" or the "B" stood for. When Peter answered her, she knew she had the right one.

"I think it's Atlanta, Jessie," Peter said.

Atlanta! So far away! So far! Jessie opened her eyes as another thought came. "But, Dad, if it's Atlanta, wouldn't the letter on the hat be an "A"? Don't all of the teams have their city's letters on them?"

Peter thought for a moment and came up with the only answer he could think of. "Well, yes. The real caps do, but probably not those that are sold in the stores. I'm guessing, but I think the team usually has the club insignia on them. It could be just the initial of the club or the club's full name."

Jessie closed her eyes again, but could only envision the hat through a haze. She tried harder, and that's when she saw the bear.

And the tiny hand that clutched it.

She opened her eyes quickly when the bear turned into a bright light. "Ouch! That hurt!"

"What hurt, Mom?" Kevin asked, concerned.

"A bright light," Jessie explained. "I thought it was a bear. I must have concentrated too hard."

She knew there was a young person with the man she had "seen", but she didn't know if it was a girl or a boy. The person with the man had been almost as big as Kevin, but had it been a boy or was it a girl?

"Would you like a cuddly bear some day, Kevin?" she suddenly asked. She glanced at her father, thinking that she must really sound crazy with her line of questions.

"Plush toy?!" Kevin blurted. "Yuk! Not me! Boys don't play with stuffed toys, Mom. Only girls do that!!"

"So, boys don't play with stuffed toys, don't they?" Jessie said, trying not to sound like a mother, but failing to bring it off. "I seem to remember you playing with one, young man."

"Yeah," Kevin said, defending himself, "but I was only little. When boys start going to school they want bikes an' robots. Things like that."

She knew that Kevin was right. He'd stopped playing with stuffed animals around the same time that he'd told her not to leave the night lite on in his room any more. He'd said he wasn't a sissy, and only a sissy had to have a light on at night.

Well now. I did see something. Only for a second, but something was there. But it hadn't been a boy's hand clutching the bear after all; it had been a girl's hand.

"You ready to go now?" Peter asked, interrupting Jessie's puzzle. "I want to get back to the house before dark."

"Sure, Dad," Jessie said, trying not to think any more on the subject. "Let's go."

Her ears were ringing, and her eyes were still sore from the bear episode so she didn't try using her mind for anything else. She didn't tell her father about the ringing in her ears; he would want to take her home and pack her head in ice.

When they were almost to the cave, Miss Muffet started growling. With the hair on the back of her neck standing straight up, she bared her teeth in a vicious snarl. Jessie knew she was in attack stance, and was surprised to see the dog like that. She was always so gentle, even when she'd been hurt. Peter stepped back and took the rope from Kevin, holding the dog back.

"You think she remembers the cave, Jessie?"

"I don't think so, Dad, but I don't know what else it can be? Maybe we better tie her out here until we leave."

Good idea," Peter said, agreeing with his daughter. Peter tied the rope around a tree and started towards the cave. Kevin bounded ahead as usual, and then disappeared into the dark opening. Peter and Jessie heard a yelp, and then nothing.

"Kevin?" Jessie called, "Are you all right? Answer me, Kevin!"

Jessie waited, and when Kevin didn't answer both she and Peter dropped their rifles from their shoulders to their hands, advancing on the cave. They had only gone a few yards when they stopped, staring in widening disbelief.

"Okay, folks," a man warned. "Drop your weapons right there or the boy is gonna get hurt!"

CHAPTER TWENTY-SEVEN

"What cha doin', Steve?" Jackie asked.

Steve was pouring over the maps, trying to find the easiest route to Oregon. They had to stay away from big cities as much as they could or they very likely would run into trouble. "Planning our trip, Jackie," he answered. "You wanna help?"

"Sure," Jackie said. "How?"

"Well, this is where we are," Steve told her, pointing to the map, "and this place—way over here—is where we are going. We have to find the easiest way to get there, but we have to stay away from the big cities."

"Why?"

"Because, if we try to go through big cities all the roads will be blocked, and that's where we'll meet up with more crazies."

Jackie turned pensive, and Steve was tempted to delve into her young mind. He still didn't know what her last name was—and she hadn't told him—but he would let her do that in her own time. The power he had could be a great help at times, but it could also be a curse. He must learn to curb his curiosity.

"Oh!" Jackie answered. "We don't want to do that, not ever again!"

Steve traced out a route with a pen he found in one of the drawers and thought that Jackie must have had a hard time of it. She had been alone for a long time, and she must have seen some terrible things. He would ask her about it some day, but he would let her tell it and not take it out of her mind.

"Now, this is where we are," Steve continued. "If we take number twenty it will eventually take us into Alabama. Oh-oh, we have to go through Birmingham, but maybe we can...yes. See this road here? It's a bypass. Maybe it will be clear enough to—"

His eyes began to water; so much he couldn't see what he was doing with the pen. A dull throb started at his temple, and a grim scenario unfolded in his mind. He was looking at a cave, and what his mind saw made his blood run cold. Jessie! His Jessie was being threatened!

There were three men with guns, and another man was holding the boy prisoner. The boy was struggling but he was no match for the strong arms that held him. He "watched" helplessly, and saw Jessie and the older man she was with lay their weapons down on the ground. He saw Jessie start toward the boy.

He saw that one of the men had raised his rifle, and he watched in horror as the man's finger tightened on the trigger. Then he saw, in his mind, the deadly projectiles actually leaving the barrel of the gun. His mind pushed out, trying to protect Jessie and the boy from being struck. But he saw he was too late, he just didn't have that sort of power!

The bullets struck Jessie in the head and chest as she scooped the boy up into her arms. Steve was so angered by the foul act of the murderer he wanted to kill. He pushed harder, and to his amazement saw Jessie and the boy stand, seemingly unhurt.

Steve saw Jessie raise her arm, pushing at something. She pulled her hand back, as if stung, then collapsed to her knees. A part of Steve's mind turned to the man still holding the gun, and saw the deadly rifle fall to the ground. Saw the wide-open eyes and the look of utter confusion on his features, as though the gunman were in a trance.

Panning his inner vision around, he pushed again and saw the other men drop their weapons. The discarded rifles were smoking, and the ground was burning where they had been dropped. The man who had been with Jessie quickly retrieved his rifle, holding it in front of him as he went to Jessie. Steve knew who the older man was now, and he was relieved. The boy was Jessie's son, and that's why she had risked her life like that. The older man was a doctor, but he was also Jessie's father.

Steve slowly backed away; he didn't know what would happen if he relinquished the force too quickly that he had created. He watched as Jessie's father approached her, watched as the older man stopped in front of her, waiting.

Steve's temper faded when he saw Jessie stand again then walk to her father. She was holding onto her son's hand, and now Steve knew both of the names of the men in her life. He now knew that her son's name was Kevin, from when he'd enveloped both of them, and now he also became aware that her father's name was Peter. This came to him when Jessie and her father embraced.

Steve waited where he was as they embraced each other, and pulled all the way out when he knew they were safe. A tug on his arm brought him out of his trance, and he looked down at the beautiful, but frightened, eyes of a child.

"Steve? What happened to you? Why did you scream? You got that headache again?"

He looked down at the terrified girl, noting the tears in her eyes. He smiled at her, telling her he had been daydreaming, and that he was all right.

"But how come you screamed?" Jackie was insistent. "An' why is your fist closed? Were you going to hit someone? An'…an'…an' what happened to the map?"

Steve looked down at his clenched fist then opened it. He saw three objects in the center of his hand. At first he thought they were coins, but a closer inspection told him what they actually were, what they had to be! He had seen things like these before, and the memory of them came into his mind.

He and Garcia had been in on a hostage-taking incident, and that had been the day Garcia had died. She had taken the bullets that had been meant for him, and had been killed in an alley behind an apartment complex. Another cop shot the psycho who had shot Garcia, and the psycho had died, too. But he'd emptied his gun into the concrete wall when he'd gone down, and that's where Steve had seen the slugs before.

God, how he had loved that dog! He had trained Garcia from the time she'd been only a pup. Although she had been a female dog, he'd named her Garcia. It had seemed like a good idea at the time. He'd stayed drunk for a week after that incident, he remembered, until Paterson's goon squad had dragged him home.

But why had that particular memory come back to taunt him? And where had "home" been then? When had that been? Did this recall have to come back to tell him he was holding three flattened bullets in his hand? But…how they had arrived there? Somehow, when he'd pushed a thought screen between Jessie and the oncoming bullets, it had stopped them, had actually flattened them. But how had something—as tangible as lead—traveled back to him on a thought wave?

Steve stopped thinking about it before he went mad, and looked down at the map, wondering what Jackie was talking about. What he saw then astounded him. Birmingham didn't have a by-pass any more. In fact, Birmingham didn't have anything; it was gone! In its place there were two holes that looked like they had been burned with a torch. The implications were staggering.

Oh my God! What have I become? Is it possible for me to destroy something like that? Just by thinking about it? And what about innocent bystanders? Would they also suffer like this map?

The more he thought about it, the more he knew he would have to curb more than his curiosity. Now, he would also have to keep his anger in check. He must never hate again or innocent people might be hurt. Even destroyed! He had to put it out of his mind, and so he returned to the map, wondering what he was going to say to Jackie.

If they could fly, they would get there faster. Even if they had to follow the roads, they would at least be above the snarled traffic. He thought he had a way that he could find the password—a way to make the ship fly—but it would be risky.

"Jackie?" Steve looked around when she didn't answer, and saw that she was curled up in a corner, sucking her thumb.

"Jackie?" he said again, slightly confused. "What's the matter?"

She wouldn't answer, prompting Steve to walk toward her, intending to help her up. When he reached for her she scrabbled back. Steve stopped, realizing now that she was frightened to death of something. "Are you all right?" he asked. "Are you afraid of something?"

She nodded, sucking harder on her thumb.

"What is it? What are you afraid of?"

She pulled the thumb from her mouth and finally told him. "You. I'm afraid of you."

"Me!?" Steve said, appalled. "Why are you afraid of me? I thought we were pals?"

She wouldn't answer, and Steve decided this was one of those times that he would have to look into her mind. He was about to do this when she started to cry.

"You made fire, Steve!" Jackie blurted. "Don't like it when you make fire!"

"Fire?" Steve asked. "What kind of fire?"

"Your eyes," she said. "You made sparks come out of your eyes! I seen them, an' I was afraid for you. That's why I pulled on your arm; I didn't want you to get hurt. Then I'd be all alone again!"

Then…it was true. He had burned the map, but the fire had come out of his eyes. Another tangible object that had something to do with the strange power his brain had been endowed with. Hank had been right about his brain, but Steve didn't think Hank had meant these kinds of powers. He had to tell Jackie something, but what?

"Oh, Jackie!" he began, "nobody can make sparks come out of their eyes. Maybe you saw the light reflected in them."

This seemed to make her think back, but it didn't decide anything. "Then what made the map burn?"

He had to find an answer or he would have to tell her everything, and that wouldn't be a good idea right now. Besides, how could he explain something like that to an eight-year-old girl? Even one who had seen far too much for her years?

"Maybe…maybe the map light got too hot and burned it," he lied. "Maybe the ship got a power surge, and it made the lamp too hot."

Jackie stopped crying, a questioning look on her face. "A power surge? What's a power surge, Steve?"

Now what? How was he going to explain about electricity when he didn't know how it worked himself? He remembered something his eighth grade teacher had told the class one day, about a special plug that had to be installed before they could use the VCR

"Well," he began, "electricity is something like water, but it flows along a wire instead of a pipe."

"I know that!" Jackie suddenly exploded, her fear forgotten momentarily, " I ain't stupid, y' know! Whoever heard of pluggin' a kettle into a water tap? My mom never—"

Steve stifled a grin. "Wait, Jackie, I'm not finished yet."

My, my, what a temper! It was easy to see that she wasn't afraid now, but Steve could see that this was one peeved little girl. If she ever grew up and found a husband, well, he sure felt sorry for him.

With daggers still coming out of her eyes, Steve continued. "I meant that only as an example," he explained. "When you open the tap a little, only a tiny bit of water comes out. But when you open it all the way, lots of water comes out. The more you open it, the more water you get and the faster it comes out."

Jackie still had a disgusted look on her face. If he were to peek into her mind now, he wouldn't stay there too long. "When you plug into electricity, the tap is always wide open. Sometimes too much comes out, and whatever is plugged in gets too hot. And that's what a power surge is."

Jackie chewed that one over in her mind and her face brightened, losing the peeved look. "That happened to my mom once," she said. "She plugged in the toaster, an' the toast flew out right onto the floor."

"There, you see? That's what must have happened to the map light," he lied again.

"Don't turn it on again, Steve," Jackie implored. "Let's bring the map up to the front where we don't need the map light. Okay?"

Steve smiled. "Sure thing, Jackie. We don't need that old light anyway. We've got lots of light up front"

Steve helped her up, and then they walked to the consoles at the front of the ship. "Uh, how about taking a nap? And when you wake up, maybe we'll get out of here."

It was the wrong thing to say again, and he cursed silently. Would he never learn to choose his words more carefully?

"I don't need a nap!" Jackie fumed. "I'm not a baby, y' know!"

Steve had to smirk a little at the look on her face, and hoped it wouldn't set her off again. "Oh, I know that. You're a big girl now, but I have some studying to do before we go. Maybe when you wake up I'll be able to fly this thing."

Jackie turned, a strange look on her face. "I thought you said you didn't know how?"

"Well, I don't yet," Steve said truthfully. "That's why I have to study."

Jackie turned back to the consoles, saying nothing. She climbed up to the bunk, and Steve reached up to tuck her in. He stepped back down and sat at the console, pretending to study it. When she went to sleep he thought he would really get into the workings of this computer.

"Steve?"

"Yeah, Jackie?"

"My mom didn't buy a new plug, y' know."

"A new plug?" Steve asked, more than slightly confused.

"Nope," Jackie said. "She bought a new toaster."

Steve didn't know what to say, and told her to go to sleep. Before she nodded off, however, Jackie had one more question. A question Steve would have been hard pressed to answer.

"Steve? How come this motor home can fly?"

Before he could come up with an answer, Jackie thankfully drifted off into slumber land.

CHAPTER TWENTY-EIGHT

Sergeant Grimes still had ten minutes to go before the allotted time would expire. He was starting to have second thoughts about his good luck now, and wondered why the colonel wanted him for an officer. He was still wondering about it when Pilke showed up.

"Okay, Grimes," Pilke said, as sarcastically as he could. "Let's get our asses in gear and get going. We don't have two months to find those suckers, we only got two days."

"Yes, sir."

Pilke looked at him, a mirthless smile on his face. "Don't sir me, you dummy," Pilke roared. "I'm not an officer, and neither are you yet!"

He flinched when Pilke roared at him, and vowed to put this bastard in his place when he became an officer. But for now, he would play it cool and try to stay out of his way.

Pilke strode toward the motor pool, where an A.P.C. was waiting and ready to go. Both men entered by the rear hatch and Pilke told Grimes to take the controls. Sergeant Grimes loved to operate machinery and didn't have to be told again.

"Which way, Sergeant?"

Pilke glared over at his companion, a sneer on his face. "Look, you asshole," Pilke said. "My name's Pilke and yours is Grimes. That's all we use. You got that?"

"Gotcha," Grimes said nonchalantly, ignoring the blast.

"Okay," Pilke said, a pleased look on his face. "Now, we gotta go toward Portland first. Somethin' I gotta take care of before we go find them jerks."

Grimes moved the machine out in the direction Pilke indicated. He was curious as to what Pilke had to do, but he'd be damned if he were going to ask him. Four hours later they reached a fork in the road, and Pilke told Grimes to veer left. Grimes obliged him, stopping when Pilke told him to.

"What in hell we stopping here for?" Grimes asked, forgetting his self-promise.

"Shut up, stupid," Pilke griped. "Pull into that yard and wait for me."

Grimes did as he was told, and pulled up to the house. Pilke reached over and put his beefy hand on Grimes shoulder, smiling. "Maybe I was wrong about you, Grimes," he said casually. "Maybe you will make a good officer. Uh, I'll be about ten minutes. Be a good time to get out and stretch your legs. Could be the last time you get to do that for a while."

Pilke went out the hatch and Grimes followed him. Grimes thought he heard an engine of some sort, but passed it off. Everything was dead all over the place, so there couldn't be anything still running.

Once outside, Pilke started towards what appeared to be a barn. Grimes put his feet on the ground and watched him go; paying no attention to the huge silo that flanked the new building. Pilke disappeared inside the big doors, but Grimes didn't even notice that these doors were exceptionally wide and high.

What in hell is going on with Pilke? Not ten words in four hours, and all of a sudden he wants to get chummy? Probably wants to get on my good side so I won't screw him when I'm an officer. Well, screw him. He wants quiet; I'll give him quiet.

If Sergeant Grimes could have seen the smirk on Pilke's face, he would have thought differently. If he could have also seen what was in the silo, he would have messed his pants. Further, if he could have known what lay in the basement of this house, he would have thrown up, and then run like hell.

After Pilke disappeared into the shadowy barn, Grimes turned to look at the house. They had passed many homes such as this, but they had all been derelict, some of them burned out husks. This one looked to be untouched, and this prompted him to investigate. Maybe there was something left inside that he could use. He looked back towards the new barn, saw no sign of Pilke then walked toward the house.

He tried the door, and to his surprise found it unlocked. A push was all that was required and he walked in. Once inside he closed the door, and then stared at one of the largest living rooms he had ever seen. It was a combination living and dining room, and on the huge dining table he saw some objects that didn't belong. There was a peculiar odor in the room, but he shrugged it off. Probably the place had been closed up for months, he decided as he walked over to the table.

He picked up one of the objects and turned it over in his hand. It was a sidearm, similar to the others on the table, but this one was inlaid with ivory. He wondered idly if it was really ivory or only common bone. He checked the clip and found it to be fully loaded. When he replaced the clip, he saw some initials on the butt and his mind registered them.

The letters G.T. were stamped into the butt of the gun. They seemed familiar, but he couldn't remember where he had seen them before or when. He opened his tunic and tucked the gun inside, deciding he would keep this one for himself. When he became an officer, he would replace the drab army issue with this fancy gun.

He glanced at the rest of the weapons, noting they were the same as his own. He counted them, registering that there were twelve, thirteen counting the one he had taken. It never once dawned on him that this was the same exact number of officers who had presumably been ordered back to Arizona. He left the table and looked at the rest of the room, his eyes lingering on the expensive furniture; every stick in the room oozed money.

Grimes left the room and walked into the kitchen, smelling something rotten as he did so. He expected to see a dead body rotting away, but the kitchen was empty and spotless. Next, he checked the refrigerator, thinking the source of the odor was coming from there. When he opened the door and the light came on, he knew he was wrong again and wondered where the hydro could be coming from. After checking the cupboards, he left the kitchen. He would check the rest of the house fast and get out before Pilke missed him. Maybe

Pilke would take some of the canned goods with them when they left; the cupboards were full.

As he left the kitchen, the smell worsened, and to his left he saw what appeared to be a closet. On closer inspection he saw that the closet had double sliding doors, and when he pushed them back the stench grew stronger. Inside the closet, on hangers, he saw army uniforms. On the floor of this walk-in closet he saw rows of boots, and finally his curiosity started alarm bells going off in his head.

After checking them all out, he found that all the uniforms had belonged to officers. Officers whom he had known personally! He parted the uniforms and saw a door behind them. He opened it and found the source of the odor.

"Grimes!" the voice was loud and demanding.

Frightened now, Sergeant Grimes turned around. He found himself looking down the bore of Pilke's .45, and he finally realized that the foul odor coming from the dark basement wasn't the only thing that smelled. Pilke returned his gun to the holster at his side, however, and Grimes breathed a sigh of relief. He had let his imagination go wild, thinking only the worst.

"I didn't know who was in here, Grimes," Pilke said. "Thought it might be one of those crazies. Phew! Smells like shit in here!"

Grimes swallowed hard, thanking his lucky stars that he had guessed wrong. It would have been better if he had trusted his first instincts. "You see what's in here, Pilke? All these uniforms? And the guns on the table out there?"

Pilke looked surprised, and walked towards Grimes. "Uniforms?" he asked innocently. "What kind of uniforms? Where?"

Grimes turned back to the closet he had came out of. "They're in he—"

A hammer blow to the back of his head stopped him from finishing what he started to say, and he crashed into the closet. He had been moving towards the closet when he'd received the blow, and that was the only reason his neck hadn't been broken. Dazed, and tangled in the uniforms he thrashed around. Two hands seized his hair and yanked him out of the maze. He felt a hand fumbling at his sidearm, and then he was set free. He spun around, losing his balance and fell to the floor.

His vision cleared a little, and he looked up to see Pilke's enormous face looking down at him. There was genuine pleasure showing on the grizzled countenance, and Grimes knew he had just made the mistake of his life. As his terror-filled eyes cleared more, he saw Pilke step back and level his own .45 at his head. Then, grinning, Pilke tossed the lethal weapon on the floor behind him. Grimes could see that Pilke's own weapon was still in the holster, and he could see his own gun ten feet away, but it might as well have been a million miles!

"Now! Mister Officer! Sir!" Pilke said, the sarcasm plain. "All you gotta do is get that gun, an' then blow my head off. If you don't, I'm gonna tear yours off, bit by stupid bit!"

Grimes was terrified, but he surprised himself when he found his anger greater. He was angry that he had put himself in such a position. He had a very low pain level, and knew he couldn't beat Pilke, because he had seen him in action when he had put the two grunts away at the same time. He had to talk his way out of it, had to save himself from being beaten up!

"Why are you doing this, Pilke? How are you going to explain this to the colonel? If you stop now I'll forget it ever happened. I won't even tell the colonel about it!"

Pilke laughed, an obscene sound. "You stupid fuck!" Pilke said, a grin creasing his features. "How did you ever even get to be a sergeant? The colonel ordered me to do this, not that I mind. Did you think, for one fucking minute that he was going to let you get away with what you done? Because of you, those jerks stole his special A.P.C. Now come on, asshole. Get up and take me!"

Slowly, Grimes rose to his feet. He knew he couldn't beat Pilke in a fair fight, but then again, Pilke didn't know the meaning of the word. He was surprised Pilke had let him get this far. His only chance lay in getting that gun, so he would have to somehow incapacitate Pilke long enough to get to it. And then he remembered the .45 in his tunic.

Grimes backed away, needing time to pull and fire the fancy gun. He reached into his uniform, fumbling, and Pilke rushed him! They crashed into the wall together, and Grimes felt pain in his elbow. Pilke heard the snap and laughed. Grimes' arm was still inside his shirt when Pilke rushed him, and Pilke's weight had broken his arm.

Grimes hadn't been able to find the gun in his tunic, and now he had a broken arm to boot. The pain was maddening, but all too soon now he would know greater pain. Grimes hoped he would lose consciousness fast; it was his only salvation now.

Pilke grabbed a handful of Grimes' hair and pulled him up. The huge right hand closed in a fist, and like a trip-hammer exploded into Grimes' face. Grimes' felt his teeth go, felt the impossible pain, then Pilke hit him again. When his jaw shattered, Pilke laughed. Grimes felt the new pain. His brain refused to believe there was pain that intense, and it mercifully shut down. Grimes never knew it when his nose exploded, making a bloody mask of his ruined face. Pilke let Grimes fall and walked around to his right side. He delivered a vicious kick to the downed man's side, smiling when he heard the ribs crack! Not finished yet, Pilke spread Grimes' legs apart and forever ended any chance of him ever fathering a child; the heavy army boots did their work well. Pilke laughed again, and dragged the limp body to the basement stairs that were inside of the closet doors. With a sneer of contempt, he dumped the body into the dark hole, and then closed and locked the doors.

"Okay, Mister Officer," he cried. "Hope you're not superstitious. You can be with your fellow officers now, all thirteen of them."

Colonel Francks and Pilke had murdered all of the officers, and had left their bodies in the specially built basement of the house. That was the raw odor Grimes had detected. Pilke hadn't been worried about Grimes finding them, because the colonel had ordered Pilke to murder Grimes as well. For Pilke it had been a pleasure.

Pilke left the house and roared out of the yard in the A.P.C. He had to get Tanner, but he knew almost exactly where he would be. The last time Tanner had been out on recon, Pilke had followed him. Pilke knew about the cave, and had destroyed everything Billy had left there. He had arrived back at the Dome before Tanner, and that's how Francks knew that Billy had been lying.

The one thing that Pilke didn't know was that Grimes wasn't dead. Almost, but not quite. It was the one mistake Pilke made, and he would pay for it in a big way.

CHAPTER TWENTY-NINE

Billy and his friends left the A.P.C. about a thousand feet from the cave and scrambled the rest of the way on foot. Billy reached into the engine compartment before they left and disabled the vehicle; he didn't want it to be used by anybody but them, and then they had camouflaged it as best they could. When he and his friends entered the cave, Billy knew right away that they were in trouble. He stopped dead in his tracks and swore.

"What's the matter, Billy?" sarge asked.

"Someone's been here, Sarge. All the stuff I trucked in here is gone." Billy checked the bedding, discovering it had all been ripped to shreds.

"This ain't been ripped, Billy," sarge said. "It's been cut."

Billy tried to remember the times he had been here, when he'd stocked the cave. He couldn't remember seeing or hearing anybody, not even a sign that anybody had been around. And that had only been... "We gotta go back!" Billy said quickly.

"You crazy, Billy? We can't go back to the Dome now! Francks would give us all to Pilke, one at a time!"

"Not to the Dome, Sarge," Billy corrected "Back to the A.P.C. We gotta get some supplies and guns from it. All the stuff I had here is gone."

Billy still had the automatic weapon he had stolen, Ray had the .45 and sarge had his sidearm, but that was the extent of their weapons.

"But, Billy, I never seen any guns there? All I seen was a few cans of food and some whiskey!"

Billy smiled, and then he winked at Ray and Jerry.

"How in hell can you smile at a time like this, Billy?" sarge said. "Don't you know they'll be comin' for us? Prob'ly on their way right now, an' they'll likely know right where to find us."

"Probably will, Sarge," Billy said. "But we'll give them a hot old reception when they get here."

"How, Billy?" sarge asked. "You gonna piss on em? Dammit, Billy. One of these days your cons are gonna land you in more trouble than you can handle. Of all the—"

"Take it easy, Sarge." Billy sobered momentarily. "I know where to get some guns."

"Where, Billy? Where in hell you gonna get any guns now? I sure as hell don't see any gun stores around here? Next thing you're gonna tell me is this cave once belonged to the three—."

Billy laughed, but the pain in his face erupted again. He put his hand to his mouth, trying to stop laughing. "Dammit, Sarge, don't make me laugh. Hurts like hell when I do that."

Sergeant Neville stared at him, still angry.

"The A.P.C. is full of stuff, Sarge," Billy explained. "Automatic rifles, some grenades and even a rocket launcher. There's food there, too"

"No way, Billy," sarge said. "No more cons!"

"It ain't no con, Sarge. I know what's there, 'cause I put it in there."

"I never seen nothing in there, Billy, an' I looked."

"You ever been on a bus, Sarge?" Billy asked "You ever seen where all the luggage goes?"

Jerry and Ray were standing to one side. They knew what was coming next, and Ray smiled. Ray touched Jerry in the side. Jerry couldn't smile, but he was laughing inside.

"You mean under—"

"Yeah," Billy interrupted. "Under. You was sitting on it all the time."

There came a look of utter astonishment on Sergeant Neville's face, turning his complexion from pink to purple. "No, Billy! Don't tell me my ass was sittin' on that stuff all the way out here? Grenades an' rockets? An' all that bouncin' around we did?"

"It was all well-packed, Sarge. Guess we know that for sure now."

Sergeant Neville shook his head and walked away. He mumbled something, but Billy couldn't make it out.

"Grab a rock, Sarge," Billy said "We'll go get the things we need. Maybe you should rest for a while."

Sergeant Neville didn't even let on that he heard, and plopped down with his back to a tree. Billy almost laughed at the dejected look on his face. When they came back, their arms loaded with supplies and guns, Sergeant Neville was sound asleep. They entered the cave, deposited their burdens on the cave floor, and then Billy whispered to his friends.

"I'm afraid the sarge was right about one thing, guys. Whoever took all the stuff I put here probably knows me. Could be Francks had somebody following me. Maybe Pilke. Yes, it had to be Pilke. That would explain how the colonel knew I was lying so fast."

"But what are we going to do now, Billy?" Ray asked. "We can't stay here too long or they'll get us for sure."

"You're right there, Ray," Billy said. "We'll pack up tomorrow, and then get as far away from here as we can. Maybe when Francks gets his A.P.C. back he'll forget about us for a while. We'll take as much as we can carry, but we'll make sure they can't use the A.P.C. against us."

"Sure thing, Billy," Ray answered, "but we better post a guard tonight."

"Yeah," Billy said. "I'll take first watch."

"Good idea, boys," a voice from the mouth of the cave said, "but we can't leave the A.P.C. here." All eyes turned at the sound of the voice and homed in on Sergeant Neville at the cave mouth. "And if Pilke is involved, the only way we're gonna get rid of him is to kill him. He never lets go once he gets something in his head."

Billy looked at the figure in the shadows, and for the first time in his life he couldn't come back with something smart. Ray came to his rescue.

"Sorry we got you mixed up in this, Sarge, but like Billy said, you would have died at the Dome. At least out here we've all got a fighting chance."

Sergeant Neville looked at the arsenal on the cave floor and whistled. He walked over to the rocket launcher and nudged it with his toe, whistling again. "You got some rockets for this?"

Billy found his voice. "A dozen. Should come in handy, don't you think?"

"Yeah," sarge agreed, "If we get a chance to use it. Tell me, Billy, how'd you know about all this stuff? I didn't even know about it."

Billy was smiling again, his former silence forgotten. It was not a happy smile, more like a wry grin. "Well, Sarge, when the officers and Francks went out in the A.P.C., I was told to load it in there. Now, I don't know where they went, but I don't think they'll be back. I think Pilke and Francks killed all of them."

"But why, Billy?" Sarge couldn't understand the reasoning. "Why would Francks want everybody dead? Seems to me he'd want people around to defend the Dome, and him, too, for that matter."

Billy then told them what Francks had told Pilke, when they had both thought he was unconscious. "Francks told Pilke that next week they were gonna put us all where they put the officers an' somethin' about a silo. You know anything about a silo, Sarge?"

Sergeant Neville looked down at his toes, then back up at Billy. The three friends looked at sarge, waiting expectantly when he didn't answer right away. Finally, something seemed to settle in Sergeant Neville's brain and he started talking. Billy saw the tension in the man's eyes, but everybody heard the tremor in his voice.

"There is a place, Billy, a brand new farm, supposedly. It's somewhere around Portland, an' it was built to hide a special silo. The government, using one name or another bought this place an' flattened the existing buildings. Then they had a new place erected, complete with barn and silo. There were four men there, supposed to be brothers, but they never grew a damned thing."

"Where'd you learn all this, Sarge?" Billy asked, impressed. "I mean, I did a lot of snoopin' around the offices when I could, but nothin' like this ever turned up?"

"I'm gettin' to that, Billy. Y' see, none of us were supposed to know about it, but I overheard the colonel and the officers arguing about it one day."

"Why in hell would they argue about some farm?"

As soon as Billy said the words, he knew what they had been arguing about. Not the farm or whatever it was. It was about the silo, and whatever was stored *in* that silo.

"There ain't no corn in this silo, Billy, but there sure is a lot of death and destruction. That's what all the yellin' was about. There's a nuclear missile in that silo. Francks wanted to arm it, but Captain Taylor and the other officers was dead against it. I'll go along with your idea that Francks killed them."

There was total silence in the cave. Billy had guessed what had to be in the silo, but Jerry and Ray hadn't.

"You never told us how you learned all this, Sarge?" Billy asked, intrigued.

"True, Billy. I never told nobody about it; I was afraid to. If Francks ever got wind that I knew about it... he would have served me to Pilke on a platter. It was all hush-hush stuff, an' I knew it. I was passin' the main conference room one day, on my way to sign off the duty roster. You know how Francks felt about proper procedure an' all. That's when I heard all the yellin."

"The door was closed?" Billy asked.

"Yeah, but I recognized Captain Taylor's voice. He was sure pissed off."

"This Captain Taylor," Billy interrupted, "is he the one who was always so neat? The one who had the fancy .45 on his hip?"

"That's him, Billy. That piece had real ivory on the butt, not just bone."

"But he was always so peaceful," Billy remarked. "I never seen him lose his cool?"

"Well, he did that day. I guess something finally happened to make him blow his stack. And now I'll tell you why we can't leave the A.P.C. here, an' why Francks and Pilke ain't ever gonna quit chasing us. Y' see, Billy, that computer in the A.P.C. can set the damned missile off! The missile can be armed and fired from there, but it can also be aborted from there, too."

Billy tried to whistle, but his mouth had gone dry and his face hurt too much. He didn't know much about computers, but he did know there would be safeguards built in to that kind of program. There were firing codes, and there would be a password that would have to be entered before anything could happen, probably more than one.

"But, Sarge," Billy said, "there's gotta be some kind of password you have to use before it could be armed, much less deployed."

"Oh, there is, Billy, but they're really simple. Even I could do it."

Billy was surprised. He had never seen sarge use a computer before. "You, Sarge?"

"It ain't hard, Billy. And I don't even know how to type. Once you find the codes and the password, the rest is easy. The computer asks you what you want, an' then all you have to do is punch the right keys. At least, that's what Captain Taylor told me."

"Uh, you know the codes and password?"

"Think I do," sarge admitted, "but it ain't in English. Oh, the letter's is English, but they're all mixed up. Captain Taylor showed me how it was done one day when he ordered some boots, said it was some kind of code that only computers understood. He said the code was something called *Binary*. There's a bunch of ones and zeroes, or they could be letters; it's called *input-output*. Then there's a bunch of yes-and-no things you gotta put in, but the computer only understands it if you use true or false. If you want to select something, you put an equal sign behind the one, and then you type true. If you don't want it to come up, you type in an equal sign then you type in false. Anyway, one turns things on, and zeroes shuts them off."

Billy thought for a moment, unable to understand any of it. "And you know how to bring this program up?"

"Shouldn't be too hard, Billy, but first I gotta have a pencil and paper to figure out the words. I can't do that in my head too good."

Billy was amazed that the sarge could be capable of doing something like this. He'd always thought that the sarge was next door to being a dummy. "Okay, Sarge. When we leave here tomorrow, we'll take the A.P.C. Just maybe we can throw a crimp into Francks' plans."

They made camp in the cave, taking turns on guard duty. The next day they heard someone out in the forest, and they'd almost been caught sleeping. Billy kept his head and brought them together, staying in the cave and sending the rest of them out among the trees. Whoever it was would now be hopefully caught in a cross fire.

Billy grabbed the boy when he rushed into the cave. He wouldn't have hurt the boy, but the bluff had worked. The woman ran to the boy after she dropped her rifle, and Billy released him. Billy yelled to the sarge to hold his fire, but the sarge was so excited he pulled the trigger without wanting to. What happened next defied explanation.

Billy was sure the woman would be killed, but as Neville fired, a mist swirled around her and the boy. Billy heard the splat of the bullets, and expected the woman to be hurled by the impact, but she never moved. Billy watched in perplexity as she first tried to push at the mist, and then sank to her knees.

When Billy looked at the sarge again, he saw a look of pure stupidity on his face, as if the man's brain had shut down. Then his own gun had gotten so hot he was forced to drop it. The strangers' guns were not hot, however, and now the old man had the drop on them. By the looks on the old man's face, they were not going to have to worry about the army catching up to them.

"Okay, you bastards!" Peter yelled. "Get down on your knees and pray!"

"No, Dad!" Jessie yelled. "Don't! Don't kill them!"

Jessie ran to her father and embraced him, stopping any further action.

Peter stared at Jessie, the terrible anger in his eyes making him look ugly. "But... Jessie?!" he pleaded. "They tried to kill you?"

"I know that, Dad!" Jessie cried. "But they're not crazy; can't you see they're not like the other ones?"

Peter looked at the men, at the army uniforms, finally coming to rest on Sergeant Neville. "That one, Jessie." Peter pointed with the gun, indicating the sergeant. "The one that shot at you. He don't look too damned bright."

The sergeant's eyes were vacant, his opened mouth drooling. Peter looked at Billy then gestured to Neville again. "Is he crazy? Was he outside when it happened?"

Billy looked at the sergeant, wondering what in hell *had* happened to him? The smoking guns puzzled him as well. "No, sir," Billy said. "Outside, sir? I don't follow you?"

"When it happened," Peter yelled. "Don't play dumb with me, boy!"

"But I don't understand *what* happened, sir? Nobody does, not even our C.O."

These people were the ones Billy had been watching, he knew, but now up close they seemed to be normal. Maybe if he played dumb a little longer he would find out what had really happened.

"The sun, man!" Peter exploded. "Something happened to the sun! Maybe a solar flare or a sun spot, I'm not sure what happened."

Billy knew that communications were out all over the globe. If it was the sun, the other side of the world would still be all right, but he knew it wasn't. "You must be mistaken, sir. If it had something to do with the sun, it would have affected only that part of the planet it was shining on at that time. But it also affected that part of the world that was in darkness."

Peter mentally chastised himself. He'd been so sure it was the sun. He hadn't thought about the other half of the world, the half that was facing away from the sun. This army man was right.

"Young man," Peter said, "I don't know what in hell it was, but right now it doesn't matter. Why did you try to kill us? And if that sergeant over there isn't crazy, then what in hell is wrong with him?"

"It wasn't our intention to kill anyone, sir," Billy said. "We thought you were...were someone else."

"Someone else?" Peter's voice blasted across the space between him and Billy. "Who in God's name were you expecting, private? And might I inquire why you, and not one of the officers over there, is doing all the talking? I should think that an officer would be in charge."

Billy was thinking all of the time that the old man was talking to him and he decided to tell him everything. The old man seemed to know his uniforms, and if they were going to get out of this with their skins intact, it wouldn't hurt to have some help.

"Uh, they're not officers, sir," Billy explained. "They're grunts, like me!" Billy told Peter the whole story then, leaving nothing out. Jessie was listening intently, knowing now that she *had* seen something that day. When Billy finished, Peter was astounded.

"You say this Colonel Francks intends to use the missile?" Peter asked, unable to fathom any reasoning behind the officer's plans. "On what, for God's sake? There isn't anything left to use it on!"

"I don't know, sir," Billy said. "Maybe he wants to use it as a threat. Maybe there's something he wants."

"And that is?" Peter asked.

Billy didn't answer. He simply looked over at Jessie, and then back at Peter. Jessie caught the implication and paled.

"Are you implying, young man," Peter said, his mind churning at the impossible theory, "that this colonel would use a nuclear missile to threaten what is left of this miserable world? For a woman? The man must be mad!"

"Yes, sir!" Billy was quick to agree. "He is that, all right. We have reason to believe that he murdered all of the officers because they opposed him on arming the missile."

"Oh my God!" Peter mumbled. His mind was wandering, trying to decide what to do when Jessie spoke to him.

"Dad? If we can't stop him, I think I know someone who can."

"Oh, come *on*, Jessie," Peter said. "This is serious! This is not a game anymore!"

"You still don't believe me, do you, Dad? You didn't see the mist around me? You didn't see that mist stop the bullets, either, did you?"

"Don't be silly, Jessie," Peter scoffed. "The man missed, that's all"

"No, sir," Billy said. "He didn't miss. I saw the mist myself, and I heard the bullets flatten out when they hit it."

Peter was annoyed at this upstart for siding with Jessie, and then his daughter hit him below the belt. "I touched the mist, Dad, and it was alive. I got the same feeling from it that I got from my hair dryer when it shorted out, but this mist pushed my hand back. I felt that it didn't want to hurt me."

Kevin was still holding fiercely to his mother. He was sniffling, but his fear seemed to be gone. "I felt it, too, Granddad," he vouched, "an' it sorta tickled. It didn't hurt me, an' I could see right through it."

Peter thought for a moment. He knew he wanted an answer to all this, and then his mind caught the elusive thought. "Well, well!" he snorted. "If these bullets flattened out, then they should be right around here, shouldn't they? But I sure don't see any sign of them!"

Jessie's hand clenched into a fist, angry that her father had refused to believe her. How could they find bullets that had probably caromed off into the forest somewhere? She knew that without those bullets her father would never believe her. She felt something in her hand and looked down. She opened her hand, palm up, and stared at the cylinder there. It was pointed at one end and almost flat on the other. She saw the lettering, and brought it to her face.

Peter's smug look vanished when she showed him the object, and after he read the letters he began to wonder. There were two groups of lettering, the first he recognized, but the second he did not. "Where did you get this, Jessie?"

"It was in my hand, Dad, but I don't know where it came from. What do those letters mean?"

Peter was still studying the second group of letters, but could make nothing out of them. "This is an Air Force pen."

"Air Force?" Jessie asked, confused.

"Yeah," Peter answered absently. "The first four letters spell that out. U.S.A.F. Damned if I can recognize the other letters, though."

Peter turned the pen around, and found another set of letters on the reverse side. He had seen this group of letters before, but it was a short form for a whole word. Miss Muffet started to whine at that moment, not caring to be left alone. Peter handed the pen to Jessie, and cautioned Billy not to move. He untied the rope, and led the dog back to Kevin.

"Hang on to the rope, Kevin," he warned. "Don't want her getting rabies from biting one of these lunatics."

Jessie glared at her father, a frown on her face. She shook her head, but said nothing. She looked back at the pen, and then read the word out loud. "Proto? What's that mean, Dad?"

Billy perked up. "Uh, could I have a look at that? Maybe I can make it out."

Peter grabbed the pen and pointed it at Billy, but didn't give it to him. "You know something about this, mister? Is this your pen?"

"Uh, no, but that word stands for prototype and we have all kinds of pens like that one in our vehicle. Probably not the same lettering, of course. But our vehicle is Army, not Air Force."

"Your vehicle is a prototype?"

"Yes, sir, it is," Billy answered. "It was built for the maneuvers we were sent here to do, but Colonel Francks wouldn't let us use it. Claimed it was for officer use only. All we ever did with the A.P.C. was to provision and clean it."

"A.P.C.?" Peter asked, slightly astounded. "You have an Armored Personnel Carrier?"

"Yes, sir," Billy replied, "but it's a big one, sir. Not like the other little ones. That's why it's a prototype; there aren't any others like it."

Peter finally handed the pen to Billy. "You know what these other letters mean?"

Billy took the pen, rolling it around in his fingers. He handed it back, shaking his head. "Never seen anything like that before," he said truthfully. "The last two letters could stand for *Armored Vehicle*, but I'm not sure. Uh, would you mind if my friends stood up, sir?"

Peter looked around and nodded. He had forgotten that the two men in officer's clothing were still kneeling on the ground. When he glanced at the sergeant, he saw that the man was still staring at the ground.

"Better see what you can do for your sergeant," he told Billy. "Looks like he swallowed some stupid pills."

Billy walked to his friends and spoke to them. He continued on to check on Sergeant Neville. After a moment he returned to where Peter and Jessie were standing.

"Something happened to the sarge when that mist showed up. I think something stopped his brain. Now we won't be able to stop Francks from arming that missile."

Peter stared at Billy. "Him? He can stop the missile?"

Billy told them about the computer and the codes. "But sarge was the only one that knew the password to get control of the missile, and now he's a mindless idiot."

"Dad? Would you have a look at him?"

Peter raised his eyebrows. "Jessie, sometimes I wonder if you're my daughter. This man tried to kill you, and now you want me to fix him up?"

"Oh, Dad! I'm sure he didn't mean to. When I ran to Kevin, he probably got excited."

Peter said nothing, shook his head and went over to look at the sergeant. After examining the man he returned. "Can't do much for him, Jessie," Peter said. "Looks like he's received some kind of shock. It's probably going to take another shock to bring him out of it, but I'm doubtful if that will ever happen. I saw men like this in Nam, and some never came out of it."

"You're a doctor, sir?" Billy asked.

Peter fixed Billy with his most intimidating stare. "Young man! When I was in Nam, I knew which end of a gun the bullets came out of! My advice to you is that you remember that! And, yes, I am a doctor. At least I was before the world went nuts!"

Billy smiled. "Yes, sir."

"Now, what can we do to disarm this damned missile?"

As the two men talked, they were unaware that other eyes were watching. When these eyes saw Billy and his friends pick up their weapons, their owner decided against showing himself.

Sergeant Pilke had found the large A.P.C. and had circled around it. He had left his smaller machine out of sight and had crept through the forest to the cave. When he'd heard the automatic rifle firing, he'd advanced cautiously. He hadn't seen the smoking guns or the mist, having arrived only in time to see that the old man from the farm had the drop on them. Sergeant Pilke smiled inwardly, and had almost decided to walk up to them when he saw Tanner's two buddies pick up their weapons.

He'd sworn soundlessly, knowing that somehow Tanner had made friends with the man. He'd retreated then, going back to his machine. He would follow them, and at some point along the way he would get his chance. As he retreated, he saw them picking their way through the forest towards the stolen A.P.C.

I'll get my chance, Billy Tanner. You and your friends are gonna get yours, but I'll get mine, too. Francks promised to turn the woman over to me and I know what to do with her. Yes, indeed, I know exactly how to make women behave.

CHAPTER THIRTY

The commander resided in a world of shadows, ever alert for a summons from his captain. He was not alone, for many others such as he were in this place of confinement. All of them were receiving data from their charges, entering into collaboration, but only he would report to The Co-Existent Planetary Commission. With his receptors open he received the impatient summons. His captain was in mind-maze, and seeking his wisdom.

More news, Captain? the commander asked.

I fear we are in grave danger, my Commander!

Of what nature, Captain? the commander posed the query. *Does it concern the powerful one?*

We do not know, sir, the captain replied with definite hues. *We were forced to intervene, as a collective unit to save the woman from being injured! We were tardy in our intervention, but something else was swift! We did succeed in stilling the brain of the attacker, but only after he had loosed his projectiles!*

The woman is safe? the commander's colors became fused.

Yes, sir! the captain averred. *A thought wave was energized around her, but it was not of our doing! Without this barrier, I fear she would have been grievously injured!*

Did I not tell you, Captain, that his powers were great? the commander beamed. *And that these powers would elevate still more?*

Yes, sir. But we did not expect powers of this magnitude. Even beings such as we cannot achieve this, and we have wires implanted in our brains.

Ah, the commander replied, *but so does he. Very special wires that even he has forgotten about, but they are not in his brain. When these wires in his body are connected properly, he will become the most powerful inhabitant in his world. Even more powerful than their worst weapon, but he must be taught how to use this ability.*

And you will teach him, Commander? the captain asked, approaching confusion.

No, Captain, I will not. But you will.

But… I am not worthy of such an undertaking, the captain was clearly appalled. *How will I know enough to teach one such as he?*

This you already know, Captain. Do you not enter into colloquy with the mechanical mind that governs your ship?

Yes, but the mechanical mind uses color for thought waves. Does the powerful one use color as we do?

I suspect not, Captain, the commander replied. *But we will convert our color to his thought waves. We will not contact him for some time yet, so you will have much time to prepare. I will be there to assist when this is done.*

The captain was relieved at this, and his commander immediately knew it. None of the captain's level could hide their thoughts from the commander, but the great one chose not to take their thoughts, merely to accept those that were directed at him. For this reason he was well respected.

The wires in this one's brain are to be utilized for our purpose? the captain inquired.

His wires are not in his brain, Captain, the commander repeated. *Do not forget this. They are in the appendages that propel him. These must be attached to the mechanical mind that runs his ship.*

The captain was confused, the colors in his mind swirling. They cleared when he pushed a clear thought. *But…how can this be? All of our wires are wound through our brains. This is what gives our color meaning, and enables us to direct our thoughts at others.*

Do not fear, Captain! the commander supplied. *These wires are connected to the powerful one's brain, but by a different path.*

And the purpose of this mingling will become clear?

Yes, Captain, the commander returned. *These wires in the appendages are connected to the nerve endings that reach into his brain. They are merely extensions of the brain. One side is positive, while the other is negative, and that is what will be required if we are to be successful. At this time, I am forbidden to enlighten you further. When these instructions are set into motion, then will you understand.*

Yes, Commander, the captain beamed. *I will follow your instructions.*

Now, Captain, the commander questioned, requiring more information, *what of the unfortunate that was placed in The Raptures?*

He is well, sir, the captain explained. *His colors are even brighter than before, and he is back at his station.*

Very good, Captain, the commander replied. *And now, I will leave you. We will not converse again until the powerful one has been contacted.*

The captain was alone in his thoughts now, remembering the magnificent color in his commander's mind. Perhaps he would become a commander in the future, and then he would also inquire about lesser beings, and show his beautiful new color to all!

CHAPTER THIRTY-ONE

The screaming, screeching agony was endless, the nerve endings driving their pain-laden messages into his brain. In retaliation, his brain shut down, unwilling to accept such torture. A little later the messages came again, but this time awareness came with the pain and found a quivering blob of humanity to feed on.

Soon he would wake up from this punishing nightmare. The pain would recede then. The realization that the pain was real, and that he was awake brought a scream to his lips. His scream stopped abruptly when the broken jaw grated together, sending new waves of excruciating pain into his already tortured body. A low moan escaped his lips, and he brought his hands up to soothe his fire-torn jaw. He found out this was a mistake as well, for the broken right arm sent a needle of anguish streaking into his brain, telling it to shut down again. When the broken ribs moved, he passed out once more, mercifully choking off the fiery attack on his senses.

An hour later he felt something on his face. He lay still, trying to remember what had happened, and then it came to him. Pilke! Something was sniffing at his mouth now, and he felt a sharp pinch. He started to raise his hand to ward off the furry thing nibbling at his face, remembering in time that his arm was broken. He raised his left arm and swatted at whatever was on top of him, feeling new pain when he touched his broken nose.

The rat scrambled away, its vicious teeth shredding the prize it had ripped off.

Through the haze of pain, Sergeant Grimes looked around and saw a patch of light. His brain was working again, and he knew where he must be. He was in the basement, where the rank odor had been coming from, and now he knew what the odor was. He was lying right in the middle of dead men; dead, rotting officers, maggots and rats, and God knew what else. He had to get out of here! But how?

He began to move, ignoring the pain in his side. He knew he must have some broken ribs, but if he was very careful, he thought dully, he might be able to stand up. Carefully, he turned and rose to his knees. His crushed testicles screamed a protest, and he knew what Pilke must have done to him.

He moaned, his brain screaming to the world what his mouth was incapable of. He vented his anger silently, knowing if he did otherwise that he would only suffer more. When the tirade was ended, but not the anger, the hatred he felt towards the animal that put him in his present state enabled him to stand.

Pure, unadulterated hatred emanated from his eyes and stifled the mind-boggling pain coming from his senses. He felt something sharp in the small of his back, and reached with his left hand, wanting to know what other atrocity Pilke had visited upon him. He traced the outline of the object, finally discovering where the fancy gun had disappeared to. This brought more silent cursing. He pulled his shirt up, and then grasped the weapon that would have saved him all the pain and torment.

At that moment, he heard a squeak and saw more rats. His eyes accustomed to the darkness now, he waddled painfully over to the basement steps. He pushed the .45 against the wood, cocking it. And then, ever so carefully, he turned and fired. The large bore gun bucked in his hand, jarring his pain-drenched body. He was elated when he saw the dark splash against the wall, knowing he had killed one of the evil bastards! His terrified, almost insane brain told him he had killed the rat that had taken a chunk out of his nose, but the sane part told him it was only wishful thinking.

He fired again, blasting more rodents to mush as his throat made insane sounds. His broken jaw started sending messages again, and the new pain brought him back to his senses. The rats scattered, afraid of this strange animal and his terrible fire stick. Most of them burrowed under the white gleaming bones they had picked clean, but some lay splattered over the dank cement walls.

Some semblance of sanity returned to Sergeant Grimes, and he knew he was in serious trouble. The stairs looked formidable, but he would have to try to navigate them. He knew he could barely walk, and when he tried to lift one leg his whole body cried out! His ruined manhood would not permit his leg to be lifted, and he suffered abominably every time he bent his knee.

He turned his head to check on the rats, finding only the ones he had killed. As his eyes followed the contour of the wall, he saw something he hadn't seen before. There, to the left of the slaughtered rodents, his eyes picked out what looked like the outline of a door.

But...why was there a door down here? It couldn't lead outside, for the basement is below ground. Intrigued, he shuffled painfully over to it, fumbling for some kind of latch. He cursed when his hand found the padlock.

He knew if he tried to shoot the lock off that shrapnel would fly around, maybe even tear his head off. But what the hell. He was as good as dead anyway If he didn't get out of here. The noise was deafening, more so than when he had shot the rats. As he suspected, shrapnel from the lock did fly around the room. Pieces of the lock pinged from the low ceiling, but he escaped, miraculously unscathed, until he touched the almost obliterated lock. It was hot and he burned his fingers when he touched it.

He tucked the gun in his pocket—berating himself for his stupidity—and used his shirt as an improvised glove. He removed the broken lock and pulled on the handle. The door opened, but he had to shut his eyes against the bright light that flooded the dark basement.

He opened his eyes slowly, squinting as he did so. He retrieved his gun and went through the opened door, losing some of the terror now that he could see again. He was in a tunnel of some kind, and as he shuffled along he heard a familiar sound; the same *whump-whump* that had delivered the canned air back at the Dome.

When he'd shuffled for about five minutes he came to the end of the tunnel, and there in front of him stood another door. There was no lock on it, nor was there a handle. He put his good shoulder to it and the door moved soundlessly. The *whump-whump* noise became louder, however, and when he had the door opened all the way he stared in awe at what he had stumbled on, but he couldn't believe what he was looking at! He was looking at more devastation than he had ever seen before. The shining silver covering and the sleek shape told the story. His brain said the words his lips dared not utter. A nuclear missile! Was this why Pilke had stopped here?

He moved around the lethal projectile, looking for a way up and out. He could see the railing above him, a railing that ringed the missile but he couldn't see any steps going to it. He was almost all the way around before he found what he wanted.

Thrusting the .45 into his pocket again, he started up. The ladder was all steel, and he pulled himself up until his feet were resting on the first rung. He only had one hand that he could use to pull himself up with, and now he felt pain starting in his good shoulder. There was only eight feet separating him from reaching the top, but each step he took was pure torture. He never would have made it if his hatred had not been so acute

He stopped to rest when he was three rungs away from gaining the top, and this was when he made a solemn promise. *I will survive; I will live long enough to get even with Pilke.* This thought consumed him, taking over his brain. The name Pilke added fuel to his hatred, and this hatred in turn was what gave him the strength to make it to the top.

He rested after he pulled himself onto the floor then peered around. His eyes told him that this wasn't a barn after all. It was a warehouse, and now he knew what the noise was. A dozen tankers had been driven in, and that was what fueled the huge generator that was pumping power into this building.

No more of your devastation, Pilke! This time you're going to be the one who suffers. You and that bastard, Francks! If it's the last thing I do on this earth, I'm going to see you crawl, hear you beg! Sooner or later you'll be back, and I'll be waiting for you!

CHAPTER THIRTY-TWO

Steve waited until Jackie went to sleep, and then searched through the desk. He was looking for information on the computer—information that would tell him how to find the special words or numbers that would unlock the airborne mode of the ship. The only thing he found was gibberish to him. Lots of numbers and letters, equal and plus signs; the words begin and end, true and false mixed up with them but it told him nothing.

He learned that the advent of the microprocessor was what had enabled the computer companies to make computers smaller, but little else. Now instead of using up a small room, the whole mess could be packed into a space a little larger than a shoe box.

He was out of options. He would have to probe into the computer with his mind.

He brought the program up on the screen that would enable the ship to become airborne, but stopped when he could advance no more. The electronic brain was asking for a password, and this was where he had to stop. Taking a deep breath, he closed his eyes and pushed his mind into the bizarre world of logical thought.

His mind's eye opened wide, trying to take in all of the wonders at once. Wonders that were so complex, so strange! Tiny explosions of light were everywhere, small specks that reminded him of stars. He lingered at the brighter explosions, marveling at the many different colors, so exquisite he wanted to enter into them, be them. He rounded a bend, and there, stretching out in front of him, stood infinity! He was dumbstruck at the characters he was looking at, extending excessively out as far as his mind could see! *Was this the ultimate number? Was this forever?*

He progressed further into this amazing world, noting that some kind of current was passing through these characters, making them look like twinkling stars. He wondered if they were numbers or letters, for there were only two kinds and could be either. Were they ones and zeroes, or were they the letters I and O?

In the distance, he perceived a section that was super bright. He pushed again, speeding to the brilliant area and found unimaginable hues. Colors so fantastic, so deep his mind had trouble looking at them. His mind tried to enter, but a force drove him back. He tried again, but was repelled once more. His mind knew then what this was; he had arrived at the password.

He knew where it was now, but he still didn't know *what* it was. He looked again, deciding these were numbers and started counting them. He could find no rhyme or reason to them, for although they were all the same, the numbers of zeroes were less. Until he passed the brighter letters, and then they reversed. There were more zeroes then than there were ones.

It was a mystery to him. He couldn't see any pattern. And then he thought of a way to convert the numbers to letters! Letters he could use on the keyboard!! He counted them and slowly backed out.

Steve opened his eyes then tried the letters he had converted. They didn't make sense to him, but maybe they would to the computer. He whispered the letters out loud as he punched them in, using the proper sequence. B.C.P.W.F. He entered them, and his heart fluttered when he saw the words on the screen.

    PASSWORD ENTERED IS INCORRECT
    PLEASE TRY AGAIN

Damn—he had been so sure! He went to the desk and picked up a pen. He wondered idly what had happened to the other pen that he had been using, but thought nothing about it. After all, there were plenty of pens here.

He returned to the instruction sheet and penciled the alphabet in on the back of it. He remembered the ones he had counted, and put a check mark under the corresponding letters. He had used the twenty-six letters of the English alphabet, and had counted each one as a letter, so the numbers 2-3-16-23-6—the numbers he had counted at the brightly-lit area—converted to B-C-P-W-F.

He was positive he had punched these letters, but tried it again, using instead the actual numbers. He received the same answer from the screen. Thinking that maybe he'd missed something, he turned the instruction sheet over. He had not read the whole thing completely, but what did it matter which company had made the computer?

He read this now, and his eyes opened wide as he continued. He devoured the rest of the words greedily, and then learned where he had gone wrong.

He had been right after all, but he had used the wrong letters. This whole system had been designed, built and installed by a company that used their own code. When they had programmed the computer, they had used the English language, but had changed it into a code.

The letter Z was taken from the end and placed in front, creating a completely new language. After the Z came the rest of the normal alphabet, finally ending in the letter Y. Then the whole thing was converted to something called binary, which were the ones and zeroes he had seen. They were also used as letters, for the booklet made mention of something called an I/O rack. This, he learned, was an abbreviation for input/output. Steve consulted his new alphabet, and found out that the corresponding letters now made sense. He punched in the new letters, but was disappointed when he received the same "error" message. He consulted the manual once more, and learned that each letter was case sensitive. Checking further, he learned that he had used all capital letters. He was so sure he had used the proper letters in sequence and tried them once more in lower case. He watched in fantastic glee as the screen changed.

The screen now showed a picture of the ship, and even as he watched the picture kept changing. Short wings were issuing out of the ship's sides, and a tail section was forming at the rear, where the body of the ship curved upwards. When the wings were all the way out, and the vee shaped tail was complete, the picture of the ship became smaller.

Words appeared on the screen now, informing the viewer that the ship was in flight mode. The picture of the ship moved to the upper right hand corner of the screen, and all of the specifications and limits were shown. The ship itself showed that the wings were level; looking like it was in a bubble. He thought this would be an immense help to him when he was actually flying.

As Steve watched, instructions came on the screen as to how to safely operate flight mode. He found out that it took off vertically and landed the same way, and that the same controls were employed that were used for surface travel. He thought it would be relatively simple to fly.

Following the instructions, Steve punched in the commands that would take the ship up to one hundred feet. He heard nothing, but saw that they were rising, the ship on the screen showing that it was rising evenly. An altimeter appeared on the screen now, showing their altitude. At one hundred feet the ship stopped rising and hovered silently, waiting for further instructions.

Steve sat back, a pleased look on his face. An immense feeling of well being permeated his whole body, radiating out to his very outmost extremities. In this relaxed and exuberant state, he didn't see the blue eyes looking down at him.

"What cha doin' Steve?" a sleepy voice said. "Did you have a nap?"

Steve looked up at the long hair hanging over the edge of the bunk. He rose out of the chair and extended his arms to her, intending to help her down. She declined his offer and used the ladder.

"I'm not a baby, y' know!" she exclaimed loudly.

Steve chuckled, and motioned to the screen set into the control panel. "See that?" he asked, proud of his endeavors. Jackie looked where Steve was pointing, and then back at him.

"Yeah." she said, not impressed. "So? It's only a dumb clock! What's so good about that?"

Steve chuckled again. He supposed that he should never ask a woman questions right after she's woken up—or little girls, especially this little girl. "Look again, Jackie. It's not a clock, it's an altimeter."

She looked again, a frown on her face. Then she looked back at Steve. "What's a 'timeter', Steve?"

"Altimeter, Jackie," Steve corrected. "It's a meter that tells you how high you are, like they use in planes."

Jackie looked at the screen again, a smirk playing at the corners of her mouth. "Huh!" she scorned. "Must be broken, Steve, 'cause it ain't doin' nothing!"

"Come over to the window, Jackie, and tell me what you see?"

Steve watched as Jackie's eyes opened wide, pure wonder shining in the large blue orbs.

"Oh—wow! We're off the ground! How'd you do it, Steve? You said you didn't know how!?"

"Yeah," Steve remarked, trying not to be smug. "But I really studied when you were sleeping, and now I think I know how. Would you like to go for a practice flight?"

"Yeah!" Jackie was all for it. "But don't crash us, Steve!"

"Oh, don't worry, Jackie. I won't."

Steve sat down in the seat, swiveling around to the keyboard. After consulting the screen, he punched in the command that would give the ship forward thrust. The screen changed, the computer now offering options.

DO YOU WISH AUTO MODE? YES/NO

Steve punched in no then waited for more instructions. When the screen displayed manual mode, he punched in YES. He wanted to be in control, at least until he knew more about this strange craft.

DO YOU WISH TO INITIATE FLIGHT YES/NO

Steve punched in YES and a final message came on the screen.

YOU ARE CLEAR TO PROCEED

Taking a deep breath, Steve depressed the two red buttons on either side of him and slowly pushed the joysticks forward. The ship moved ahead, and now another "clock" was showing on the screen, but this one was showing airspeed. He moved the controllers more, and released the buttons when his airspeed reached fifty. He took his hands away from the controllers and beamed when the airspeed remained constant, the ship moving ahead unerringly. Steve took control of the ship again, easing the "sticks" back until the ship stopped, hovering as before.

"How did you like that, Jackie?" he asked, unable to keep the pride out of his voice.

Jackie's eyes sparkled. "Yeah! Great! That was fun!"

Steve consulted the flight manual again, and discovered that only the Starboard (right) controller governed the speed, while at the same time giving the ship forward thrust. The Port (left) controller was used to change altitude. This controller, when pushed forward, would tilt the nose down. When it was reversed, the ship would climb higher, but only if the port button was not depressed.

He had been lucky. He had depressed both buttons, and had nullified the Port controller. The Starboard controller had done the work, and the Port controller—a slave to the Starboard controller— followed the dictates of the master controller. After reading this, he continued on until he read it all. The ship had limitations, but none that would concern them.

"Would you like to try it, Jackie?"

"Oh, Steve!" she complained. "I don't know how?"

Steve smiled. "Well, look. You use this stick, and I'll use the other one. If anything goes wrong I'll be right here to take over."

A little afraid—but wanting to try—Jackie sat in the chair. At Steve's instructions, she pushed the starboard controller and the ship leaped ahead. Steve used the port controller to gently climb higher, finding that it worked as the instructions said it would. He eased the stick ahead and leveled off. They were now one hundred and fifty feet up, and cruising at fifty-nine miles per hour.

"There. You see how easy it is?"

"Oh, wow!" Jackie murmured softly. "I'm really doin' it, ain't I? I'm really flyin' the ship!"

"You sure are, young lady," he beamed.

They kept flying until Jackie had to go to the bathroom. Steve took over both controls, and a little later Jackie returned with an old friend. She put the harmonica to her lips and started blowing on it. Steve leveled off at one hundred feet and stopped the ship. He turned, smiling at the young musician. Jackie took the mouth organ from her lips, smiling.

"This is what saved me, Steve," she explained. "They would have killed me, but they stopped when I made music. I was with them the day I found you, an' that's why I don't ever want to shoot these awful guns!"

Steve's smile disappeared. "Jackie, I don't want to use the guns either, unless it's necessary. But I would use them to save you."

She looked down at her toes. "You must like me pretty much, Steve," Jackie mumbled. "These guns make an awful noise, you know. That's what made the crazies run away that day. I did, too, but I only hid. All I wanted was some place to sleep that night I climbed through the hole!"

Steve didn't say anything. He was sure now that she had been through more hell than he had. "Okay, Jackie," Steve relented, "you don't have to use the guns. But you will have to learn some new tunes on that thing."

Steve was rewarded with a smile, and that was worth more to him than anything else. The only other thing he wanted was to see Jessie, face to face and in person. He now had the means to do that, and he wasn't going to waste any more time. "Why don't you sit in the co-pilot's chair over there and learn some new tunes. Better strap yourself in, though, 'cause we're gonna go faster than we did before."

Jackie nodded, and for once did as he asked.

"Ready?"

Jackie nodded. "Uh-huh."

Steve applied more thrust, and soon they were streaking across the Georgia sky at more than one hundred miles an hour. He estimated two days or more to get to Oregon, but would have pushed the ship harder if he had known what was unfolding there. When next he received a plea for help from Jessie, he would push the ship to its screaming limit!

CHAPTER THIRTY-THREE

While Steve and Jackie were winging over Georgia, and the people-laden, large A.P.C. was being navigated towards Portland, Colonel Jeremy Francks was carrying out his insidious plans. He had lured all of the remaining soldiers to the recreation room, and under the pretense of having a party had proceeded to murder them.

Francks had wheeled in a cart loaded with bottles and decanters, and then had produced a bevy of foam cups with which to drink. After he had assured them that they would soon be able to resume outdoor activities—and that this was what this party was all about—he had excused himself. Once away from the cheers and laughter of the assembly, he had gone straight to his private stock and poured himself a drink, using a real glass. Sipping it once, he'd smiled. He had lit a cigar, thinking of what was going to happen.

The poison that would kill all of the remaining men was not in the alcohol, but in the foam cups that had been impregnated with it. The alcohol would draw the poison out and sit like a time bomb, waiting to explode.

Francks poured another drink and went to his video library. He chose the film that contained his latest home movie, and the star of the show was the woman at the farm. Pilke had expressed a desire for her, and Francks had promised her to him, but all Pilke was going to get would be a large hole between his black eyes. He shut the machine off after watching the video for about twenty minutes, reveling in the grace and beauty of the woman. He returned to the recreation room to check on his handiwork and was not disappointed. He saw the rigidity in all of them, each mouth opened in the silent rictus of death.

Chuckling now, he advised Soames that his services were required in the recreation room. He would let the good doctor live, at least for the time being. He would need someone to dispose of the bodies, and Soames was good at that. Of the few operations he had attempted, Soames had a success rate of one-hundred-percent. Not one had survived.

With this accomplished, the only other inhabitants of the Dome were deep in the bowels of the building. These were the four scientists who were responsible for the manufacture, and monitoring of the life support systems. The lower reaches of the Dome were completely self-contained, and the four scientists were content to remain where they were, as long as they had their experiments to keep the boredom at bay. Colonel Francks had to know if he could get along without the members of these key personnel. Especially Doctor Koessler.

In the event of a nuclear strike, the Dome was capable of taking samples from outside while keeping the inhabitants of the structure safe from harm. There were test animals, all caged, and all subjected to the outer elements. The scientists were trying to determine what had happened to the environment. Air, soil and moisture samples would be introduced to the animals before any human was subjected to it. The only exception had been Billy Tanner.

He took the elevator down to the basement of the building, intent on questioning the people there. If he could, he would get rid of all of them, but first he had to be sure of what was going on. He stepped out when the elevator stopped at the bottom.

It had been a long time since he had been down to this section of the Dome, for all of the communications with this area had been done by phone. There was a direct line to his office, and he had spoken to Doctor Koessler many times but had never actually met the man.

Koessler had been at the Dome since day one, had supervised everything that was installed, and was the only other person who knew about the chopper. This was only one of the reasons that he wanted to get rid of him. He had welcomed the other scientists when they had arrived, and had given them instructions as to where they would find their superior, Doctor Koessler. Since that time he had spoken only to Koessler, but had seen nothing at all of the people who resided in their intellectual labyrinths.

He inserted his I.D card into the slot and entered the main control room, but found it deserted. His gaze zeroed in on the many computer screens, but he didn't know what it all meant. As he watched, the screens changed, now depicting something else. He froze when he heard a voice behind him.

"Colonel Francks?!"

He turned; looking at the figure that had spoken to him. His eyes took in the usual laboratory smock, but the similarity to the other three scientists ended there. The lips parted, showing perfect white teeth. When the lips smiled, so did the eyes. "Well, Colonel," the figure said, "we finally meet. You seem a little surprised."

"But…but…you're a…a—"

"A woman?" the voice finished for him. "Does that make you uncomfortable?"

"Uh, no," Francks said, totally unprepared. "Yes… I mean, I thought you were a man."

Colonel Jeremy Francks was delighted when he surprised others, but when someone did the same to him he usually became angry. He recovered quickly and smiled back.

"Doctor Jan Koessler, at your service, Colonel. I'm afraid you were duped into thinking something else, but I was chosen for this position because of my credentials, not my gender. When I talked to you on the telephone, I used a device that would make my voice sound masculine."

"I see," Francks recovered. "And you programmed all this?" He swept his arm around, indicating the screens and controls.

"I'm afraid I did, but it all seems so useless now. There doesn't seem to be much of a world left."

His mind whirling, Francks decided to play dumb. He couldn't let this woman know that everything outside of the Dome was clear. He wasn't sure about the water, but he had a way to test that. Good old Doctor Soames. What he had to know now was this operation, and this woman.

"You seem awfully young for such an operation, Doctor," he said, turning on his charm.

Jan smiled, knowing where this was leading. Another male ego was hurting. It had happened before with Tom. She thought of Tom, and knew he must be dead. "I'm almost thirty, Colonel, and I had training for all of this. I naturally took to computers, and I'm really quite good at it, you know."

"Yes," Francks said, totally out of his element. "I can see you must be."

Damn! Why had they put a woman in charge of all this? And such a beauty.

"Uh, what I came down for was a tour of the place. I really don't know where all of our life support comes from, and I would appreciate it if you could perhaps explain it to me." Jan had heard stories about Colonel Francks from her colleagues, stories that had apparently come from a Doctor Soames. As she had heard it, Soames was a hazard to the medical profession, and when Colonel Francks had asked for him the Army had Okayed it. Due to the nature of the Dome's existence, which Jan knew to be the arming and firing of a certain missile, this had presented no problem. But now—with world devastation—there was no need for such a weapon. She wondered again about the stories relayed to her, and decided to be very careful around him.

"Certainly, Colonel," she cautiously answered, "but there really isn't very much to explain. Everything is run automatically, and the computer is totally in charge."

Colonel Francks was silent, listening intently to her. "Everything?" he asked slyly. "There is nothing that has to be done? No changes have to be made at all to the program?"

Jan Koessler was an exceptionally intelligent woman; she didn't care for the excitement she picked up from the colonel's words. She decided to give him something to worry about. The lie she told probably saved her life.

"There is one problem we are working on," she lied. "One that must be solved."

"Oh?" Francks asked, interested. "And what would that be, Doctor?"

"Well, we have a glitch in the main computer," she lied again. "If it isn't sought out and corrected, we could have a very serious problem on our hands."

Colonel Francks' plans were falling apart, the turmoil in his mad brain nearing the breaking point. With a tremendous surge of will, he stopped the thought process that was threatening to destroy him. And then a new thought came to his depraved mind. He would still have the woman at the farm. But now he would have two of them, and he would have this one today. Immediately.

"Uh, you will keep me informed, Doctor?"

"Certainly, Colonel Francks."

"Well, that's it then," Francks said. "Oh, before I go, would you be so kind as to show me around? Sort of a guided tour?"

Jan nodded, unsure of herself now. *Could she have been wrong about the colonel? He seemed so pleasant, so calm.* "What would you like to see, Colonel?"

He smiled. "If it's not an imposition," he said softly, "I would like to see your facilities, Doctor. Recreation room, living quarters, things like that."

Jan pointed to the banks of computer screens. "Are you sure you wouldn't rather see some of the programs we—"

"Oh, no!" Francks complained. "No, I'm afraid all the screens and things in here are far too complex for me to understand. My limited knowledge would only confuse me more if you tried to explain *that* to me!"

He wanted to take her right then and there, but some part in his brain told him to be patient. He would try to make her a willing participant, but he would use force if necessary. The terrible fire that his thoughts had started in his loins must be quenched, and this woman had caused those thoughts.

"Very well, Colonel," Jan said. "Would you follow me, please?"

Jan led the way and his eyes glued to her form. He almost took her then, his need greater than ever. With a gigantic effort, he somehow controlled the blood that boiled in his body.

She showed him the recreation room, which—except for the dead bodies—was identical to the upper hall. From there he followed as he was shown through the small galley-type dining room.

"We take turns doing the cooking," Jan explained, "and each of us cleans up whatever mess we make. Consequently, the whole place stays relatively neat."

They passed through the dining room and entered a hallway,

passing two washrooms. Further down the hall they passed several closed rooms. Jan explained as they walked. "There are nine rooms here that could be used to house others, but the last five are being used for storage. One of us sleeps during the day, in case something goes wrong at night."

She turned to face him, but he turned away so she wouldn't see the bulge in his crotch. He couldn't wait much longer. "And one of these rooms is yours, Doctor?"

Unwittingly, Jan told him that hers was the first room, and that it also housed a small computer.

"Could you show me that? The computer, I mean."

Jan hesitated, not wanting him or any man in her bedroom. After she and Tom had split up, she had been devastated. The only thing that had any meaning now was her work. "Um, it's only a P.C., and I can't make any changes from there. I usually use the main computer."

"That would be appropriate for me, Doctor," Francks said. "Something small to start on."

Apprehensively, she opened the door to her quarters and started in. She was almost immediately spun around, and found the colonel's body pressed up against her. Taken by surprise, she was unable to escape his embrace. Warning bells clanged in her brain when she felt his male hardness thrusting into her abdomen.

"Come on, woman!" Francks insisted. "You must want this as bad as I do. But maybe you're already getting it? The night man, maybe?"

Jan was appalled at the utter lack of respect! She had not lured him into her bedroom, would not have, even if he were the last man alive! And now he was trying to impose his will on her!

"Colonel!" she cried, "Have you lost your mind? Let go of me this instant or I'll—"

"You'll what, bitch?" Francks roared. "Scream? Go ahead."

He let go of her, and with his left hand he grabbed her hair, forcing her face to his. When his lips touched hers, she bit down hard!

"You bastard!" Jan cried. "If you don't let me go you'll be sorry!!"

He surprised her then, releasing her and putting a hand to his bleeding lip. Then he smiled and hit her with the back of his hand. She screamed and backed away. Francks advanced on her, seeing the drops of blood falling from her nose. Jan unknowingly backed into her bunk, and her knees bent, toppling her onto her back. She screamed again as her legs went into the air. As he advanced towards her, knowing that he now had her softened up, a voice behind made him stop.

"Doctor Koessler? Jan? Are you all right?"

The gun appeared in Francks hand as if by magic, and Jan looked on in horror as a hole materialized over her colleague's left eye. The man crashed back into the hall, and Colonel Francks calmly walked to the door, closing and locking it.

"Now we're going to play some games, bitch. Look at me when I talk to you!"

Jan curled up in a fetal position, her terror on the verge of panic. She didn't move until she felt her smock parting and heard the buttons popping off. She came to a sitting position and tried to stop him, but cringed back when the gun pointed at her face. She knew she was only inches away from death as the lethal weapon steadied on her forehead.

"Now!" Francks said viciously. "You know I need you to work on that computer, but I'm sure you don't want your other two friends to get what I gave this one. If you don't do as I say, I'm going to knock you out and take what I want. Then I'll kill the other two. Is that what you want on your conscience?"

Jan's brain was beginning to work again, and she knew the colonel would do exactly what he said. She had no choice but to do what he wanted.

"Where are your boy friends? I'll find them if I have to, but you won't know about it!"

Through teary eyes, and choking sobs she told him that they were in the laboratory, and then she was roughly pushed back. She cried when her smock was ripped open, and her heart broke when her panties were removed. Jan wore only undergarments when she had the smock on, and she groaned in shame when her brassiere was taken from her. She lay passively, waiting for, but not wanting the terrible onslaught she knew would be perpetrated on her now vulnerable and nude body.

Francks removed his clothing quickly, keeping the gun in his hand. He bent over her; his tongue flicked a nipple, teasing it. Jan's body betrayed her and the nipple hardened, making him believe that she liked what he was doing. He lowered his lips and bit down. Jan's body arched at the new pain, bringing her body up to touch him.

Francks lost all control then and completed the rape. His mouth closed over hers, effectively shutting off the scream that originated in her soul. His teeth nipped her upper lip, and again her body bucked in pain, sending her uncaring, totally indifferent body up to meet the terrible juggernaut that was invading her body!

It was too much for him, and Francks dropped the gun. He grabbed Jan's hair in both of his hands and pulled her face into his, glaring into her pained, but now uncaring features. When the heinous act was finished, he stood on the floor and picked up his gun, looking down at the body he had used. Her eyes were open but unseeing, and this prompted him to bend over and slap her face. Jan screamed and tried to cover her nudity when she realized what had happened. He laughed at her and slapped her again.

"Get your ass in gear now, lady, and get some work done on that computer." Francks laughed harshly. "I think you enjoyed that. Do you want some more of me?"

This thought brought her all the way back, and she vaulted from the bed, searching painfully for her clothes.

Francks grinned. "You better go clean yourself up first, lady," he leered. "You're a fucking mess!"

He laughed again, and started to put his own clothes on. Jan brushed past him as he was doing this, and he slapped her bare bottom as she passed.

She made a solemn vow that somehow she would exact payment from this animal! She would not be subjected to any more grief from this sadistic bastard! She would kill herself first! Nothing could assuage the remorse she felt over being raped. She felt dirty—a soiled woman. She must bathe; scrub this feeling out of her body and her soul!

Jan opened the locked door, but shrieked when she saw her dead colleague. She felt guilty that she hadn't been able to save his life, as she had the two scientists in the laboratory. She stepped over his inert form, conscious of her nude and pain-wracked body.

She turned on the shower as hot as she could stand it. The pain from her chewed lip and shattered nose were almost unbearable under the hot water, but she reveled in the cleansing power of the spray. She scrubbed her womanhood until she had rubbed it almost raw, but she still felt dirty.

Never again would she let a man use her body, of that she was sure. She would never again be able to enjoy the sex act.

But the future would prove her wrong. As wrong as she had been about saving her colleagues' lives. She didn't know that Colonel Francks had sought out the two scientists, and while she had been feeling sorry for herself, their valuable brains had been blown out through their ears.

CHAPTER THIRTY-FOUR

The large A.P.C. parked at the rest area, and everybody was out enjoying a long forgotten pleasure; they were having a picnic. It wasn't much, but they all delighted in the idea of sitting at a picnic table again. Kevin and Miss Muffet were romping around, exploring the little wooded area. Sergeant Neville was still not back to normal, but he was at least now able to feed and cleanse himself. He was now also capable of controlling his bodily functions.

"Dad? You think these washrooms are still operational? I know there won't be any water or hydro, but a person could probably sit on the throne, couldn't they?"

Peter was spooning cherries from a can, stopping every once in a while to wipe the juice from his chin. He looked at his daughter, and grinned at her serious countenance impishly.

"You got something pressing on your mind, Jessie?"

"I gotta go pee," she whispered. "It sure beats leaning against a tree!"

"You know, Jessie," Peter said, a slight smile on his face, "I been thinking about something. This man you claim to be talking to all the time? The one in your mind? Well, I wonder if he can see that pretty rump of yours when it's stuck out, all shiny and bare. Why, a thing like that might even make a blind man see again."

Jessie blushed, and her ears turned red. "Oh...Dad!" she scolded. "That's awful!! He wouldn't do that! He's a perfect gentleman, I know he is!"

Peter chuckled, smirking at the red in her face. "Wouldn't be the first man to have his head turned by a pretty face."

Jessie left the table, fuming over her father's offbeat humor. She stalked off towards the now deserted washrooms, fire coming from her eyes. She couldn't escape her father's laughter as she walked away.

Damn men to hell! Even here, they put the girl's facilities farther away than the boy's room.

Still angry, she entered the room and looked around. She checked out the stalls and chose one. Her panties were almost down when she remembered her father's words, causing her to stop. And then she giggled.

Her father had been kidding her; she'd known that from the start. She had gotten angry, but now that she was thinking clearly, she knew she hadn't been angry with Peter. She'd been angry with herself, angry that her father had guessed what was in her heart. Jessie had searched her soul, and had found that she wanted this man to see her body. Her father had unknowingly stumbled onto the truth of what had been troubling her, and that's why she had been angry.

She pulled some tissue from the roll that had somehow miraculously survived whatever had happened to the world and finished her task. She was still thinking about her dream man when she left the building, and didn't see the skulking figure until it was too late.

Pilke grabbed her, his beefy hand stifling any scream she might have uttered. The scream that he couldn't hear—the one that went streaking across the disease-plagued heavens—was the one that would cause Pilke to doubt his sanity and give him a taste of what he had given to so many.

Ten seconds after he grabbed Jessie, and dragged her kicking body behind the building, Pilke received a blow to his head that would have felled a lesser man. It staggered him, but he was determined. He still had her in a grip of steel when he felt the fire in his brain, but had to release her to clasp his hands over his ears. The man who had never before known fear now had a taste of it, the fear that his brains were about to melt and run out of his ears.

Jessie turned when she was released and screamed. Pilke was on his knees now, thinking that someone had put a bullet in his brain. When the pain left him he opened his eyes. What he saw then mesmerized him, and he stared until he heard the shouts of the men rushing to Jessie's aid.

Sergeant Pilke did something then that he had never done in his entire adult life. He crashed chaotically through the trees that surrounded the rest area, blinded to everything except escape. He had tasted fear; raw and unadulterated, mind-numbing fear!

When he'd grabbed the woman, Pilke had planned to knock her out and creep up on the rest of them, killing them all except Tanner. He would *do* Tanner with his fists, and that would please him as much as any woman ever could. He would then take the woman with him, using her when he chose to. All of his plans had caved in when he'd seen the mist that had surrounded the woman, and the blue fire that had almost immediately surrounded the mist!

Peter was the first man around the end of the building, his weapon raised to fire. He stopped dead in his tracks when he saw the blue fire that enveloped his daughter and advanced slowly. He stopped six feet away when he found he could not get any closer.

Kevin and Miss Muffet were next to arrive on the scene, and the dog slid to the ground, whimpering. Billy and his friends were next, but Peter motioned them to stay where they were. All of them stood rooted to the spot, seeing, but unable to believe.

Jessie was encased in a ball of blue fire, a shimmering, sparkling halo that disappeared into the ground. Her eyes were closed, but she was smiling, her features so calm and serene that Peter thought his daughter had finally lost her mind. The only other emotion he could think of—when he looked at her face—was one of pure pleasure, akin to something really wonderful, tasted for the very first time. This latter thought was the correct one, as Peter would find out later, but it would cause him great discomfiture.

After what seemed like hours—but in reality was only a few minutes—Jessie opened her eyes. Peter gestured to Billy then whispered something to him. Billy left, and returned with Sergeant Neville in tow. When the Sergeant looked at the spectacle in front of him, intelligence returned to his eyes, and Peter mistakenly thought this shock was what made the sergeant *see* again.

They all stared in awe as the presence around Jessie began to dissolve. When the last vestige of mist disappeared, a sharp *ping* was heard and Jessie walked toward them. She first hugged Kevin, and then her father. Miss Muffet came to her, demanding the same treatment.

"Jessie?" Peter asked immediately. "Are you all right?"

"Sure, Dad," Jessie exclaimed vociferously. "I feel great."

Peter rested his hands on his daughter's shoulders and looked into her eyes. They seemed different, brighter and more alive than he had ever seen them before. "You want to tell me what that was all about?"

Jessie smiled radiantly, blue fire emanating from her eyes. "When that man grabbed me," she began, "I tried to scream, but he had his hand over my mouth. Then when I—"

"Man?!" Peter asked. "What in hell man was that? There wasn't any man here? Only you and that blue…blue—"

"But there was a man, Dad!" she cried. "A big man, very strong! An Army man, by the look of his clothes. He was going to hurt me, that's why Steve sent—"

"Steve?" Peter asked, unable to follow the conversation. "Who in hell is Steve?"

But he realized who *Steve* was. Her imaginary friend, the one in her head. The New York City cop from the paper clipping. He had no choice now but to believe his daughter after what he had seen. But this also meant that his daughter wasn't crazy after all—didn't have a brain tumor—and wasn't suffering from some mind disease.

"Okay, Jessie," Peter said, before Jessie could say anything, "I think I know who this Steve is, but who in hell was this other man? The one who attacked you?"

Billy interrupted before Jessie could answer. "Jessie, did this man have short hair? Brush cut? Blonde? Dark eyes?"

Jessie nodded. "Black eyes, they looked like, but maybe only dark brown. I really didn't get a good look at him, but I do know that he was awfully strong."

Billy looked at his friends and nodded. "It was Pilke! That bastard! He's been following us, probably waiting for the right moment to kill us all. The only reason he hasn't already shot us is because of…"

"Why, Billy?" Peter asked, when Billy said no more. "Why hasn't he already killed us?"

Billy told Peter and Jessie what kind of man Pilke was, and what he was capable of.

"Damn it, Billy." Peter reprimanded, "He almost got us, too! Would have, if it hadn't of been for Jessie's—"

What in hell was he doing? Here he was—a grown man, and a

medical man to boot—talking about an imaginary man who really wasn't there! Even though he had seen what had happened with his own eyes, he still had trouble believing it.

"Uh, Billy," Peter continued, "we better post a guard from now on. Just in case your friend Pilke shows up again. We don't want to get caught like that again."

Billy knew it was hard to swallow, especially for a scientific mind such as Peter had. But he had seen it, too, not only once, but twice. And he had felt the impossible heat in the guns. Their guns, not Peter's and Jessie's guns! This whole family had an advocate; a champion, and it was all directed at Jessie, for Jessie, and for her loved ones. He felt sorry for the person or persons who tampered with these people, especially with Jessie. He sure as hell wasn't going to bother this family any more. What had happened back at the cave had happened again, only now it was more potent, stronger.

Billy said, "I'll take the first watch, Peter."

"Okay, Billy." Peter turned to talk to his daughter. " Jessie? Could I speak to you privately?"

Billy went back to the picnic area with Jerry and Ray. Kevin followed them, knowing he was still too young for some adult themes. Sergeant Neville didn't move, seemingly back to the land of the living but lost in thought.

"What happened in there, Jessie? What was that blue fire?" Peter was intrigued when his words caused Jessie to blush, more than she had before. More so than at the picnic table. He knew her eyes were brighter, but otherwise appeared normal.

"Um, well," Jessie said, her cheeks flaming, "he saved me from that man, that Pilke. Then he told me about his machine, and about the little girl; her name is Jackie. He's on his way here, and should be here by tomorrow or the next day. His machine can fly, but he's still learning how to do that." As Jessie talked, her voice took on a dream-like quality, and her eyes seemed to glow.

"That's all he told you?"

"Um, yeah."

"Then what in hell made you blush? I never seen you blush like that since you caught your, ah, your boob in the fence that time. Had to cut the whole damned square out to get you free. You remember that?"

Jessie's blush deepened, and Peter thought that if her ears got any redder they would start to smoke.

"You can tell him, Jessie," a voice said.

Both father and daughter turned, and looked into the intelligent eyes of Sergeant Neville.

"He was in my head, too," the sergeant said, "an' now I don't have the worms crawlin' in my brain no more. Only a sort of tickle that feels nice."

Jessie turned back to her father and told him, still blushing. "He, um, oh hell! Steve made love to me!!"

"He what?!" Peter was astounded.

Jessie was still blushing, but now she was angry. It had been a very personal thing, something that only she should know about. "Oh, it's not what you think! It happened in my mind! It wasn't a physical thing; it was so much more than that. A tender melding of minds, so intimate and complete that I don't think the physical act could even compare to it!"

Sergeant Neville moved off to join his friends, but Peter stood with his head lowered. He had gone too far. All of his life he had spent delving into unexplained events, trying to unravel the strange, and often bizarre enigma of life. It was the reason he'd joined the medical profession, but now his damned inquisitive mind may have alienated his daughter to him.

"I'm sorry, honey. You should have told me to mind my own business. I had no right to question you or your motives. Please, forgive me."

Jessie had never seen this side of her father, only the practical side. She knew it had taken a lot for him to accept what had happened today. She took his hand in hers, squeezing it gently. She was happy to have her father back again, even though at times he was a pain in the rear. But one thing for sure, when Steve and her father met each other, there would probably be a real clash of wills.

CHAPTER THIRTY-FIVE

Steve stopped the ship over Shreveport to check out a shopping Mall. He thought it was a good idea to re-stock the ship's stores, but he didn't want to run into any more crazies. Jackie was sitting in the co-pilot's seat, her young eyes roving over the radar screen. She had almost driven Steve crazy with questions he couldn't answer, mainly because he didn't know how the radar worked. And that had been only the tip of the iceberg.

There were other screens and items he didn't recognize or remember. He did remember vaguely how the sonar worked, but that was because when he was a boy he had been infatuated with submarine movies. With sonar, a signal went out from the vessel to the bottom of the sea, and a pinging *beep* was heard. If there was anything between the vessel and the bottom, the pinging was different, like an echo. At least, that's how it had been in the movies.

Steve had shut the sonar off, because neither he nor Jackie could stand the constant pinging noise. There was a compass, and he'd explained it to Jackie as best he could. She had watched it for a while, but had gotten bored when it hadn't moved too much. Then she spotted other sensors, and something called a C.D. that he knew nothing about.

Patiently, he'd tried to explain what he knew, but he was at a loss. "I think one of those is used to find out how far away you are from a certain point, but you have to know exactly where you are before you can use it properly."

She had looked at him then with wide eyes. "You don't know where we are? Are we lost?"

Steve had chuckled, and had then told her that they were not lost. "We are in Louisiana, Jackie. And right now, we're going to use that other screen. See that one marked C.D.? The one with the crazy swirls in it?"

"Yeah," Jackie had answered. "Looks like what my mom used to make."

Steve puzzled over this, until Jackie told him about her mother mixing stuff up in a bowl. It turned out to be a batch of peanut butter cookies. It reminded him that they were all out of the gooey stuff, and that was one thing he was going to stock up on.

"That C.D. means to Come Down," he lied," and that's what we're going to do right now. We are going to go down to that Mall and get some supplies."

"But... what if there's bad people down there?"

"I didn't see any signs of anybody around, but I'll take the shotgun in case there are."

Jackie frowned, reminding Steve that she didn't want to kill anybody. "Don't worry, Jackie, I won't hurt anybody. The gun will let them know that we're armed, and maybe they won't bother us."

Steve brought the ship down and they foraged until they found what they wanted. A case of peanut butter lay on the floor of the ship, and Steve also found shells for his shotgun at a sporting goods shop. They had lunch, and Steve was preparing to lift off when the terror laden scream came from Jessie!

His mind's eye saw Jessie being attacked! He pushed out a thought and saw the man lurch back, but still hold fast to his prize. He knew he could disable Jessie's attacker, but he had to be careful. If his anger was aroused, there was no telling what would happen.

The molten fire that Pilke had experienced was only a thought, but to Pilke it had been real. He'd released Jessie to clamp his hands over his ears, and Steve had moved in, pushing a thought field around her to protect her from any further danger.

Jessie had been terrified by the attack, and this had prompted Steve to enter her mind, calming her and telling her of many things. He'd told her of Jackie, and the ship. As he was about to leave her mind, she had clung to him, her mind holding his. He could have broken the hold easily, but he'd remained with her, caressing her and soothing her fear. And then a wondrous thing had occurred.

Without conscious effort, his mind had become one with hers, locking onto Jessie's most private thoughts and cravings. They had soared then, bound together in a mind embrace that had ended in the ultimate of ecstasy! This was what had created the blue fire, but Steve was not solely responsible for it. The blue fire happened when both minds coalesced with each other, becoming one single thought. A wall was created that would repel any and all things, resulting in a force field of pure love that Steve and Jessie had created together.

When it was over, and Steve had started to withdraw from Jessie's mind, he'd sensed a whirling maelstrom of twisted thoughts and had sought them out. He'd found them in Sergeant Neville's near-defunct brain; a gelatinous mass of worm-like creatures that were smothering the thought processes. Steve had left a tiny speck of himself in Sergeant Neville's brain when he'd erased the offending parasites, but had left a bigger part of his mind with Jessie. This was the reason for Jessie's eyes being so much brighter than they had ever been, and was also the reason for the "tickling" sensation in the sergeant's brain.

The part of his mind that he had left in Jessie would serve him as a homing device, and he could use it to find her. He would find her sooner now, for the ship was hurtling along at more than two hundred nautical miles per hour, testing the ship's very limits. Steve was not following the roads and highways now; he was zeroing in on Jessie, on the spark of love he had left in her mind.

CHAPTER THIRTY-SIX

Doctor Jan Koessler finished feeling sorry for herself, was all cried out over the unnecessary and wanton killing of her colleagues, and was now planning her revenge. Her mind was not hers to command any more; she had joined the ranks of the insane over the degradation forced upon her.

Under the pretext of repairing the supposedly bad program, she instead initiated another program that she had installed a long time ago. A program she had designed to disable enemy factions should the Dome ever be breached.

She had set her broken nose, and stuffed both nostrils full of gauze. She could now only breathe through her mouth, but this suited her psychiatrically disordered plans admirably. The program she was about to call up—if all of her plans went well— would end the Colonel's raping days. She had only to enter the program now, and the beginning of the monster's end would begin.

Jan went into the Laboratory and released all of the animals, opening the outer doors of all the cages. She then called Francks on the phone, promising him a repeat performance. It was a terrible lie, but she used it to get Franks into her realm.

Smiling insanely now, trembling, waiting for his arrival, Jan opened her case and removed the special mask. She turned her back to the door, and when she heard him enter she did two things. First, she pushed the enter button on her keyboard, and then brought the mask to her face, breathing raggedly through her mouth.

When the door closed behind Colonel Francks, the lock clicked. The computer had locked it, and only through the computer could it be opened again. An odorless substance issued out from the vents, and almost immediately the Colonel's hands went to his throat. Jan knew he couldn't breathe now, and turned to face him. When he saw the mask over her face, he clawed for his gun.

She knew he wouldn't make it, for the gas that was coming from the vents was asphyxiating him. She smiled mirthlessly when he fell to the floor, unconscious, and then she entered the program that would stop the flow of gas and went over to him. Jan took his gun first, making sure she had the upper hand, then waited for the green all-clear light to come on. When the air in the room was breathable again, she removed her mask and dragged his body to a sitting position. She tied his hands behind him with electrical plastic wraps, and let his body slide to the floor, being careful not to bang his head. She wanted him very much alive when she revived him, and this she did when she was ready.

When Colonel Jeremy Francks was revived, he was totally nude. He tried to rise up, but found he couldn't. He looked down at himself to find that his legs were spread wide, and both of his feet were lashed to the steel frame that supported the computer screens. And then he smiled when he looked up.

Standing over him, her hands behind her back, a very nude Jan Koessler stood. She knelt down, stroking him, exciting him. He squirmed; trying to raise his head and found there was a chain around his neck, holding him down. Then he saw Jan's other hand come into view and he screamed!

"Why, Colonel," a near-insane Jan asked softly, "don't you like what I'm doing?"

Colonel Francks could say nothing. His eyes were riveted to the wire cutters in her hand!

"All I'm going to do is cut you out of there so we can have some fun," Jan told him. "Wouldn't you like that?"

Francks nodded, unable to speak. He breathed a sigh of relief as her hand started away from his genitals, heading for his hands. When the wire cutter took the vee-shaped wedge out of his upper lip, he screamed in pain!

"Why, Colonel?" Jan asked softly. "I thought you wanted me to cut you out of there? Don't you want to have some fun with me? Like you did before?"

The blood flowed down into his mouth from the wound that Jan inflicted with the wire cutters, and she flicked the piece of flesh onto his bare chest. Then she rose up, her empty hand searching for something on the desktop. She knelt at his side again, both of her hands full now.

"What I want you to do now, Colonel," she whispered huskily, "is to open your mouth, nice and wide. We can't very well make out if your mouth is closed, can we?"

Colonel Francks had a low pain threshold, and had already passed its peak. This had not bothered him when he administered pain to others, but now that he was on the receiving end of something he'd ordered so nonchalantly before, he started begging, pleading for a mercy that he had not shown to any.

"Please! No more," he whimpered. "I promise not to bother you again!"

His thoughts were very different from his words, and his mind was thinking what he would do to this bitch when he was freed. He would have her in every conceivable way he could think of, and then he would send a .45 slug into her ear!

"Oh?" Jan asked, innocently and insanely. "Did that hurt you? Isn't that what you did to me? Now open your mouth, Colonel, nice and wide. If you don't, I'm going to light this shiny new propane torch. And then do you know what I'm going to do with it?"

Jan brought the torch up so he could see it, and then laid it on the floor. Her hand empty now, she grasped his defeated and limp organ, pinching with the nails of her thumb and finger. Colonel Francks flinched, closing his eyes and opening his mouth. The stretched lips were opening the wound wider, causing more pain.

"Very good, Colonel," Jan cooed. "Now we can have some fun."

The first tooth she pulled was too much for him, and he lost consciousness. Jan carried on, sticking the torch head into his mouth to pry the jaws open. When she finished, she was sweating from the exertion, but she had sixteen pieces of ivory sitting on his chest. She had not been able to extract the molars.

Jan stood up and flexed her knee, hoping she had not hurt it when she'd held the colonel's head down. She reached into her case and brought out another item. She waved it under her patient's nose and stood back, smiling irrationally. The colonel snorted and woke up, but wished immediately that he hadn't.

"Oo uckin' itch!" he tried to scream. "Wha hab oo one oo ee?"

"What have I done to you, Colonel?" Jan asked. "Is that what you're trying to say? Well, I'll tell you. I've done what anybody would do with a wild animal that bites."

The fire in his mouth consumed him, the hatred in his eyes plain. He was sure she had used the torch on him, so intense was the fiery feeling behind his ravaged upper lip.

"Now that you can't bite," Jan continued, "you're a safe little animal. Are you ready for some more fun?"

Francks shook his head; the hatred in his eyes now replaced with a look of abject fear. Gone were his thoughts on what he would do to her when he was free. He thought now that she was going to kill him, but the woman he had so violently raped had other plans for him. Jan's demented brain told her that death would be too easy; too quick.

Jan reached into his nose with the cutters and clicked the handles together. Blood gushed out, and she was surprised that he had not fainted again. She pushed gently up on his nostril and the cutters clicked once more. She had neatly snipped out another wedge of flesh, and this she deposited on his chest as well.

The colonel's eyes were glazing over now, and Jan slapped him in the face with an opened palm. She wanted him awake for what she was about to do and the slap brought him back. His tear-filled eyes opened, and he watched in complete horror as she squeezed his left nipple to an erect position.

When the cutters clicked again, another bloodstained lump of flesh lay on his chest. Jan had sheared the nipple even with his breast, but Francks had only experienced a slight sting. He didn't know it, but his body was going into shock. When she told him what his final humiliation would be, and what she planned to do after that, his mind told him it would be better if he were dead!

"Now, Colonel," Jan said, "I'm going to tell you the rest of what I plan to do. I'm sure you will pass out again, but it would be so nice if you didn't! So nice to hear you beg and scream!! Oh, I'm not going to kill you. That would be too easy, and much too humane."

Jan told him then, and he tried to speak, to plead. In the end, as he'd had his way with her, so she also had her way with him. As she predicted, his brain did shut down, but not before she made the first cut.

His terror escalated to panic when he saw the razor knife, and when she lit the torch his mind went numb. He thrashed around, trying to free himself but only succeeded in tearing the skin from his ankles. He didn't feel the pain from his torn limbs, but he felt nothing but pain when Jan made the first incision. His brain ceased all functions then, and he would wake up much later, wishing that death had claimed him.

Jan cried when she finished her grisly task. He'd made her do it, made her seek revenge. She looked over at the unconscious form and stopped crying.

Colonel Francks had destroyed her life, had stolen from her that which she would have gladly given to the right man. He had paid for it dearly, for the rape and the suffering he'd caused. She glanced at the blackened, burned area where his manhood had been, and walked shakily toward her quarters.

He would never again sexually molest any woman. Colonel Jeremy Francks had been castrated, and his member had been surgically removed with the razor knife. The torch had been used to effectively cauterize the wound, stanching the flow of blood. Jan had wanted desperately for him to live, to suffer even more.

She called Doctor Soames from her quarters, and told him that the Colonel was hurt, and that he would need medical attention. It was an understatement, but Colonel Jeremy Francks would be the first person ever to be saved by Doctor Soames. It would turn out to be a medical wonder.

When her mind cleared, Jan left the Dome, taking a Jeep, intent on incapacitating the missile. She wasn't able to put her brassiere on because of the chewed nipple, but this gave her a feeling of freedom. She tossed Francks' .45 on the seat and drove out, enjoying the cleansing effect of the pure air blowing through her long hair. She never looked back.

CHAPTER THIRTY-SEVEN

Sergeant Grimes prowled through the house, checking the loads in all of the guns. He had bandaged himself as best he could, but he wasn't much to look at with a broken jaw, broken arm and ribs, not to mention the injury to his masculine parts. All in all, he counted himself fortunate that he could even walk.

He was swollen badly from forehead to pelvis. He knew he needed help, but where could he go? The Dome was out of the question, even if he could get there. And where else was there? What more could he do to help himself? Hell, he couldn't even open a damned can of soup without the use of both hands. He went to the window again, and what he saw made him wonder if he wasn't already dead.

A Jeep! There was a Jeep coming up to the house. An Army Jeep, and an angel was driving it! He could tell it was an angel, because of the long blonde hair. Grimes tucked the ivory handled .45 into his sling and opened the door. The Jeep drove up and stopped abruptly, the angel not moving.

He stumbled out, hardly able to move because of the swollen testicles. The angel in the Jeep bent to the right then opened the door. He couldn't talk, but he waved his hand in greeting. When the angel leveled the .45 at him, his hand went to his chest, close to the sling.

"Who are you, mister?" Jan asked. "What are you doing here?"

Grimes saw the beautiful face, saw the slender hand holding the gun and decided they didn't belong together. Angels didn't kill. They were supposed to help. What was this one doing with a .45? He tried his voice, and something guttural came out.

"Ant awk!" he slurred. "Oken aw!"

He pointed to his lips, then at his jaw. The angel just stood there, looking at him. He made a cup out of his hand and pushed his broken jaw into it, and then he repeated what he had managed before.

Jan Koessler looked at the apparition in front of her. The man had part of a sheet wrapped around his chest, and his arm was in some kind of a sling. He was speaking in some kind of foreign language, and could hardly walk. She lowered her gun, deciding that he was no threat to her. She glanced towards the barn, and then turned back to the man. She was looking down the bore of his own gun, and she cursed herself for being a fool!

The man motioned for her to drop her weapon, and then waved her into the house. Jan looked for a chance to escape, but the man was careful to keep his distance. To her amazement, once the man had her inside the house, he thrust his weapon into his sling, stumbling over to a desk.

Jan stood still, assessing how she could overcome this crazy man when he produced a pencil and pad. He waved her over to a huge dining room table that seemed to be a munitions depot, and he dropped the pad onto its shiny surface. Laboriously, he printed something and passed it to her. When she read it, she understood what was wrong and breathed a small sigh of relief.

"Broken jaw? And ribs? And your legs; what's the matter with them?"

Sadly, and slowly, he pointed to his masculinity. Jan's eyes opened wide, and fear entered her mind until he printed another message. After she read what he'd printed she went to him. Jan kneeled in front of him and pulled his trousers down, flinching when she saw his injury. She knew now why he couldn't walk very well, but without an ice pack she couldn't help him at all.

"We need some ice," she murmured. "But where—"

Grimes was so surprised at what she did that he couldn't move. He knew the woman wasn't a real angel now, but she had sure looked like one to him. If he had seen her in action just a few short hours ago, he would have thought quite differently. When his trousers were pulled up and the woman had fastened them, he tapped her on the shoulder.

Sergeant Grimes pointed to the kitchen, and then he led her there. He pointed to the fridge, waddled to it and opened the door. When the light came on inside, Jan knew that the whole place was still powered up. She opened the freezer door, and a lump caught in her throat. There were three trays of ice, exactly what this poor man needed to give him some relief. Jan brought one of the trays out and placed it on the counter, and then she searched the drawers for a towel.

"Where is the bathroom…mister…uh—"

She realized she didn't know the man's name, but he understood what she wanted and again pointed the way. As she left the kitchen, she smelled something corrupt but kept on going. Jan found the bathroom and the towels that she wanted and returned to the kitchen. On her way back, she noted that there were two bedrooms, and that the bathroom adjoined them. One of the beds looked like a cyclone had hit it.

She plopped the towels down on the counter beside the ice cubes, and then felt a hand on her shoulder. She turned, taking the pad from the outstretched hand. As she read the words he had painstakingly printed, Jan found out more than she wanted to know. But she also learned that she had been much too easy on the colonel.

The note read: *My name is Grimes. Sergeant Andrew Grimes. The Colonel's aide, a Sergeant Pilke, did this to me. Colonel Francks ordered him to do this, but I think he was supposed to kill me. If you smell something strange, it is likely coming from the dead officers in the basement. Colonel Francks and Pilke murdered them and left them here to rot. Just like he meant me to do.*

Jan knew that Francks was a bastard, that he had murdered all of her colleagues, but she hadn't realized just how crazy he was. To have murdered every officer at the Dome proved it. She knew now that she had been fortunate to have escaped with only what she had received from him. All of her injuries would heal, except for the one in her mind.

"Andrew?" Jan said, her mind reeling. "May I call you Andy?"

Grimes nodded.

"Okay, Andy," she continued. "What we have to do is pack your, um, your injury in ice. It will pain considerably at first, but in a little while numbness should set in. Hopefully, the swelling will diminish, and you will feel much better. Maybe we can still save your, um, your jewels."

Jan felt the flush on her face, but she welcomed it. Maybe there was hope for her after all. Maybe in time she could forget what had happened to her, and more importantly, what she had done. She'd had second thoughts on the drive out here, but now she knew that she had not been harsh enough with Francks. She thought it ironic that she would now try to save what she had totally destroyed just hours before.

Jan led Grimes to the "cyclonic" bed, and stripped it down to the bottom sheet. She removed his boots and trousers and told him to lie on his back. He groaned when she moved his legs so she could administer the ice.

"I'm sorry, Andy, but I think the worst is over."

Grimes nodded, knowing she was trying to help. Jan returned to the kitchen and came back with an ice-cube-filled towel, spreading his legs tenderly so she could position the ice pack. She couldn't help remembering doing this very same thing only hours ago, but she hadn't been as caring.

"Your shorts seem to be stuck on something, Andy, so I don't think it would be a good idea to take them off. Your, um, your...you must be ripped down there, and I don't want to cause any more damage. When the swelling goes down, we'll get some nice warm water and bathe the area, then we'll see what the problem is. There's more ice, and I'll change the pack later."

Grimes looked at her with adoration. Already he could feel the soothing numbness creeping into his crushed maleness. The fire was not so intense there now, and his eyes thanked her for helping him.

"I want you to rest for a while now, Andy," she said when she finished. "I'm going to go out and put my Jeep in the barn."

Grimes shook his head.

"You don't want me to hide the Jeep?"

He shook his head again, and raised three fingers up. His arm went into the air until his rib complained, and then his hand described a half moon arc.

"Do you know what's in the barn, Andy?" Jan asked, guessing that Grimes was trying to describe a rocket with three fins.

He nodded.

"Is it a missile, Andy? A nuclear missile?"

He nodded once more.

"Were there any flashing lights on it? On the missile panel?"

Grimes thought for a moment then shook his head. His broken jaw started sending pain messages to his brain again, and he moaned. Jan saw his anguish and decided not to ask him any more questions. She would see for herself.

"Try to get some sleep now, Andy. I'll be back in a little while to check on you."

Jan went out then, and pulled the Jeep into the barn. She hadn't known about the tankers and the generator, but she supposed the army had put them there. Somehow, Francks had kept the power alive, enabling him to retain control over an insane world. She knew that Francks could send the missile up, could even cause it to explode where it was, but she had nullified that threat. At least for a while, maybe for all time.

Jan entered the silo, and was amazed at the size of the missile. She had never seen the missile before, had, in fact, never seen any missile. She expected something bigger, but was positive it could do what it was designed for. When the Dome had been built, she had merely supervised the installation of the computer panel and had installed the program. But now she had to change the program. She knew that the missile could be fired from almost any computer if the right buttons were used, but there was also an access code in place. She used the panel then and found out that the missile was already armed, but she could change that. This she did, and then she made sure it couldn't be deployed or armed again. If this thing were to somehow explode where it was, neither she nor Andy would ever hear it. They would just be part of a huge hole in the ground.

Jan changed the first password from what it was to STOP. She continued on through the program and made the second and final password FIRE. Now if the missile were ever to be armed and deployed, the computer would have to be told to STOP FIRE.

Jan returned to the house when she changed the codes and was satisfied with her work. She looked in on Andy, and smiled when she saw that he was sleeping. The poor wretch probably hadn't had any sleep for a while, not since Pilke had beaten him up.

She checked the ice pack, being careful not to disturb what it was resting against. She thought that Pilke must be a real bastard, too. To do a thing like this to another human being, for no reason at all was a terrible act. What she had done to Francks was bad, but now she felt vindicated. Francks had deserved what he'd reaped, and more.

Jan rummaged in the kitchen until she found the canned goods, selecting beef stew for herself and chicken soup for Andy. Her upper lip was shredded, but if she used a small spoon she could manage the stew. She sat the cans on the counter, and then decided to take a nap while she waited for Andy to wake up. She went to the farthest bedroom, removed her slacks but left her top on. She dropped her head on the pillow, sighing deeply at the comforting bed.

Sleep claimed her almost at once, but it was a troubled sleep. The nightmare, when it came, was almost too real. Francks was chasing her, a huge meat cleaver in his hand. He was going to fix her for what she did to him. She tripped, went sprawling on the hard floor of the computer room at the Dome, and Francks grabbed her hair and spun her around. The cleaver descended then, slicing through the air on its way to her throat. She knew it was the end for her when she couldn't breathe, and she woke up screaming to find a huge hand covering her mouth!

CHAPTER THIRTY-EIGHT

Pilke was still following the large A.P.C. He watched as they pulled into each house, checking into each barn—if there happened to be one—then leaving again. They hadn't attempted to even look into the houses, so he knew what they were looking for. Sooner or later they would come to the right place and find the missile.

He scooted past them through the trees when they turned into another driveway. Once safely out of their sight he returned to the road. Five miles later, he turned into the farm that was actually a missile command post. It was almost dark, but he didn't need lights yet. Pilke drove his vehicle up to the barn and pulled in, and that's when he saw the Jeep. He shut his machine off and clambered out, thinking that Francks had come out here to check on his work. Pilke chuckled. He was sure Grimes was dead by now; he had sure put it to him good.

He checked out the missile, but it didn't register in his mind that the "armed" lights were no longer on. He headed out of the barn then, going towards the house. If Francks was here to see him about something else he wanted him to do, well, he could go to hell.

Still chuckling over how he had "done" Grimes, he entered through the back door and saw the canned food on the counter. He wondered about the two cans, and then he saw the notebook. He looked at it, but the words didn't make any sense. When he turned the book over it did.

The words had been scrawled, printed as a child might do, and Pilke hadn't understood what it meant. When he turned the pad over and saw Grimes name, and his and Francks' implication, he knew something was wrong. Grimes wasn't dead after all, but Pilke knew he had broken his jaw, so maybe he couldn't talk too well. Maybe he was trying to tell somebody something. It sure as hell wasn't Francks, so who in hell was in the house? And where?

Pilke pulled his .45 and advanced into the living room. He passed the gun-laden table and crept over towards the hall that led to the bedrooms. Cautiously, he passed the bathroom and looked into the last bedroom. What he saw in the room started a pain hammering at his loins. The long hair that cascaded over the pillow started a fire in him, and left him light headed. His greedy eyes stared at the trim ankles, and his gaze followed the sleeping form up to the top. His black eyes slowed at the twin mounds, then continued on until he finally stopped at the most beautiful face he had ever seen.

Although he was normally a very cautious man—at times to the point of paranoia—his sexual hungers were now aroused. He threw caution to the winds and holstered his gun, and then he approached the sleeping woman, clamping his large beefy hand over her mouth. He didn't want her to suddenly wake up and start screaming before he found out where Grimes was hiding.

Jan's eyes opened wide when she discovered she couldn't breathe. Panic claimed her when she realized she wasn't dreaming after all, and that there was a real hand over her mouth. She tried to bring some air into her tortured lungs through her nose, but she hadn't taken the gauze out yet. Part of her mind knew that her breast was being massaged, because she felt the hand that ripped her blouse open. That hand was now kneading her flesh, hurting her.

Jan's oxygen starved brain was starting to dim and she knew she would soon be unconscious. When the hand left her mouth, she sucked air in greedily, her lungs crying out for more. When she could breathe easy, she started to scream, but the scream suddenly was choked off when she saw the gun aimed at her head. She was going to be raped again, and as before, she could do nothing about it. She lay back, quietly resigning herself to another terrible onslaught!

Pilke dropped the gun back into the holster. He fumbled with his pants, and succeeded in getting his right leg out of them before the leaden projectile shattered his left knee. He had been balancing himself on his left leg when it had happened, and he went down as if the bullet had gone into his brain.

Pilke landed on his back and Grimes calmly waddled over to him. He smiled—as much as the broken jaw would let him—then he blew Pilke's right knee out. The knee shattered, the bullet shredding bone and cartilage as it changed direction. Pilke howled, cursing, and Grimes aimed again. Pilke pushed himself back, trying to evade the bullet that would end his manhood, and then Grimes fired.

Instead of a boom, the gun emitted a sharp click. Jan came off of the bed then, but not before Grimes had picked up Pilke's own weapon. Jan pleaded with him not to do it, not to take Pilke's manhood away. Finally, Grimes nodded and Jan turned to retrieve her clothes.

Out of the corner of her eye, Jan saw Andy swing the gun, heard the crunch as Pilke's nose broke. She then watched in awe as Andy blew out both of Pilke's elbows. Grimes really smiled then, looking at the pain-wracked, quivering mass of animal that floundered on the floor in front of him. He'd promised the woman he wouldn't destroy Pilke's manhood, but that was all. He lowered the gun when Jan came over to him, and let himself be led out to the kitchen table.

Jan left Andy there and returned to the bedroom for her slacks. She was surprised that Pilke was still conscious, but she was more surprised when he leered at her almost nude body. She thought of bringing Andy back in to finish what he had started, but instead calmly walked out of the room. She'd had enough revenge for one day.

Jan dressed in the bathroom, finding a pin to repair her torn blouse. When she returned to the kitchen, she found that Andy's eyes were glazed. She flicked the lights on but didn't say anything, searching the cupboards until she had found two small pots. She opened the cans and dumped the contents of them into the pots, and then she turned the stove on. While she waited for their supper to heat, she found some bowls and spoons. She looked, but could find no straws. Andy would have to use a spoon.

"You all right, Andy?"

Grimes nodded, wiping at his eyes with his good hand.

"Then why the tears?" she asked softly. "A no good bastard like that doesn't deserve them."

He motioned for the notebook. When she read what he printed, Jan knew what had been bothering him.

"Oh, Andy, it wasn't your fault?"

He nodded his head and printed again.

"SHOULD HAVE KILLED HIM. WANTED HIM TO SUFFER. SHOT TOO LATE. HE HAD HIS HANDS ON YOU."

Jan read it and shook her head, then she returned to the stove. With her back turned to him she faltered, and then told him what had happened to her at the Dome. What she had done to Francks, and who she was. When she turned to look at him, he had a look of incredible astonishment on his face.

"That's why I didn't want you to maim that animal," she concluded. "I was wrong in doing what I did to Francks, and I didn't want you to make the same mistake as I did."

Grimes printed again, telling her she hadn't been wrong.

"Yes, I was," she demanded. "Don't you see? It brought me down to his level; an animal, just like him!"

Though she tried as hard as she could, no amount of arguing would convince Grimes that she had been wrong. As far as he was concerned, Francks had received what he deserved. When his mind envisioned Francks—his male parts cut out and plopped on his chest like a choice cut of meat on display—he smiled to himself. The other parts Jan removed were as nothing compared to that.

"You hungry, Andy?"

Grimes nodded. With the news he'd heard about Francks, he found that he was ravenous.

Jan poured the contents from the steaming pots into the bowls and brought them to the table. She sat down across from Andy and smiled. Jan picked up her spoon, and then turned quickly to the window. A huge machine was bearing down on them, its terrible lights blinding her!

Jan saw the lights come to a stop, but she couldn't see anything except shadows because of the glare. She moved back from the table, yelling at Andy to do the same. Before the words were out of her mouth, however, a man barged in, the weapon in his hands ready to spit death. Jan was dumbstruck when she saw the man's face and a name from another time came to her mind. The man looked her over quickly, but then turned his gaze on Andy.

"Grimes?!" Billy said. "Is that you?"

Grimes nodded, taking his hand away from the sling when he saw who Billy was. At one time, Grimes had wanted this man hurt, even killed, but not now.

"What in hell happened to you?" Billy asked in surprise. "Pilke do this?"

Andy Grimes nodded again, smiling. Billy looked at him as if he had two heads. "What in hell are you smiling about, Grimes?" Billy asked. "Where—"

Grimes pointed over his shoulder with his thumb.

Jan finally found her voice and spoke up. She'd been shocked when the man had showed up, had thought that he was Tom. Although the resemblance was uncanny, she saw now that she was mistaken. Besides, Tom had hated guns, but this man seemed to be right at home with his awesome weapon. "You know this man, mister—"

"Tanner, ma'am," Billy said. "Billy Tanner. I'm sure sorry for coming in the way I did, but when we saw the lights we thought—"

"Yes, Mister Tanner?" Jan asked. "What did you think?"

"Uh, I'm sorry," Billy apologized. "But we thought maybe this Pilke, the one who beat up Grimes here, was in the house."

Jan smiled. "Oh, he is here, Mister Tanner," she said, a slight smile playing at the corner of her mouth. "But I doubt you'll need that gun for him now."

More people came into the kitchen then, and Jan was surprised to see a woman and a young boy. The woman smiled at Jan, and she smiled back. Billy started introductions, but he didn't know who Jan was. When he found out who she was, and what she was doing in the house, it was his turn to be surprised.

"You mean to tell me that there was a woman at the Dome all this time? And such a damned fine looking woman to boot!? Are you sure you programmed the—" Billy stopped, his flow of words cut off as if he had lost his tongue. He smiled sheepishly over his candid assessment of Jan's beauty.

Jan smiled at his discomfort. Billy's face turned three shades of red, stopping at crimson. For all his cons and tricks, Billy was really a shy person. Hell on wheels when it came to facing a man, but unable to function if there was a woman involved.

"It's all right... Billy," Jan said "Thank you for the compliment. A lot of men have made the same mistake about my abilities, though, so don't worry about it." Jan caught her tongue just in time. She had almost called him Tom. "Now, this Pilke you were talking about? Would you like to see him?"

Billy could only nod.

"Andy?" Jan asked. "Do you think you could make the trip?"

"Andy?" Billy came out of his trance at the name.

"Sergeant Andrew Grimes, Mister Tanner," Jan supplied. "Have you men never met?"

"Well, yeah," Billy said, "sure, but I never knew his first name." Come to think of it, Billy thought, he didn't know Neville's first name either. He had always referred to Neville and Grimes as sarge.

Grimes was only too glad to lead the way, and after Jan helped him to his feet, he stumbled to the bedroom where they had left Pilke. Jan went with them, putting lights on as she did. She left the last light for Andy to flick on, and when he did, Billy saw the unconscious, bloody form of the man who had caused so much terror and pain.

"He tried to rape me, Billy," Jan said. "He would have, if it hadn't been for Andy."

"Is he alive?" Billy asked, staring at all the blood on the floor.

"Barely," Jan said. "He was awake a while ago, but I imagine that shock has set in now. He's lost a lot of blood. I tried to stop Andy from doing all this, but—"

"I'll be damned!" Billy said, impressed. "What did Gr... uh, what did Andy do to him?"

When Jan told him, Billy whistled once and turned to leave. "There's some friends of mine who would like to see this. You mind if I send them in?"

Jan didn't mind in the least and Billy sent Jerry and Ray in. Peter went with them, his curiosity aroused. He wanted to see the man who had attacked his daughter. When he saw the mess the man had been left in, his medical mind took over. He returned to the kitchen, his eyes blazing!

"Good God, woman!!" Peter admonished "What in hell did you do to him? And why are you letting him bleed to death? Don't you have any idea what—"

Jan turned, her eyes on fire. "Why, I didn't do anything to him.

Andy merely gave him something called a "pay back"! Yes, that's what I think it's called!"

"Do you know what in hell happened to that man in there?" Peter asked, enraged.

Jan smiled, but only with her mouth. Her eyes were dead. "Well, yes, I do," she said, her words cutting. " Andy shot out both of his knees, and then he did the same to his elbows! He also broke his nose! He wanted to shoot his balls off, too, but like a fool I talked him out of it!" Jan was angry now and she let Peter have both barrels.

"I understand that you are a medical man, sir?" Jan asked Peter.

Peter was quick, but he would regret it. "Yes, I am!" he spat. "And I have never seen such cruelty since I was in Nam! Over there it was war, but this…this—"

Jan's eyes gleamed. "Well, Doctor," she said, her voice nearing hysteria, "how would you like to save the lives of the thirteen officers who are rotting in the basement of this house? Men that bastard in there murdered?" She had a full head of steam now, and Peter was the one who became the unfortunate recipient of her anger. "Why don't you have a look at Andy? His broken ribs! His broken nose and his broken jaw! Better yet, have a look at his testicles! They were the size of a football when I found him, and I don't know if they will get any better!"

Jan was crying, but she had more to say. "That bastard in there… that bastard was about to rape me when…when Andy stopped him! The other bastard at the Dome *did* rape me, but I fixed him better than Andy fixed this one!"

Jan broke down completely, sobbing uncontrollably. Jessie came to her, wanting to comfort her, and Jan leaned on her shoulder. She had cried when Francks had raped her, had cried again when she had seen the putrid gray matter on the laboratory floor, which had once been her colleague's brains, but not like this.

Everybody came back into the kitchen when they heard the commotion. When Grimes saw the dire straits his angel was in he waddled over to her. Jessie looked over at her father and smiled wanly. She wanted to comfort him as well, but she couldn't. And then, as Jan's sobbing slowed, Jessie saw something that only she could see. Peter saw Jessie's eyes glowing brightly, and knew something was about to happen.

The house trembled, and then the whole area outside lit up as bright as any sun could make it. Jan stopped crying and Jessie left her, heading for the door. With her hand on the handle, she turned and spoke to her father. "Ohhhh... Dad," she breathed, "he's here! He's finally here!!!"

Jessie opened the door then and went outside. Jan's first thought was that the missile had exploded, the noise was that terrible and the light so bright. And then she knew that it had nothing to do with the missile. This close to the center of a nuclear explosion, she knew, a person would not see or hear anything, not ever again. The flesh would have been torn from their bodies, and even their bones would be pulverized into radioactive fallout.

Jan looked through the kitchen window, but could only see a bright light. When she turned back to face into the room, she saw that all of the others were following Jessie outside. She took Andy's hand and led him, following the others. Once outside, the terrible noise was close to being unbearable, the air pressure almost enough to destroy eardrums. The light was close to the ground now, and she could see the outline of something huge, the likes of which she had never seen before.

It was a craft of some kind, and Jan saw huge pipes retreating into nothing. It created an awful wind, and dust was still flying through the air. Something in this strange machine seemed to be winding down, and the awful din was now replaced with a slight hum. She and Andy followed the others, catching up to them when they all stopped.

Everybody was silent; the only sound a slight humming coming from the craft. On the side of the great ship a door swung up and out, followed by a set of steps that flowed to the ground. As they all stared, a diminutive figure came down the steps, slowly, as if unsure. Then a man appeared, carrying a plush bear.

Jan and the others watched in utter perplexity, all except Jessie. With a yelp, she ran to the small figure, picking it up and whirling it around. She set the figure down again, beaming, then turned towards the man. Jessie walked towards him, her steps deliberate, and Peter could have sworn that his daughter's feet never once touched the ground.

Kevin was terrified by the noise and ran back to the A.P.C. He returned with Miss Muffet in tow, and his small hand crept up into

Jan's. It startled her at first, and then she grasped Kevin's hand, squeezing it gently. She felt the trembling in the small hand and tried to reassure the boy, but found it wasn't needed when the other small figure approached and spoke to him.

"Hi, Kevin. I'm Jackie."

Kevin was growing up—had matured in the last couple of days—but he was not ready for this. In front of him now stood a girl, even though she looked like a boy. Kevin looked at the ball hat that perched sideways on her head, then at the long golden hair that reached past her shoulders. She had called him by name, but he had never seen her before in his life!

"Hu...hi" he stuttered. "Uh, how did you know my name?"

"Oh, that's easy!" Jackie blurted. "Steve told me."

"Steve?" Kevin said, still confused.

"Yep," Jackie answered. "That's him over there with your mom. But don't ever, ever make him mad!"

Jan was listening to the exchange between the two children, and though the girl seemed younger, she sounded much older. Jan smiled inwardly in spite of herself, wanting to hear more.

"Why would I want to do that?" Kevin asked deliberately. "An' anyway, what would it matter?"

"You'll see if you ever do!" Jackie said solemnly. "The last time he got mad he burned up a whole city, an' he only used his mind."

Jan was watching the man and woman, but was listening intently now to the young people at her side.

"No way!" Kevin was unwavering. "Nobody can do that! It ai...isn't possible."

"It is so!" Jackie became defensive. "I seen it! When that man over there shot at you an' your mom, Steve got so mad he burned up Birmingham! I can show you the burn holes in the map, an' he never even knew he done it!!" Jackie was still pointing at Sergeant Neville, and Kevin just stared at her.

"Where...who...who told you all this?"

"Nobody told me, silly," Jackie said. "Steve put the pictures in my head. It was great. Just like watchin' a movie, only my eyes was closed."

Jan wasn't smiling any more. If this child was telling the truth, then she had just described something wonderful—and quite possibly—something very dangerous. She had to know. She untangled her hands and left both Andy and Kevin to fend for themselves, and then she walked towards the man and woman. They were holding hands, but not speaking. The woman was nodding now, as if in reply to something, but nothing had been said. Jan put a greeting in her mind, something she planned to say to this man, and staggered back when she heard a booming voice in her head!

"It's true! My God, it's true! The girl wasn't lying!"

Steve relinquished Jessie's hand and spoke. "I'm sorry," he said, his voice deep and resounding. "I didn't mean to do that; it just jumped out at me."

"You…you…you can read minds?!" Jan squeaked. "And…and put your thoughts in other minds?! Why…that…that's preposterous!!"

Steve smiled thinly. "I see Jackie has been telling everybody about it." Steve had known that she would, especially Kevin.

Jan didn't know what to think, and then she decided not to think anything. At least not when this man was close to her. "No, not to everybody. Just the boy; I overheard it. Is it true about Birmingham? About the map?"

Steve smiled again, more warmly this time, and Jan saw the brightness in his eyes. Steve slowed his smile. "Yes, I'm afraid it is. It's the reason I must never become angry again, not really angry. I don't know what would happen if I ever did."

Jessie reached for Steve's hands. "Maybe we should all go inside. I'm sure everybody is just dying to meet you, especially my father."

Steve turned to Jessie and they left the ship. As they neared the waiting group, a wave of pain drove into Steve's brain, causing him to stop. "That man," he pointed, indicating Sergeant Grimes. "The one with the bandages, he is in much pain."

Jan told Steve that indeed he was. She told him the nature of Andy's injuries, and how he had received them. Steve reached into the man's mind and destroyed the pain, but could not heal the hurt. He left a small trickle of himself in the man's mind, but as had been the case with Sergeant Neville, he was unaware of it.

"His pain is gone now," Steve advised, " but not his injuries. I'm afraid that's all the help I can give him."

Jan looked at Andy, at the wonder in his eyes. She was so amazed at the transformation in the heretofore-crippled body that she didn't feel the probe in her own mind.

"You will feel better now, too, Doctor Koessler. Your physical injuries were slight compared to the man, but your mental anguish was intolerable."

Jan looked at Steve in wonder as Jessie started introducing him to the throng. He knew them already, but suffered through the introductions as though he didn't. When Jessie introduced Steve to her father, she gave Peter such a blistering look it made the doctor wince. Steve smiled, knowing what an inquisitive mind Jessie's father had.

When the introductions were complete, and they were all in the house, Steve made an announcement that floored all of them, and Peter finally learned what had happened to the world.

CHAPTER THIRTY-NINE

Steve brought Pilke's pain down to a level that was not screaming into his heightened senses. At Steve's insistence, Peter bandaged Pilke and Pilke was tied to the bed that Grimes had originally occupied. Steve knew without a doubt that Pilke was a dangerous and vindictive individual. He'd learned that when he'd entered his mind.

Jessie was constantly at Steve's side now, ever since the mind-boggling announcement that he had made the night before. Jessie cried when Steve finished, but Steve lifted her up out of her agony. As they walked through the relatively burned out woods behind the house, she thought back to the night before.

"I'm sure you all are wondering what has happened to the world," Steve had said. "Well, I wondered about that, too, but now I know."

Steve had told them then of the experiment that had almost destroyed the ozone layer, and of the aliens who'd caused it. "These aliens contacted me yesterday, when I was on my way here. Apparently, these gases—that were brought back with the ozone layer—must be moved or destroyed. Failing that, they will surely destroy us."

"What happened?" Peter had interrupted. "How can we do anything?"

"I'm coming to that, Peter; please be patient. These gases are still with us, intermingled with our planet's protective layer. This is the reason we haven't had any rain, and the reason for the oppressive heat. This is also the reason that I was "directed" to the ship I came here in, and one of the reasons that I am here. It is the reason that the missile must be fired."

There had been total uproar, but Steve had silenced them again. "The aliens tell me that it is the missile that must be used to rid our planet of these wayward gases, and it is my brain power that will provide the magnetism that will enable the missile to accomplish this, utilizing the ship's computer."

There had been a murmur, and Jessie had reached for Steve's hand. Steve had glanced at her, his eyes losing some of their brightness. "The aliens have explained to me that I could be harmed in some way when this is attempted. Perhaps killed." Steve had squeezed Jessie's hand then, but hadn't looked at her. "In three days this will be attempted," he had continued. "Then maybe the world will return to normal. Only then will it rain, and only then will things start to grow again. We are losing precious oxygen even as I speak, because of the lack of trees and grass, and now we have only about one mile of oxygen left. Before this happened, the oxygen went up about three miles. You can see what we have lost."

As Jessie's thoughts came back to the present, tears filled her eyes. Steve knew what she was thinking and he wanted to help her, but he also knew that she must accept what he had to do.

"I have to do this, Jessie."

She smiled through her tears. "I know."

"Maybe everything will be fine," Steve said, trying to reassure her. "Maybe nothing will happen to me at all."

"Sure!" Jessie became angry. "And maybe you'll die! Your brain and soul lost forever. Traveling through endless space, never stopping!"

Steve wanted to go into her mind and soothe her, console her, but he remembered Jackie's words when he'd finally had to tell her the truth.

"That's not funny, Steve!" Jackie had warned. "It ain't nice to peek at people like that. People don't want anybody looking at them when they go to the bathroom. Did you do that to me?"

"No, Jackie," Steve remembered saying. "I don't do things like that. I only try to help, to ease some of the hurt in people's minds."

What Jackie said next had slowed him down, and he'd known then that she was much older than her years. "Y' know, Steve, sometimes you take memories away. What happens then? Are those memories gone forever?"

Steve hadn't been able to answer her and he had apologized.

"Steve?" Jessie broke through his thoughts.

"Hmmmm?" he asked, returning his mind to the present.

"Would you do something for me?"

"Anything, Jessie. You know that."

"Would you make love to me? Real, physical love? I want your baby, Steve. I...I need it." Steve was almost speechless!

"But...Jessie!" he murmured explosively. "What if something does happen to me? You'll be all alone to—"

"No! I won't!" Jessie cried. "I'll have part of you with me all the time then."

"Why don't we wait, Jessie?" Steve almost pleaded."

Jessie shook her head violently. "Don't you see, Steve?" Jessie begged. "We may never get the chance."

Steve wanted Jessie, but not for only the moment. He wanted her forever and a day. He didn't want it to be this way, but maybe she was right. Maybe he would live on in his and Jessie's child. But then again, maybe he wouldn't die after all.

They made love under the trees, tenderly, passionately. It was a love that engulfed them completely. Later, when Jessie cried, Steve was at a loss. *Had he hurt her? Had he done something to make her cry? Although he wanted to find out, he didn't want to go into her mind. He was more perplexed than ever when she turned to him and smiled, and then kissed him.*

They returned to the house shortly after, and Steve showed Jessie his ship. He explained what he could, and showed her the computer banks. Jessie cried again, knowing that in two days Steve's brain would be inside, reaching for the stars!

CHAPTER FORTY

The alien captain had contacted the man, had converted color to thought and had been successful. He now had information for his commander, information that might prove very productive. He pushed his special colors out now, brilliance that would find his commander.

You wish to confer, Captain? the answering colors formed.

Yes, Commander! the captain replied. *I have some thoughts that may be beneficial to all concerned!*

Please elaborate, captain.

The diminutive captain of the alien vessel pushed his colors, informing his commander of his dealings with the man. If the commander would have had eyebrows, these would have shot up in surprise.

This is very good, Captain! You have devised a solution for all concerned! You have advised the powerful one of this change in procedure?

No, Commander. I wished to receive your great authority to proceed. If it is your wish, then we will do so.

The commander was not awed easily or often, but this was one of those times. His captain had showed promising capabilities, and this thought of his was bordering on magnificent, but it must be handled correctly.

You have done well, Captain. Very well, indeed, and you deserve a rest. You will contact the powerful one now, and have him assemble all in his ship.

I will communicate with them all through the screens on the ship, and we will proceed with your great plan.

The captain had not expected this. It was unheard of for a commander to deal directly with others. *Yes, Commander! It will be as you instruct!*

The commander was aware that his captain was dismayed. The captain had devised an excellent avenue of escape for the powerful one, and it held splendid chances for his survival. He had hoped to save this powerful one, for his leadership would be invaluable. But he would supervise now, for nothing must go wrong!

You will contact me when all are assembled, Captain, and I will apprise them of this plan. If this thought of yours is completed satisfactorily, then I see no reason for you to captain this vessel any longer! If all goes well, you will progress to commander level.

CHAPTER FORTY-ONE

Jan Koessler and Peter Lindell had been talking almost constantly since they met. After he had been *taken down a peg* by her, Peter had found out all sorts of things, and this had fed his insatiable curiosity to capacity. Peter had known about the Dome, of course, but had never understood that it had been merely another government ploy.

It was common knowledge now what Jan had suffered at the Commanding Officer's hands in the Dome, and of the punishment she had meted out in return. It had been considered a just sentence by all, except Jan herself. She had regretted that she had inflicted that particular brand of pain and suffering on Colonel Francks; her only consolation being that she had been partially insane at the time. Steve had taken the mental anguish away, but the memory was still there.

"You have to forget it, Doctor," Peter said. "You have to go forward now, we all must."

Jan looked at the man who had remonstrated against her. "Please, Doctor, call me Jan. And may I call you Peter?"

Peter smiled. "That's a deal."

Everybody knew now what was going to happen, but not one person was very happy about it. Peter had talked to Jessie and Steve, and knew what they had been doing. A blind man could have seen what was going on, but he was proud that his daughter had seen fit to tell him.

"What has to be done now, Jan?" Peter asked. "How do we get Steve hooked up to the computer?"

Since Peter had finally accepted Steve at face value, and since talking to Jan, nothing else the world threw at him would be a surprise. He didn't know it, but he was about to be surprised again. They all were, including Steve.

"It's simple, really," Jan said. "The way Steve explained it, all we have to do is run some input wires from the computer on his ship to the wires that were implanted in his ankles, and the rest of the operation will be automatic."

Peter nodded. "You know, Jan, it's still hard to believe. Aliens, our ozone layer contaminated by some strange life form. Steve, himself."

Jan smiled. She knew what it cost Peter to say the things he was saying. "It is fantastic, isn't it? But then, so is his ship. Did you know that Steve has never used computers before? He doesn't even know about the printers; he said there was a whole lot of stuff in there that he never used. I find that just short of amazing."

It was Peter's turn to smile. "I'd say that Steve is a human computer now, and I think he could almost do what he wants without using a programmed mind."

Jan nodded, and was about to say something when Jessie walked into the house. It was the first time she had been seen alone since Steve landed, and both of them wondered where Steve was. Jessie and Steve had been "joined at the hip" ever since he'd arrived.

"Dad? Doctor Koessler? Steve would like everybody to come to the ship."

Peter was mildly amused, for the only one that was permitted on board was Jessie. Even Jackie had been relegated to the house.

"Oh?" Peter said, unable to resist a barb. "I thought you and Steve wanted to be alone?"

Jessie blushed, and Peter grinned impishly.

"Steve has been in contact with the aliens again," Jessie said, trying to ignore her father's humor, "and now the aliens are going to "speak" to everybody through the computer on the ship."

Peter was dying to see the interior of the ship, and now he was going to get his chance. He knew his curiosity would get the best of him some day, but he couldn't help being what he was. "What about Pilke?"

"Steve said to leave him here, Dad. He was very enigmatic about it, but he was smiling when he told me that. He said Pilke would hear all about it."

Peter left to collect the others, leaving Jessie and Jan alone together. Jessie smiled thinly. Jan wanted to ask her something but curbed her wondering. Jessie was a grown woman, and it looked like she knew what she wanted, but Jan couldn't help but wonder where it would all end.

When they were all in the ship, including Miss Muffet, Steve spoke to them. Jan noted with satisfaction that Jessie was at Steve's side, her arm around him.

"As you all know," Steve began, "tomorrow is the day we attempt to fire the missile. It was planned to use my brain—through the computer—to boost the missile, but this was not the reason for me to be connected to the computer."

Jessie looked at Steve, as did all the others. He held his hands up, soliciting silence. "The real reason I was supposed to be hooked up to the computer was for the positive and negative forces in my body. This is what must be used to neutralize the threat to our ozone layer, and to our planet. The aliens have contacted me again, and now they will speak to all of us. If you will all watch the screen, I'm sure you will understand."

All eyes turned to the screen that Steve pointed at. At first, all that could be seen were colors, every hue of the rainbow. And then the beginnings of words emerged through the twisting, whirling vortex. Total silence reigned, and as all eyes watched the words, a voice boomed gently in each mind.

We are from an atmosphere much like your world, existing side by side with your world, but on a different plane. To you, it is thought of only as the fourth dimension, an unproven, and, as yet, undiscovered existence.

We—in our infinite wisdom, we thought at the time—attempted an experiment. We wanted to bring our two worlds together in the past to enable us to visit your world in the future.

Due to our obstinacy—and somewhat unwise meddling—your world's own protective layer was stripped away. It was a temporary setback for our race, and we returned your world's ozone layer to its rightful place. But in our ignorance, we also brought back another life form, and now we are presented with the insurmountable task of repairing that which we destroyed.

Steve clasped his arm around Jessie, bringing her trembling body to his. All eyes were on the screen, all brains "hearing" the words!

It was in this man, this powerful one that we found a champion. Our brothers thought he was the only being capable of completing this task, but now we find this is not so. With his advanced mind, this powerful one is able to transport thought and objects, and for this reason we entered into continuity with another of your kind. This other is not so gracious as the powerful one, but has expressed a desire to visit the stars. In his own vernacular, he is now nothing more than a "basket case", a state in which he does wish to exist.

The words melted from the screen, and the booming *voice* stopped, but the swirling, impossible colors remained. In Jan's mind, she knew that the alien was speaking about Jeremy Francks. When the booming resumed, she and all of the others present found out who the *chosen* was. Steve had known all along, but wished not to impart this information, knowing that the aliens would convey this to all.

This being's appendages will never support him again, and this is the reason he wishes to depart this world. His brain is the capacitor that will be sent into the heavens, and from there into the universe. The powerful one will be but the catalyst. Here are the instructions that must be carriedout. Beware; there is still a danger to the powerful one, but this has been decreased greatly!

Everybody watched the screen intently, especially Jan and Peter. They knew that they would make the proper connections, knew they were the only people that could, with the possible exception of Steve. Both of them realized that Steve's mind was capable of almost anything.

Jan reprogrammed the missile computer and changed the explosion sequence. She set the amplifier at maximum and connected the extra wires. They had all learned from the *voice* that the ozone layer was now stretched out. Was, in fact, no more than three millimeters in thickness. It would not take much to breach it; they were advised, to utterly destroy it. The nuclear explosion must occur before the missile actually reached it. If the ozone layer were destroyed, Jan knew, all life on the planet would cease. This was why she changed the firing sequence. She hoped her calculations were correct, and now only that ancient enemy of man would decide. She returned to the ship, and watched as Peter worked on his project.

When Pilke awoke—they were told—if he ever did, he would feel nothing. Thanks to the power of Steve's mind. The two electrodes that Peter had connected to Pilke were being coupled to Steve's wires;

the wires that had been implanted in his ankles so long ago; the wires that were hooked up to Steve's nervous system, and, ultimately, to his brain.

When Jan gave the computer command that would fire the missile, Steve would push Pilke's mind into the ship's computer. This would take Pilke's positive and negative forces out to the missile and from there soar up to the heavens. Pilke's mind and soul would be free of his body then, blasting up to the gaseous-entangled ozone layer.

At the precise moment that Pilke's being was one with the missile, Steve would withdraw. If Jan's calculations were correct, the missile would explode well below the ozone layer, sending Pilke's life force through. His positive and negative factors would collect the offending positive and negative gases and pull them out into the far reaches of deep space. The matter—that originally separated the gases—would pick up debris along the way, building a wall that would forever keep the lethal gases apart. If the ozone layer escaped intact, the world would be safe again. Then the awesome task of rebuilding would begin.

What would happen when Pilke's being blasted through the ozone layer was pure conjecture, but it was hoped that his mind would soar to the stars. If his mind survived the trip, perhaps he would travel the time tunnels to the very creation of the cosmos. His would be the first human mind to unravel the mystery of life.

Oh, what an event that would be! To see the cosmos being invented. Over, and over again, to actually be a part of it! Jan shivered just thinking about it.

"We're ready here, Jan," Peter said.

Steve opened his eyes. Jessie was holding his hands, and would continue to hold them until he returned or be taken with him.

"Are you sure you want to do this, Jessie?" Steve asked.

She smiled. "I've never been more sure of anything in my life! Whatever happens, we'll be together."

Steve smiled back at her, knowing that his body wasn't going anywhere. Jessie would be safe. Steve lay back then, trying not to think, but he was startled when Jan spoke to him.

"Are you ready, Steve?"

"Ready," Steve answered.

Jan punched in the command to the missile computer, and Steve closed his eyes, pushing. In the silo, rockets erupted and the great bird rose. The guiding fins on the missile opened when it was clear of the confining walls, and man's greatest adventure had begun.

Steve pushed, sending Pilke's mind and being out to the missile. He was surprised at the positive and negative show that he encountered along the way. Although he didn't know what they were named, he was looking at protons and electrons, and, on occasion, positrons. It was beautiful, so much so that he didn't realize what was happening to him. He realized that he wasn't pushing any more; he was being pulled along, and both he and Pilke were one with the missile.

The heat inside of the great bird was tremendous, and although he used his greatest effort, he could not break the hold that Pilke's demented brain had on him. Pilke was dragging Steve along with him, refusing to relinquish his hold. Jessie felt the straining in Steve's hands and screamed, but Steve never heard her.

Peter realized that something was wrong, and rushed to Steve's side, trying to bring him out of whatever trouble he was in, but nothing seemed to work. Finally, in desperation, Peter pulled the wires from Steve's ankles.

Jan yelled to Peter, trying to stop him but she was too late. Steve was gone now, Jan knew, for he had no way to return. Even if he could separate from Pilke, he had no way to get back. Those two slender wires had been his umbilical; his brain's only ties to his body. With the connections broken, Steve's mind would be lost. Steve's psyche would never be able to return to his body.

Unknown to all present, Steve had finally pulled free of Pilke's demented brain, but it hadn't been his doing. Pilke's heightened awareness wanted to be alone now; he didn't want Steve or anybody else around when he roamed the universe. In death, as in life, Pilke was a self-centered individual who cared only for himself, and for this reason had relinquished his hold. Steve wasn't being dragged now, but he still couldn't find his way out of the missile. This wondrous event happened only because Peter unplugged the wires that had been implanted in Steve's ankles.

Although Steve was out of the missile and away from Pilke, he was stranded. All around him, his mind's eye saw only the twinkling stars and he knew he was lost forever. Like Pilke, he would travel the heavens until the flame in his mind dimmed, and finally *wink* out.

Jessie had both of Steve's hands in hers, squeezing and pumping them, trying to bring him back. Jan plugged the wires back into Steve's ankles, but she knew it was too late. They had lost him!

Peter took the stethoscope from Pilke's chest, shaking his head. Pilke's body was dead now, his being on its way to the stars. Peter touched the stethoscope to Steve's chest, brightening when he heard Steve's heart still beating. When Peter had yanked out the wires connecting Steve to Pilke, he had saved Steve's life. Pilke had died at that moment, but Steve hadn't been connected to him at the time and had escaped with his life.

"He's alive; Jessie," Peter said, "but I don't understand it. Pilke is dead, but Steve is still alive."

Jan tried to think of something, but nothing came. She had done everything she could and it hadn't helped. And then, as she was about to resign herself to the fact that Steve was gone forever, a helping hand was extended.

"Doctor Koessler?" a voice broke the silence. Jan looked up. It was Sergeant Neville. "Uh, maybe I can help."

"You, Sergeant?" Jan asked, her mind in turmoil. "How can you help?"

"Uh, well, y' see, I still have the tickle in my head from when Steve took my worms away and—"

"Worms?" Jan asked. "What worms?"

"Uh, yeah, guess you don't know about them. That day back at the cave, something screwed up my brain. Well, later on at the picnic table, when we stopped, I felt something else in my brain. It took the worms away, an' I was all right again. That something is still in my head, an' it must be something Steve left in there. I thought if maybe you hooked up some wires to me an' plugged 'em into Steve he might find his way back."

Jan felt something akin to extreme anxiety entering her soul; the feeling only worsened when Andy stepped up beside his associate. Andy nodded and pointed to his head, signifying that he, too, had a part of Steve still in his brain.

A quick flash of light burst in Jan's mind, and she turned quickly to Jessie. "Hold on to his hands, Jessie!" Jan demanded. "Don't let go, no matter what! Peter, is he still alive?"

Peter nodded, wondering what was going through Jan's mind.

"All right now! Who else here has had Steve enter their minds?"

Jan counted the show of hands then whispered to Peter. "Have Jessie's eyes always been this bright?"

"No," Peter answered, "not this bright. It's only since he…since Steve made love to her that day at the picnic area."

Jan was surprised that Jessie had been so open about it and she asked Peter when it had happened. Peter chose his words carefully. He could see that Jan was looking at him in a funny way, and he thought he had better explain about it.

"It was the day that Steve saved her from Pilke. It wasn't a physical love, you understand; it only happened in their minds. A soul love, she called it. There was a blue light all around her that day, and later Jessie called it a love light. Steve wasn't physically there, you understand."

Jan's specially trained mind assimilated all the facts she had, and she thought she had a way to bring Steve back. She started firing orders around, mildly surprised when everybody did as she asked. When they were all in position, she told them her plan.

"We must all close our eyes now, and in our mind's eye create a road. A road of light stretching up to the sky."

On Jessie's right, Kevin grasped his mother's wrist. Neville was holding Kevin's and Grimes' hand. Jan was holding fast to Grimes and Jerry. Ray was attached to Jerry and Billy, and the circle was completed when Billy grasped Jackie's hand. Jackie placed her other hand on Jessie's left wrist, and each one projected their minds, trying to create a silver road to the stars.

But nothing happened, and Jan was afraid she had guessed wrong. Peter had his stethoscope on Steve's chest, shaking his head. Suddenly, Steve's mind came crashing back through the ages, travelling the lighted road back to his body. His return was so sudden that everybody received a staggering jolt. Peter dropped the stethoscope and clasped his ears when Steve's booming heartbeat almost destroyed his tympanic membranes.

If Pilke would have still had them, his eardrums would have been destroyed as well, but not from the booming of a heart. The detonation was tremendous when the missile exploded, and Jan's calculations were right on the money. Pilke's essence was blasted into, and through the precious ozone layer, and the view his mind's eye received must have been totally awesome!

As the gases and the ozone layer, together with the life saving debris intermingled, solid electrical energy streaked everywhere. The flashes were indescribably magnificent. The terminal gases clung to his magnetism as he breached the ozone layer, following him out into the heavens. If a telescope from the planet's surface could have seen the outcome of man's interference, it would have appeared as a new comet. Though the protective layer was stretched when the clinging gases tried to hold fast to both Pilke's and the ozone layer's magnetic fields, it was not destroyed. Instead, it functioned as it had been meant to. No amount of time would heal the rift that was left, but man would still be able to pursue his quest for a new and better life.

A finger twitched, an eyelid fluttered, and all was still again. Jessie's heart almost stopped. The finger twitched again, more pronounced this time, and the eyes opened fully. Jessie shrieked and pulled her hands away. She brought them up to Steve's face and looked into his bright, understanding eyes, and then she collapsed over his body.

"Hey, lady," Steve said. "You're going to smother me."

Jessie was crying, but she backed away. Her hands went to his and she pulled him up to her. Steve stepped towards Jessie and held her tightly.

Jan was smiling; she was so happy that she had guessed right. So happy that she grabbed a wondering Billy and kissed him.

"Oh, Tom!" she cried. "It worked!!"

Billy was totally unprepared for this, and it shocked him.

"Oh! Billy!" Jan cried. "I'm sorry! I didn't mean to do that!"

"Don't be," Billy said, grinning. "I liked it fine, even if you forgot my name"

Realizing what he had said, Billy felt the heat creep up his neck. He peered sheepishly around, but everybody except Grimes was clustered around Steve. Jan retracted her arms from around Billy and moved away. Grimes gave Billy a deep, dark look before he, too, moved away.

"That was a beautiful trip," Steve said, "but I'd just as soon not try it again. At least not for a while. Thanks for unplugging me; I couldn't seem to get away from that maniac. Someone here sure saved my bacon. If I hadn't followed that blue light back, I never would have made it."

Jessie was beaming. "Blue light?"

Jan was more than a little puzzled. "But... Steve," she stammered. "We sent a silver road up to you. A white light."

"Well, whatever it was," Steve told her, "I sure am grateful. I followed it right back here."

The more Jan thought of it, the more she wondered. Then, as a light had saved Steve, so now did a light come on in her brain. *It wasn't a silver road that saved Steve. It was a blue light. Jessie's blue light. Jessie's love light!*

Jan said nothing more. It had been their collective minds that had pushed the light to Steve, but it had gone through Jessie. He was back safe and sound, and that's all that really mattered.

Jackie opened the hatch of the ship and screamed. "Oh—Wow! You gotta *see* this!"

Steve and Jessie moved to the opened hatch and looked at what Jackie was pointing to.

It was raining!

CHAPTER FORTY-TWO

Jessie and Steve walked in the life-giving, splendid rain. She was her usual bubbly self again now that Steve was with her, but Steve didn't seem to *be* with her all the time. He had grown pensive lately, and she couldn't understand why. She asked him about it, but he shrugged. Something was bothering him, but even he didn't know what it was. There was still something he had to do, but he couldn't remember what it was.

The aliens had departed, but had contacted Steve before they left. They wished to thank him for saving their own way of life. Of Pilke, they said nothing, only that he had been successful, but everyone knew that he had because of the rain. What Steve told nobody about was that the aliens would return periodically to check on their charges. Steve feared this might upset some of them, and had kept this information to himself.

The evening before, Jan had gone through Steve's ship—at his insistence—checking out the ship's computers. He didn't understand them too well, and it was largely luck that had enabled him to fly it at all, he had told her.

Billy had wanted to help Jan, but she noticed that whenever Billy was around her, Andy had gone a little strange. She had decided to steer clear of both of them, at least until Andy found someone else to protect.

Jan had come across a program called, simply, C.D., and when she'd followed it through she had learned what it was. The C.D. that

Steve had guessed at—and had told Jackie that it meant to *come down*—stood for Capture Dimension. If what she had uncovered was the real thing, then the ship could become invisible. It was another fantastic part of the ship. The ship could enter any dimension, thus rendering it invisible to all other dimensions. It simply "slipped" from one dimension to another at the operator's whim.

She had followed another program through as well, intending to tell Steve about this one later. The missile sites in the entire world were listed on this program, and she had thought that Peter might be interested in this information. She knew that Peter had an insatiable curiosity about almost everything in the world, so she had told him about all of the global missile sites. The next morning, Peter had told Jessie about them, and when Jessie now told Steve about them, he stopped in mid-stride. He turned after a short minute and kissed Jessie on the nose.

"You can do better than that, mister!" Jessie demanded. "Or do you want me to bust you one?"

Steve did it again then ran. Jessie ran after him and Steve let her catch him. They tumbled to the ground, and Steve kissed her again, deeply this time.

"A man would have to be crazy to refuse a bust from you," he said, holding her tightly. "Which one was caught in the fence?"

Jessie blushed then became angry. "You're worse than my father! You know that? At least *he* does things out in the open! Nobody knows about that except—"

"Peter," Steve supplied.

Jessie was fuming! "And you darn well know it, too, mister! You only have to peek into a person's mind to find things out!"

"Oh! Is that so?" Steve asked gaily.

"Yes, that's so!"

"Well, for your information, miss smarty pants, so can you. And I didn't *peek*, as you put it. Peter told me."

Jessie calmed down in stages, wondering what he meant. "Do you...do you mean I can too?" she stammered.

Steve smiled, saying nothing, but pointed to his head. Jessie understood what he wanted, but she shook her head. "Oh-no-you-don't!" she said, becoming alarmed. "You can't make me believe that. I can't read minds or anything resembling it."

Steve went into Jessie's mind then and told her to try. He told her to close her eyes and try to guess what he was thinking. Still not believing him, but willing to try, she did as he asked. And then she knew. She knew that Steve had not been lying to her.

She opened her eyes and smiled. "Don't start anything you can't finish, mister! I'm not one to be trifled with, you know. Maybe I should tell a certain doctor that you're ready to answer all of his questions now."

Laughingly, Steve showed her that he could finish anything he started. Much later, as they were resting in each other's arms, he dropped another bombshell. "How would you like to take a little trip?"

"A trip?" Jessie asked. "Where? When? What for?"

"When you told me about the missile sites, it reminded me of what I had forgotten. Something I promised Jackie we would do if we ever got the chance. Now we all have a chance to start a new world, one without death machines. Maybe along the way we might even find some kind of preacher who has survived this mess."

Jessie bopped him, swinging at his shoulder. When Steve feigned injury, she stopped, afraid she had hurt him. When she saw the grin it was too late, and Steve rolled over on top of her.

"Now, woman!" he said softly. "You're at my mercy!"

"Oh, yeah?" Jessie asked huskily. "What are you going to do about it?"

Steve grinned again. "Not what you're thinking, at least, not right now. What we're going to do now, my pretty lady, is get back and tell everybody about our trip. We've got some missiles to disable."

The ship landed at the Dome, and Jan was escorted into the building. Billy used his card to get in and everybody except Jackie and Kevin followed him.

"Huh!" Kevin griped. "Must be adult games again!"

Jackie had a funny smirk on her face; a look Kevin had come to understand. "What's the matter with you, Kevin? Don't cha know that we're still kids yet? Besides, someone has to stay behind to guard the ship. That stupid dog of yours ain't much of a watchdog."

Kevin smiled. He knew she was trying to get him to bite, but he was getting wise to her now. "That's all you know," he said, annoyed and on the defensive. "Miss Muffet is probably the best dog around here."

When Kevin saw the glint in Jackie's eyes, he knew he had been beaten again.

"That's 'cause she's the only dog around, dumbo!" Jackie said, grinning.

When the others exited the building, Kevin breathed a sigh of relief. His grandfather had been right; you just couldn't beat a woman.

Steve and the others had learned that Francks was still alive, but only barely. They would not have any more trouble from him again. There were only two people alive at the Dome now, but all were of the opinion that only one was human. Jan felt better knowing that she had confronted her terrible deed, and vowed she would never again let anger cloud her vision.

Steve winked at Jessie. "How would you like to take her up, Jackie? I'm a little tired of flying.

When the impish gleam came into Jackie's eyes, Kevin thought he was in trouble again, but when she spoke to him he knew he would never understand the female brain. "C'mon, Kevin," Jackie said, her eyes shining brightly. "You better learn to fly this thing. Looks like this is one adult game we get to play!"